‖‖‖ ‖ ‖‖‖‖‖‖‖‖‖‖ ‖‖‖‖‖ ‖ ‖‖‖‖‖‖‖‖‖‖‖
◁ **W9-BTN-726**

> "TV'S MOST COMPLEX AND
> COMPELLING SCI-FI SERIES."
> —*TV Guide*

"We detected these alien ships approaching our space."

"I've never seen those markings before. Who are they?"

"I believe they are the Humans. I have investigated them on my own."

"They have tried to contact us, but we do not understand their language. As is our custom, we are approaching with gunports open. That is the tradition of the warrior caste, a gesture of respect and strength. They can see our weapons; they can see we approach them openhanded."

"Sir! Alien ships have opened gunports. Enemy presumed hostile! Weapons hot!"

"Hell . . . all batteries, all forward guns . . . fire at will! I repeat, fire at will!"

Also published by Ballantine Books:

CREATING BABYLON 5 by David Bassom

Babylon 5 Season-by-Season Guides by Jane Killick
#1 SIGNS AND PORTENTS*
#2 THE COMING OF SHADOWS*
#3 POINT OF NO RETURN*

BABYLON 5 SECURITY MANUAL*

BABYLON 5: THIRDSPACE* by Peter David

*Forthcoming

Books published by The Ballantine Publishing Group
are available at quantity discounts on bulk purchases
for premium, educational, fund-raising, and special
sales use. For details, please call 1-800-733-3000.

In the Beginning

By Peter David

Based on
the screenplay by
J. Michael Straczynski

A Del Rey® Book
BALLANTINE BOOKS • NEW YORK

Sale of this book without a front cover may be unauthorized. If this book is coverless, it may have been reported to the publisher as "unsold or destroyed" and neither the author nor the publisher may have received payment for it.

A Del Rey® Book
Published by The Ballantine Publishing Group
TM & copyright © 1998 by Warner Bros.

All rights reserved under International and Pan-American Copyright Conventions. Published in the United States by The Ballantine Publishing Group, a division of Random House, Inc., New York, and simultaneously in Canada by Random House of Canada Limited, Toronto.

Babylon 5, names, characters, and all related indicia are trademarks of Warner Bros. Copyright © 1996 by Warner Bros., a division of Time Warner Entertainment Company, L.P.

http://www.randomhouse.com

Library of Congress Catalog Card Number: 97-94495

ISBN 0-345-42452-2

Manufactured in the United States of America

First Edition: January 1998

10   9   8   7   6   5

In the Beginning

— *prologue* —

I had such dreams. Such dreams.

I dreamt of power and glory and followers. I dreamt of protecting my homeworld from dark invaders. I dreamt of restoring my great republic to its former glory. I dreamt of a noble death in battle, with my hands at the throat of my greatest enemy. I dreamt of love and I dreamt of redemption.

Such dreams. Such dreams. And I have achieved almost all of them. Who would have thought such a thing possible? For that matter, who would have thought possible that fulfillment of such dreams would leave me with nothing? Nothing. I sought to taste glory, and instead found only ashes in my mouth. Ashes and a sense that it was all useless. The lives disrupted, the lives lost, all useless, all wasted.

For what did anyone learn, really? What did any of us, in the final analysis, learn?

That question has bothered me greatly as of late. It is something that I have desired to attend to for some time now. You see, learning can only come from teaching. But teaching requires the investment of time on the part of the teacher who is to impart the lesson, and by the student who wishes to learn.

In this instance, however, we are sorely lacking both.

It seems, then, that I must become the teacher. But for that to happen, I must also be a student. For one cannot truly teach if one is not learning as well.

I have long made a study of the history of Humans. They are a fascinating, squabbling little race. When my people, the Centauri, first encountered them, they seemed to have as much value as a pile of rotting spoo. They were creatures to manipulate, something to distract us, something to pass the time. Something that we could, in short, feel superior to. Perhaps our involvement helped to remove the sting from the fact that we, the Centauri, had become little more than a shadow of our former imperial selves.

Oh, we could posture and preen, which impressed the Humans to no end. We sported flamboyant garb, great coats of deep purples and reds, shirts with flourishes, high boots. When around Humans many of us adopted an almost courtly swagger. We wore our hair high, in an arcing-upsweep crest style; the higher the hair, the greater the rank and office one had attained. It was symbolic, and we Centauri do so adore our symbols.

The Humans had their own history, and I admit to taking an interest that was at first merely passing, bordering on the morbid. We were, after all, an older and more knowledgeable society. The Humans seemed a rather unimaginative lot. Even their planet name was astonishingly uninspired. Earth. Named for dirt. Second in unoriginality to their designation for the single moon that orbits their world. Namely: the moon. What was there that we could possibly learn from planet-bound dwellers such as the Humans?

What could we learn indeed?

Yet as I began to familiarize myself with Earth's history, I saw parallels to the rise and fall of our own Centauri empire. Numerous parallels, in fact, and as the years have passed, there have been more and more overlaps. Indeed, these have led me to speculate that certain events are universal constants, much as the laws of physics or mathematics. Just as the planets move under certain rules, perhaps events *upon* those planets unfold in a likewise similar manner. I leave to philosophers, poets, and those wiser in the ways of the universe than I the exact reason for this happenstance. I note, however, the following oddity.

We are able to observe planetary movements, or mathematics, or other laws of physics, and we learn from them. We learn to predict an eclipse, or geologic quakes, or tides. We learn something as rudimentary as that, if we fall, gravity will pull us down.

But we can observe history as much as we wish . . . and we never learn a thing. Not a single damned thing.

We make the same mistakes, over and over, and the only thing we take from the previous generations' mistakes is a sort of insufferable arrogance. We sit in judgment of our sires and declare confidently that we are too clever, too canny, to stumble into the same traps. *This time,* we feel, *it will be different.* But it never is. It never, ever is.

This has become clearer to me in my continued investigation and reading of Earth history. I have much time for reading, you see. There is little else to do these days. Little else except to wait for the inevitable to finally overtake me.

Once . . . once I looked upon our race, and all I could see was how far we had fallen. I would look at the great palace, here in the capital city of Centauri Prime. The gleaming walls would evoke wonders of an age long gone. The city, built mostly by our ancestors, seemed to carry only reminders of our lost greatness in every curve, every decoration, every mural or statue that served as a testimony to days gone by. It pained me to see my people having reached such a state.

Great Maker, look at what has happened to us since.

The nights on Centauri are generally cool, but not this night. This night, the city below me burns. Many once-thriving areas are burned-out shells, skeletons of their former selves, while others are still in flames. The heat from the burning city radiates outward, and the air around me has a dull warmth to it. But from within me, I feel a chill. The inward chill interacts with the outward warmth, and I shiver, trapped in between. Trapped, as I have been for so many years.

Once I had a vision of massive alien ships, filling the skies over Centauri Prime like an evil cloud. Now I look out my window, and see a great cloud of smoke, shrouding our world much like a fleet of alien vessels. And there was another time . . a time when I faced a mage, and he told me he saw—and I shall never forget his words—"a great hand reaching out of the stars. The hand is your hand. And I hear sounds—the sounds of billions of people calling your name." When I asked if he was referring to my followers, he shook his head and replied with a cold smile, "Your victims."

That prophecy is driven home to me now, for as I look at the choked skies, the smoke seems to stretch out like massive, clawlike hands. My hands. My hands have brought us to this pass. By my hand. My true hand is old and withered, as withered as I. But my dark hand . . . how powerful it truly is.

Far below, there is a fountain that I remember playing around, in my youth. I laughed and wrestled with my friends. I remember Urza . . . my good friend, my dueling companion. We sparred, frisky, two young Centauri, and he knocked me squarely into the fountain. I came up sputtering and laughing, outraged and amused, all at the same time. Urza Jaddo, yes. Yes, I remember my friend.

I killed him. Years later, on Babylon 5, he died impaled on my sword.

Babylon 5. As always, my thoughts return to that . . . place. Turning, turning in the darkness, like the axis of a great set of wheels. Yes, I believe I begin to understand. Wheels of destiny, massive and invisible, the past at one end of the station and the future at the other. And in the middle: Babylon 5, through which all events of the past would be channeled to create this . . . this abomination of a future.

I wander. My mind wanders. The elderly are allowed such meanderings. And emperors . . . fawh! Emperors can do whatever they wish. So I am doubly entitled.

I was speaking earlier of Earth history.

In my perusals, I found myself drawn to the Roman Empire. Now, *there* was a time of emperors, of all sorts. Interestingly, it is the mad emperors who are the most memorable, and certainly the most evocative of those with whom I have had to deal. Our crazed emperor, Cartagia, for example, is certainly the spiritual brother of the insane Caligula. Never were my wits more tested, never was my survival instinct more pressed into service, than when I was part of Cartagia's court and had to remain two steps ahead of his madness—lest I lose my head. I was present when he was assassinated. Mine was not the hand that struck him, although it was certainly not for lack of trying.

My readings would seem to indicate, then, that if Cartagia harkened back to Caligula, then I would be kin to the Emperor Tiberius Claudius. Certainly our early reputations were of a kind. He was considered to be a fool, as was I. But his foolishness served him well, for he survived all manner of plots and schemes, and eventually acquired rulership even though it was not something that he truly desired.

He was old and weak and crippled, as am I. I cannot draw a single breath without pain stabbing my chest, and every fifth or sixth breath I am racked with coughing.

And he was a historian. He strove to teach, as I have mentioned. He wanted others to learn from the mistakes of his forebears. And in a way, I think he desired to be remembered. He wanted the immortality that fame provides in death and which the body cannot provide in life. He unspooled the histories for anyone who would listen.

I shall do so, as well. For I stand on the brink, I believe. The smell of burning buildings, of charred flesh, hangs in my nostrils, burns in my lungs. I have a body that is breaking down, I have prisoners to deal with, and I have a destiny—long denied, long craved—to finally fulfill.

But it is not right that it end without my making at least some effort to keep to the tradition of my spiritual kin. I shall produce my own history. I shall tell the story, yes. As I survey the wreckage of my world, of my dreams, I shall let all who come after me know as many of the details as I can recall.

For, as cynical as I am—as weighed down as I may be by the great burden of responsibility which hangs upon me much in the same shroudlike manner as the smoke of destruction hovers over our once-great city—I *still* want to believe that there is hope for someone to learn from what has gone before. That I may teach those who will come after me.

I sit now in my inner sanctum, my private office. There are no windows, although, in that respect, it's not all that different from the rest of the rooms in the palace. There are windows, yes, but they have been covered, ostensibly for protection and privacy. Though I'm not entirely certain, I think my advisers believe that, if I were able to look out at the devastation from wherever I may be, at any given time, I might eventually go mad. I defer to their considerations for the most part.

But one window remains. One window in the throne room, curtained, but through which I peer from time to time, looking out at the physical realization of my greatest nightmare. I keep hoping that repeated exposure will allow me to build up a merciful immunity.

The first time I ever entered this room, it was at the invitation of Cartagia, who displayed to me a line of disembodied heads, and seemed oblivious of the fact that they were dead. The heads have been long disposed of, but I can still feel their lifeless eyes drilling into me. I would not have it any other way. For that way I need never worry about building up such emotional detachment that the plight of my people might fail to affect me.

I am fully aware that the latter sentiment contradicts the former. Self-contradiction is the prerogative of women, fools, and emperors.

A history, then. Where to begin. Where to begin.

Babylon 5, I suppose. That is where the story must start. Since it was a station created by Humans, then I shall reckon the time as residents of Earth do. Twenty-one years ago, as the Humans measure it.

There is a large bottle next to me on the desk. I unstopper it and toss back a swallow, and it burns in a most satisfying manner as it dribbles down my throat. Many people claim that alcohol clouds the senses. Poor fools. When I have liquor in my veins, it is the only time that I can see matters clearly. The more alcohol, the more clear everything becomes.

I have been seeing matters with startling clarity as of late.

I was there, at the dawn of the Third Age of Mankind. It began in the Earth year 2257 with the founding of the last of the Babylon stations, located deep in neutral space.

It was a port of call for refugees, smugglers, businessmen, diplomats, and travelers from a hundred worlds. It could be a dangerous place, but we accepted the risk because Babylon 5 was our last, best hope for peace.

When I first arrived on Babylon 5, the commander was a stiff-jawed fellow named Jeffrey Sinclair. But he left after a time, under mysterious circumstances, to meet an equally mysterious fate. He was replaced by Captain John Sheridan. Sheridan was the station's final commander, and it was under his leadership that Babylon 5 was transformed. It became a dream given form . . . a dream of a galaxy without war, where species from different worlds could live side by side in mutual respect . . . a dream that was endangered as never before, by—

What is that noise?

Laughter.

I put aside the recording materials and listen carefully. Who could laugh at destruction? Certainly someone who has no regard for loss of life, who is inured to the horrors that have occurred these past days. I am intrigued to see such a being. This is not to say that I haven't met such creatures before. I saw skies full of them. I met another who was their agent, whose head I eventually stuck on a pike. But none of them ever laughed with quite that brand of carelessness or lack of concern.

Children. Yes, of course, children. At least two. I hear their rapid footsteps, their gleeful chortling, as they are running through the halls of the palace. How in the world did they get in here? Absurd question. Who is there to stop them? All but a handful of my most faithful guards and retainers are gone, and the size of this place is monstrous. A couple of small beings gallivanting about could easily slip through. For that matter, even if they had run into guards they would probably receive no more than nods and winks of mirth. Very little these days strikes anyone in the palace as especially funny. One must find one's amusements where one can.

And then I hear an adult voice, a woman. She is calling with extreme urgency, "Luc? Lyssa! Where are you?" The voice—musical, softly accented—is unfamiliar to me, but I know the names she has called out. They are most familiar to me. But from where, from where do I . . .

I snap my fingers as I realize. Of course. Luc and Lyssa. Nephew and niece of Urza Jaddo.

When I slew Urza, those many years ago, it was less a murderous act on my part and more a suicidal decision on his. Urza faced dishonor; his house was in disarray. By challenging me to combat and then dying at my hand, he put his house under the protection of the House Mollari, for all time. In later years, the House Mollari became the Imperial House, and the protection over the House Jaddo became that much more thorough. There is my answer. That is why, even if they did encounter any guards or retainers, these children would have been allowed on their way. They are under my protection, and so no harm may come to them.

I have not met these children, however, except when I officiated over their naming ceremonies when they were infants. I am a memorable individual, but I doubt that they would recall me.

I drink in the sound of their laughter, a man parched of emotion, with a soul as dry and shriveled as my skin. I hear them clattering about in the very next room, in the throne room, the seat of power. Since they are under my protection, the children have—by necessity—lived fairly sheltered lives. Urza's family resided in a home I had specially built for them, near the palace. I sought to bury my guilt in the foundation of a house. Being part of the House Jaddo, they have been raised in an environment that respected tradition and protocol.

In more recent days, I had the family moved into the

palace itself—to relative safety. The Great Maker only knows where their parents have gotten off to.

I can hear the woman who must certainly be their nurse or governess. She has just entered the throne room, and is all too aware of where they are, where they shouldn't be. A glimpse. She is young and lovely. Most Centauri women shave their heads completely, but many of the younger ones—including this one—keep a single, long trail of hair descending down their backs. Some men cluck and shake their heads, but I find the fashion attractive.

The children had been running about, but I heard them stop moments before the nurse came in. No doubt their attention was caught by the sight of the desolation outside my window. The young boy has an impish and determined air about him, his hair a bit wild and disheveled. The girl is softer and more quiet, wearing a cap.

"No . . . no, no, you shouldn't be in here," the nurse says. She speaks so softly that it is barely above a whisper. That is of no particular import to me. I have become quite skilled in listening in on any conversation that I find of interest. I managed to stave off at least two assassination attempts in that manner. I dredge my memory, to see if I can recall her name. Senta, was it? No, no, Senna. I recall now. A longtime retainer of that house. Been with the family for quite some time. Yes, it is most likely Senna who is with them. "You can't play here," she continues.

The laughter is gone. I mourn its passing. In its place I hear the sound of the boy, the one called Luc, speaking in an awed tone. "What happened to the buildings?" he asks. So I was right; they did become somber after looking out my window.

I can tell that Senna is searching for the best way to answer this fairly straightforward question. While she tries to find the best way to phrase it, I make my way from my private room. Their backs are to the throne and so they do not see me slip out from behind the curtains, stepping into the concealing shadows of the canopy. I allow my withered fingers to slide along the cool material of the chair. For so long, I wondered what it would be like to occupy this seat. Now . . . now I wonder what it would be like to be free of it. Well, if I am fortunate, I shall not have to wait much longer to find out.

Senna has found her explanation, and even for a child, it must be a most unsatisfying one. "They . . . fell down," she says. "Some bad people made them fall down. That's why," and she gestures aimlessly, "all the windows in the palace are covered, so you can't see . . ."

I can see her take the opportunity to afford herself a glance out the window. She shudders at what she sees, and I cannot blame her. As for me, however, I have long since given up my shudders. I have seen and done too many horrible things to indulge in pointless displays of physical concern.

But she has many shudders left, apparently, much as women seem to have an endless fount of tears available to them. She looks again, in the same manner that one keeps glancing at a rotting corpse. It is a terrible sight, and you are aware that you should not, but it carries with it a grim fascination. "If they find out you've been looking . . ." she says, her voice trailing off. After all, who knows what hideous punishment is reserved for the awful crime of seeing what one should not have to look at?

The boy, Luc, is the first to stir, and he looks mildly impatient. Children do not suffer fools gladly, which is why there is a sizable shortage of child politicians. "Then why is the window here, if we're not supposed to look?"

"This is the Emperor's window, Luc," Senna tells him, her voice a whisper, unaware that her every word is audible to me. "He's the only one who can look out of the palace. That's why we can't stay. We have to go, before—"

Go. They prepare to go, and suddenly my lack of company weighs more heavily upon me than I can stand. "No," I say abruptly, "it is all right." I lean into the light, away from the throne.

Senna's recognition, though her back is to me, comes in two stages. She stiffens, my voice hitting her even as she must be trying desperately to deny to herself the reality of what she hears. Slowly she turns, doubtlessly hoping that she will *not* see what she already knows will greet her eyes. She stares at me with a somewhat frozen look. Ironically, it strikes me, I very likely cut an impressive figure. I am garbed in the traditional white. The white of light, the white of virtue. Truly, the irony is rather sickening. I feel the rumbling of the hacking cough in my chest, but I suppress it. It is not right for the moment.

Yes, an attractive woman, this Senna. Not a rich woman; she is merely a nanny, after all. But she clothes herself well. Were I a younger man, I might approach her with some suggestions. Of course, as Emperor, I could likewise approach her, and my merest intimation would immediately be interpreted as imperial decree. She would have to grit her teeth and submit with a smile plastered to her face. I hate myself for even contemplating the notion, and I hate my body for what it has become. But my body is the least of my problems.

She bows slightly, her body frozen like a hinged stick figure. "Majesty . . . I'm . . . I'm sorry," she stammers. She gestures vaguely in the direction of the children, except she's not looking at them. Her eyes are riveted on me, though she is not looking into my eyes. She is likely too intimidated for that. She is staring instead at the gleaming golden breastplate that hangs about my neck, my symbol of office. I hope she finds the lustrous purity of it more to her liking than the withered, dying corpse-on-legs that it adorns. "They meant no harm, they're only children—"

How kind of her to inform me. I thought perhaps they might be sentient vegetables. I laugh to myself with mild amusement. It is not much of a joke, but it is mine, and I shall cherish it for, oh, a second or two.

"I know," I say softly. I pause, trying to recall the last occasion when peals of mirth rippled through the throne room. I believe it was when my late wife, Timov, came for a visit. She took one look at me, propped up on the throne, the imperial buffoon, fooling everyone—but not her. Never her. She chortled disdainfully, never saying a word, and she turned and walked out. I never learned what it was that she had come to accomplish, what the purpose of her visit had been. Perhaps that was all she intended to do: see me, laugh, and leave. Charming woman. Should have had her executed when I had the chance.

The recollection passes through my mind in a moment. "It has been a long time since I have heard the sound of laughter in this room," I continue ruefully. "A very long time." The children are cowering behind Senna, although with that odd combination of fear and defiance that only children can master. I indicate them with a slight inclination of my head. "Let me see them."

Senna's trembling increases. It may be that she believes some sort of punishment is imminent. That I am merely lulling them into a false sense of security. Perhaps she believes I will grab the children up and swallow them whole. Who knows what terrible stories about me are in circulation?

Actually, come to think of it, *I* do. Vir Cotto, my one-time assistant and the inevitable heir to the throne, keeps me apprised. I don't know which are more disconcerting: the stories that are utter fabrication, or the stories that are true.

She begins to back up, ushering the children toward the door. They peer out from around her skirts as she says, "We really should—"

In as calm, as unthreatening a tone as I can muster, I tell her, "It's all right. Stay." It is comforting to know that I am still capable of assuaging fears when I truly put my mind to it. Her shuddering stops, and she ceases to hasten the children out the door. I address the next words to the children, as I say, "Let me see you."

Slowly they move toward me. The girl appears sullen; the boy is trying to muster his bravery. He has pride, this one. Like his uncle. May it serve him well and, ideally, not quite as fatally. I know their names, of course. I heard Senna call out to them. But let's see how they handle directly addressing the Emperor of Centauri Prime.

"And what are your names, hmm?"

I am not surprised when it is the boy who answers. He draws himself up, squaring his shoulders. "Lucco Deradi," he says very carefully, very formally. Well trained, this one. He includes the girl with a glance as he says, "This is my sister, Lyssa."

Deradi. Yes . . . yes, that was the married name of Urza's youngest sister. I wait a moment for the little girl to say something, but her reticence continues. She does not seem particularly afraid of me, however, now that her initial trepidation has passed. Still, it would seem she has no intention of opening her mouth.

"Doesn't talk much, does she?" I ask Lucco.

He shakes his head and seems a bit sad, as if I've touched on a difficult subject. "No. She's always quiet." He lowers his voice slightly, as if he is imparting confidential information that she couldn't possibly be overhearing. "We think maybe there's something wrong with her."

I lean closer, sizing her up. She doesn't look away. Yes, definitely not afraid of me. I could use a planetful of females such as her. "Or something very right," I say, and although I am addressing the boy, I am looking at the girl. "The quiet ones are the ones who change the universe, Luc

Deradi. The loud ones only take the credit."

I'm pleased to see that the familiar use of the informal "Luc" draws a smile of appreciation, if not outward surprise, from him. I'm about to speak again, but then the cough bubbles up in my chest once more and this time it will not be denied. It seizes control of my chest, racking me with a fit so profound that I feel as if I'm about to vomit up a lung. I reach out, bracing myself against the throne. Somehow it's appropriate that I draw strength from it, at least for a moment. Great Maker knows that the damned thing has drained away enough of it over the years.

Slowly, achingly, it subsides, and I see Luc looking at me with outright skepticism. "Are you really the Emperor?" Luc asks. I cannot blame the lad. The Emperor should be something majestic. Impressive. Not a wretched old man. "I sometimes ask myself the same thing," I say, and then see the puzzled expression on the boy. I must make a mental note of that: Ironical comments are usually wasted on children. I nod and, throwing aside what passes for Mollari frivolity these days, I assure him, "Yes . . . I'm the Emperor. Here, you see . . . ?" I tap the breastplate. "This is the seal of the Centauri Republic. Only the Emperor can wear it. So either I am the Emperor, or I am in a great deal of trouble." My words ring in my ears a moment, and then I add, "Or both."

The boy cannot take his eyes off it, having had it brought to his attention. And so I remove the breastplate. I waggle a finger at Luc and say, "Come here." Senna's eyes go wide as I drape it around Luc's neck, adjusting it as if it's a perfect fit, though in truth it is hanging loosely about him. "For the next five minutes, *you* are the Emperor of what was once the vast Centauri Republic. You may give one order. Any order you desire. Make it a good one. What do you want?"

Even as I ask the question, the irony of it is not lost upon me. *What do you want?*

Years ago, more years ago than I can count, a man came to Babylon 5. People believe that evil automatically *looks* evil, but true evil is actually pleasant to see. His name was Morden, and he had a most charming air, like a salesman who knew he possessed a product that one simply had to have. And he said to me, "What do you want?"

I told him.

Great Maker, I told him and got precisely what I asked for. And the torched world outside is the result.

I think on my words to Morden, but quickly pull myself away. Instead I focus on the boy. I must prioritize. Time enough to dwell on Morden later. At least, I hope that there will be time enough.

Luc considers the moment with a gravity that I would have thought impossible for a child his age to acquire. Would that I had given the same question as much thought, decades ago. And then he says in earnestness, "Tell me a story."

The request catches me completely by surprise. I am not at all sure what I was expecting in my impulsive little game. A request for riches, or toys, or fame. Some bit of silliness or frivolity which would catch the fancy of a child. But . . . a story?

It was as if the child's entire history was laid out for me with that simple request. A day-to-day existence of neglect or lack of attention by his parents. A desire to have his imagination engaged by someone, *anyone* . . . even an old, washed-out man who happened to be his emperor.

Senna looks mortified by it all. Clearly feeling it has all gone too far, she gestures for the boy to be quiet. "Luc—" she begins.

But I wave her off. Imperial privilege, after all, even though the power is nominally in the hands of a child. In a way, I wonder if the power has not been in the hands of a child ever since I assumed the throne. "No, no, it's all right," I assure her. "He did far better with that question than I did." I study the boy thoughtfully a moment. "And what kind of story would you like to hear?"

To my surprise—to say nothing of my amusement—the girl whispers in his ear. She does so with great urgency and seriousness, and the lad seems most annoyed that she has chosen this moment to make her wishes known. He shakes his head almost imperceptibly, and I'm not entirely certain if he's addressing me or her as he says, "I want a story about great battles, wars and bravery and heroes and villains."

I go on the assumption that he's talking to me as I nod gravely. "I see. And what does your sister want?"

With that unique dissembling manner that only a child can produce, he says, "Nothing." This less-than-honest reply garners him a sharp elbow to the ribs. A blessedly silent female his sister may be (a trait that I am quite certain will evaporate once she reaches an age where males would *prefer* a little quiet), but shy in making her feelings known she most definitely is not. He sighs with exasperation. "She says she wants to hear a true story."

I understand his annoyance. To him, "true" is to be equated with a history lesson, and there is little that is more boring to a child than history. Flights of fancy are far preferable to that which is grounded in reality.

The poor, unknowing lad. He has no way of grasping that the truth can be far more horrifying, far more exciting, and far more tragic than anything that the most inventive of fiction writers could possibly produce.

And then I realize. I, the would-be historian, am having the way pointed out to me by children. Perhaps the Great Maker himself is desirous that I lay out history for generations to come. But now, here, staring into the face of my potential audience, I realize the folly of my earlier intention. I had intended to begin the story at Babylon 5. But if

I simply toss the children into the middle of the labyrinth of politics, deceit, alliances, agendas, and schemes which laced that ill-fated space station, they will never be able to understand it. It will be far too complex to untangle. I said the lad would be emperor for five minutes. Five *minutes*? To explain everything that occurred on Babylon 5, it would take me five *years*.

No, no. If I am to produce a history of the events which helped to form a galaxy—by nearly shattering it first—there is only one reasonable place for me to begin. And that is, of course . . . in the beginning.

"Very well, then," I tell them. "I will give you both what you want." This announcement piques the interest of both children, who—from their expressions—clearly believe that such an endeavor is impossible. "A story about great deeds. About armies of light and soldiers of darkness, about the places where they lived and fought and loved and died. About great empires and terrible mistakes." I pause, momentarily displaying that old Londo Mollari flair for the dramatic. "A *true* story."

For the moment, at any rate, I have their attention. Even Senna looks intrigued, momentarily putting aside her trepidation as her natural female curiosity gets the better of her. A female as a spellbound audience. Yes, that brings back fond memories as well.

"You see," I tell them, warming to my subject, "I was there, at the dawn of the Third Age. It began with the Humans, you know. They are the quiet ones I mentioned before. They changed the universe. But in doing so, they paid a terrible price. It began thirty-five of their years ago . . ."

—— chapter 1 ——

Earth is situated in a fairly uninteresting part of the galaxy. We'd never bothered much with that area before. It had little strategic or military value. Still, as a culture grows decadent, it becomes more intrigued by art, by trinkets . . . by eccentricity. And the Humans had art, and trinkets, and eccentricity to spare. But it was none of those traits that would cause so much death and pain. They have an expression: Pride goeth before a fall. And their pride was their undoing. I know. I was there.

The center of the Humans' government is in a place called Earthdome, which is in a place called Geneva, Switzerland. Switzerland is an interesting country on Earth, noted for—not necessarily in order of importance—neutrality, chocolate, curious timepieces, and cheese. I am not entirely certain which of these traits prompted them to locate Earthdome there, although if I had to bet on any one, it would most likely be the cheese.

Earthdome was one of the Humans' more impressive structures. The exterior seemed to shimmer in sunlight and reflected the stars at night. Vast and, they probably fancied,

19

impervious to attack, Earthdome was exactly what it sounded like: a mighty dome that covered a virtual labyrinth of office buildings and governmental bodies. All major policies and issues were siphoned through Earthdome, which may have explained the frequent disarray in which the Humans often found themselves.

I still remember the first time I saw the place.

We Centauri were the first spacegoing race that the Humans encountered. It was considered a major opportunity for both sides. For them, it was a means of expanding technology and getting a leg up on their own ambitions. And for us it was . . . amusement. A means of staving off the boredom that had set in upon us as a race. Although we interacted with the Humans with great pomp and posturing, the fact is that they were little more to us than a distraction.

Oh, they didn't recognize that, of course. They thought themselves valuable allies, and believed that we hung on their every word. It was as if there were a massive joke being shared, and they did not understand that *they* were the butt of the joke. As it turned out, there was indeed a joke going on—a joke of cosmic proportions. But it was the Centauri who would bear the brunt of the final punch line. But that was all to come many, many years later, and is not really germane to the story at hand.

I was first sent to Earth as diplomatic liaison to the Centauri legation several years after others of my people had made the initial contacts. We had determined the Humans to be a fairly inconsequential race. As a result, the post I had acquired was likewise inconsequential, for at the time I had very little power or influence in the royal court. I was an individual whose desire, I thought, far outstripped my knack for playing the sort of political games required for true advancement. In short, I was a disappointment to my family and my house. Considering my eventual fate, you should let that be a lesson to you, although what sort of lesson, I could not begin to say.

The aggravating thing, of course, was that the Humans had no idea that my assignment there was in truth little more than busywork given me by the Emperor. Whenever my presence was required, they would greet me with much enthusiasm and respect. Had I been a far wiser person than I was back then, I would have derived some comfort and enjoyment from that. Or at least amusement. Instead, every time they looked at me with deference, each time they hung on my every word . . . it galled me. Galled me because they treated me with the sort of regard that my peers never afforded me. As I mentioned, there was a sort of "joke" mentality when it came to how the Centauri viewed the Humans. Unfortunately, I was made to feel as if—rather than being on the outside laughing—I was on the inside being laughed at.

But I could not let that show, of course. So every day, at every meeting, I would swathe myself in elaborate clothing—purple, usually, since the Humans considered that a sign of royalty—and stride into their presence as if my being there were an important matter rather than a source of amusement to those on Centauri Prime.

I have decided that I will start at the beginning, and so I will. It began one day, thirty-five years ago, at the aforementioned Earthdome. I had only recently returned to Earth, having spent a fairly futile time on Centauri Prime, pleading with the Emperor to be relieved of my assignment. I considered the position—envoy to a race that we did not take very seriously—to be a dead end. By extension, such an envoy is not held in especially high esteem. But the Emperor felt that I was doing a good job, and it is most difficult to turn down an imperial compliment, no matter how galling. So I hid my frustration behind a veneer of civility and returned to the seat of Earth government.

Upon my arrival I found I had a slate of meetings waiting for me, as I usually did, most of them with various low-level Earth officials who tried to schedule time with me in an effort to elevate their own importance. But squeezed into a day of handshaking and pointless chitchat was a meeting with an aide to their planetary leader, the President. The aide's name was Hastur, and when I arrived he was in deep discussion with a military individual named General Lefcourt. Hastur had a fairly bland face, as if his greatest skill in life was blending into a crowd. Lefcourt was indistinguishable from most of the military-oriented Humans. He had an aggressive, no-nonsense air about him, with a square jaw and closely cropped brown hair. Furthermore, he possessed a seeming unawareness of his own mortality . . . to say nothing of his race's.

Lefcourt and Hastur rose as I strode into the room. I cut quite the dashing figure in those days, although it may be difficult to believe now. Hastur nodded briskly upon seeing me and put on an air of familiarity as if he and I were the best, oldest of friends. "Ah, Mollari! Good. I'd like to introduce you to General Lefcourt. General, Londo Mollari, liaison to the Centauri delegation."

Humans have an interesting custom. It is called "shaking hands." The idea is that you approach each other and grasp each other's right hands firmly in order to show that you carry no weapons. I've never quite understood it. To me, a handshake allows you to immobilize your opponent with your empty right hand, keep them stationary, so you can then kill them with the weapon you've concealed in your left hand.

Still, I should not single out Humans for criticism in this matter. Other races have their own traditions when it comes to greetings . . . and some of those traditions can, and did, have fatal and galactic consequences.

But I am getting ahead of myself.

I gripped Lefcourt's hand firmly and felt him grinding my knuckles slightly against one another. I sensed immediately that he was the suspicious type and apparently he didn't feel much trust for me. Whether it was something personal, or directed at the Centauri, or indeed at anything non-Human, I couldn't really tell. All I knew was that I wasn't going to show the slightest hint of discomfiture. Not to him. I gritted my teeth and smiled as Lefcourt shook my hand, and said, "A pleasure, sir."

"Please, sit." Hastur waved to several large and comfortable-looking chairs.

As we eased ourselves down, I asked conversationally, "How is your president? Well, I hope."

"Much better," Hastur said. "I just saw her a little while ago in the Red Room, and she's gotten some of the color back in her cheeks."

Lefcourt nodded sympathetically. "This damn flu's got half my staff down sick."

I reached into my pocket. News of the President's illness had been broadcast on their news network with a gravity that could easily have been ascribed to a story about their sun going nova. (They named their sun "the Sun," by the way. Truly the imagination of their ancestors was boundless.) I withdrew a small vial and said, "I suggest you give her a little of this before she eats. I brought it with me from Centauri Prime when I heard she was ill. It will completely eliminate her symptoms in two, three hours at most."

Hastur held it up to the light to study it with what I assume he thought was scientific expertise. I could see what was running through his little mind: What if this is a Centauri trick? What if it's poison? The Centauri are supposed to be our allies, but who knows how an alien mind may work? On the one hand, I almost applauded his concerns. If he really possessed such a suspicious thought process, he'd have made a credible Centauri. On the other hand, I was slightly insulted. Could he think that I would be *that stupid*—so stupid as to hand a vial of poison over to him in the guise of a flu remedy? One poisons an enemy because it can be done discreetly, in such a manner as to not provide an immediate trail that leads back to the poisoner. One isn't so obvious as to present a vial of toxin in front of two witnesses and wish the victim *bon appétit*.

Ultimately, it did not matter. I knew that they would likely run tests on it before presenting it to their president. It was of no consequence to me. If they wanted their leader to be coughing up her lungs for another few hours while they fiddled in their laboratories, that was entirely their concern.

"Thank you," Hastur said. "I'm sure she'll appreciate it." No trace of suspicion in his voice. Experienced fellow.

I bowed slightly. "My pleasure. Now, gentlemen," and I clapped my hands together in my best down-to-business manner, "perhaps you will tell me why you arranged for this meeting."

Hastur pocketed the remedy and nodded toward Lefcourt. "Of course. General?"

There was a starmap posted on a nearby wall. It was decorated with a series of graphics that indicated expansion, identified territories marked out as Earth's, noted unknown territories, and so on. Lefcourt had a degree of smug pride as he tapped it. Ah, the joy of seeing a young and confident race flexing its muscles. It's the same feeling one gets upon seeing an infant, first learning to walk, taking those initial confident and rapid strides across a room, and the expression of satisfaction on his little face just before he slams full-tilt into a wall.

"Following our victory against the Dilgar," Lefcourt said, "we've been taking advantage of the goodwill from the other worlds to expand our sphere of influence." His hand swept across the starmap to encompass entire vast areas. "We're making trade deals and mutual defense treaties with the League of Non-Aligned Worlds. Most of the races have been very receptive to our advances." And then his face darkened slightly. "Others have been downright hostile. And a few are still a mystery to us."

He paused, and I had a sense that we were about to get to the meat of the meeting. "What do you know," he asked slowly, "about a race called Minbari?"

I felt cold.

I wanted to give myself time to think, and so I walked slowly toward a bar at the far side of the room. When one is faced with a difficult situation, it is always wisest to provide a period of silence before attempting an answer. This will buy you time to come up with the least inflammatory response, and make you appear to others as if you are very wise, your opinions worth waiting for.

Understand: We had presented ourselves to the Humans as a powerful and intelligent race, and to a degree we were. But we were a mere shadow of what we had once been. A large degree of our greatness had turned to, at best, artifice.

But the Minbari were quite frightening, quite powerful, and quite genuine. They were an unknowable people. They inhaled secrets and exhaled intrigue.

In case you have never seen a Minbari: They wear robes, generally, or flowing gowns, as if anxious to disguise every aspect of their forms. They are bald and possess no eyebrows. Their ears are situated near the base of their skulls, and they have a bone crest ringing the back of their heads. The Minbari divided themselves into three distinct social castes: warrior, religious, and worker.

They were not *completely* mysterious, mind you, even then. We had our fingers poking into the affairs of every sentient race, and the Minbari were no exception. My source on Minbar was a fellow named Sonovar. Sonovar was attached to the staff of a relatively influential member of the warrior caste, a Minbari named Morann . . . and Morann in turn had close ties to the inner circle of a religious caste member named Callier. So if there was anything to be known, Sonovar had a knack for hearing of it, even though Sonovar himself was a fairly low-level member of their warrior caste.

At the time, I felt that the warrior caste was the only one that could be reasoned with. In later years, I would discover no truer friends—or more formidable enemies—than the Minbari religious caste. Two in particular: one a young Acolyte named Lennier, and the other . . .

The other was Delenn.

I will tell you of her . . . but later.

So there was General Lefcourt, waiting for my reply as I poured my drink in a most measured manner. I did not wish to hint to him that the Centauri felt in any way intimidated by the Minbari. The Humans respected strength, were taken by our swagger and confidence, and I would be damned if I did anything to undermine that respect.

Trying to sound as nonchalant as possible, I said, "We had some dealings with them in the past," as noncommittal as if the dealings had been little more than friendly card games. In point of fact, the last time we'd dealt directly with the race as a whole had been fifty Earth years before and had involved a minor dispute over territorial rights, a dispute that was quickly settled by the arrival of a Minbari fleet so daunting that our vessels retreated to Centauri Prime without so much as a shot being fired. "But nothing in recent years," I concluded. "Why?"

Hastur's hands were draped behind his back in what he likely fancied to be a self-confident manner. "We're going to send an expedition to their border to find out if they pose a threat to our program to expand our sphere of influence."

It may have been my imagination that the temperature in the room had further dropped by twenty degrees and was plummeting rapidly. I looked from Hastur to Lefcourt, seeking confirmation. The general nodded. "We understand that fully a third of their population is dedicated to warfare."

I shook my head and noticed that my hands were trembling ever so slightly. The drink splashed a bit in the glass and I fought to steady it. We Centauri fully believe in precognition, as you know. The future is open to all of us in our dreams, and to some of us in our waking moments. I am hardly a seer. But at that moment, disaster was writ in great letters across the star-filled sky. "They have a warrior caste," I corrected him. "Not exactly the same thing."

"Semantics." Lefcourt waved it off. "We need to know all we can about them."

I gestured with such emphasis that I was in danger of spilling my drink. I put it down and said urgently, "Then send one ship. One ship only. Any more than that could be perceived as a threat. If that were to happen, I can assure you that they would never return home."

With insufferable swagger, Lefcourt replied, "My people can handle themselves. We took care of the Dilgar. We can take care of the Minbari."

Up until that moment, I had felt—at most—bored with Lefcourt. Now anger bubbled just below my surface. "Ah, arrogance and stupidity all in the same package," I said. "How efficient of you."

Lefcourt's face reddened, and Hastur said, "Just a minute—"

In a way, I blamed myself. I had been so concerned about trying to maintain the Centauri air of superiority that I might have given the impression that the Minbari were not a serious threat. But I realized I had reckoned without Lefcourt's mind-set. Ignorance, you see, can be outthought. Arrogance can be outmaneuvered. But ignorance and arrogance combined are unassailable.

I knew I had to assail them, though, for I suddenly intuited that right there, in that fairly nondescript room, the future of the Human race was being bandied about, and only one of the three people in the room realized it. Unfortunately, it was the only one of the three who was *not* in a position to make decisions regarding that fate.

I could depend only on reasoning, and I knew that I had to try to provide it. I knew that I had to put aside the façade of Centauri superiority, however momentarily, so that I could make the Humans understand just what it was they were contemplating. With as much honesty as I have ever employed in my life, I said, "Listen to me: The Minbari are one of the oldest spacefaring races. Even at the height of the Centauri Empire, when we were expanding in every direction, we never opposed the Minbari. If you do not bother them, they will not bother you."

Something in my voice—sincerity, perhaps, which would certainly have been a novelty—seemed to penetrate ever so slightly, at least into Hastur's mind. "Perhaps," he allowed, but then he drew himself up and proceeded to spout the official line. "But the decision has already been made. All we're asking from the Centauri is that you give us whatever you have on the location of their military forces, so we can avoid any possible contact."

How charming. They wanted our cooperation in a spy mission. They wanted to know precisely where they could skulk about with the least danger of running into opposing forces. To give them that information—even if Sonovar were willing to provide it, and I had no reason to assume that he would be—would be a tacit approval on the part of the Centauri. This business had disaster written all over it, and I had no desire for the writing to be scribbled upon us as well.

"No," I said firmly. "This is foolish."

Lefcourt, radiating suspicion, said, "You'll excuse me for saying so, but it sounds like you're mainly concerned with keeping your monopoly on our business. If they're as advanced as you say, maybe we should buy from them instead of you."

I could not quite believe what I was hearing. Everything, as far as the Humans were concerned, boiled down to profit. In an oblique manner, there was some truth to what he said. I was trying to protect an investment of time and resources. If the Humans were obliterated, as I knew the Minbari were perfectly capable of doing should there be a military encounter, that would naturally have a negative impact on our business dealings. Corpses are rarely in a spending mood.

But this went beyond the simple financial concern. I couldn't stand by and watch a race jeopardize its existence simply because of the stupidity of its leadership. However, it seemed that there was little I was going to be able to do.

Trying to make matters clear to them, I said tightly, "Minbari have no interest in alien affairs or alien business, and I resent your implication. I have tried to help you. You have refused to listen. There we are."

I considered dropping the matter at that, but I realized that the sole hope they had for avoiding disaster rested with me. As much as it angered me, pained me to do so, I saw little choice. "I will get you the information you've asked for, and that is the end of it. Good luck with your mission, gentlemen. I only hope that in your stumbling around, you do not wake the dragon. Good day."

I turned on my heel and stalked out. I paused only the briefest of moments to glance over my shoulder, and there I saw the two of them in a hurried, whispered conference. I was hoping that they were deciding at the last minute to listen to me and would conclude that this mission should be canceled before it was too late.

They did not, of course. They didn't listen. Arrogant men never do.

Sadly, arrogance has never been exclusively a Human

trait. Considering the number of people who have tried to warn me off my own course of destruction, throughout my life, I think it safe to say I know this better than most. For that matter, arrogance travels between the stars like solar winds . . .

It was as swift as those winds that I reached Sonovar. We had an elaborate contact system, one so thorough that my calls to him, and his replies to me, were utterly untraceable.

Sonovar was a typical youthful Minbari, who wore the classic look of confident arrogance on his face. The difference between him and Lefcourt was that Sonovar was entitled to it. I told him of the situation, wondering how he would react to the prospect of the Humans stumbling about, trying to make first contact. Would he be concerned? Angry? Anticipatory?

Actually, he seemed rather bored by the notion. I was even more surprised when he gave me the key locations of the Minbari fleet, simply upon my asking. I asked him why he was being so utterly cooperative, and he smiled in a way that did not generate positive feelings.

"What does it matter if they know where we are?" he said reasonably. "They cannot hurt us. And if they did try to hurt us . . . we would crush them."

It was hardly what one would consider a pronouncement to put the soul at ease. I cleared my throat, smiled gamely, and said, "Well, let us hope it does not come to that."

"Let us hope indeed," Sonovar replied.

"Dare I say, Sonovar, that you seem in a particularly good mood."

"Your facility for observation remains undiminished, Mollari."

I shrugged. "May I further dare to ask why?"

"Shall we just say that matters are proceeding well for the warrior caste?" Sonovar said. "Some political difficulties are on the verge of being attended to? And leave it at that?"

But Sonovar would not leave it at that; I knew that beyond any question. For Sonovar was a self-satisfied and rather smug individual, basking in the inherent and perceived superiority of his clan. Some years later the religious and warrior castes would find themselves at war with each other, and that came as no surprise to me, for I could see the seeds of the arrogance already freely scattered about.

I probed with an innocuous question or two, and it took no effort whatsoever to get Sonovar to speak to me of a meeting he'd heard about—from the lips of Callier himself. A meeting which, according to him, spelled the beginning of the end of the only aspect of Minbari life which might pose a challenge to total dominance by the warrior caste. It concerned a group they called the *Anla-Shok* . . . the Rangers. A group whose very existence teetered on the edge of extinction . . . and if they were to disappear . . . one of the last lines of defense against a great darkness would be forever removed.

And no one would know until too late.

—— *chapter 2* ——

The architecture on Minbar is like none you've ever seen, I assure you, or ever will see unless you travel there yourself. A dazzling array of crystalline surfaces, oftentimes in geometric shapes, most predominantly that of the triangle. To the Minbari, everything reflects off the number three. Their caste system, their inner circle called the Grey Council, their most sacred relics . . . even their architecture, all are evocative of "three."

In their city of Tuzanor stood a temple, one of many, and a most impressive structure. To that temple, an older Minbari had come. His name was Lenonn, and he moved with a slow grace that both underscored his age and, by the same token, lent dignity to it. He felt a soft wind against his face that day, and sensed it to be a wind of change.

(Yes, yes, yes, I cannot have been privy to precisely what was going through his mind at that exact moment. You will indulge an aging emperor his attempts at poetic scene setting, and grant some dramatic license throughout, for this is my story and I will tell it as I see fit. I have a number of fairly dry history texts I could provide if you desire a

recounting of various events in a less stylistically vivid manner. Otherwise, you will kindly allow me the latitude that my rank and age have earned me.)

Lenonn was a study in contradictions. On the outside, he seemed peaceful and not particularly threatening. But when you looked into his eyes, you saw the fires that still smoldered within him, and if you endeavored to fan those fires, you would quickly discover that he had the prowess and the will to back them up. He sported a trim, white beard that only added to his stateliness.

He moved through the temple, stopping every few steps to absorb the wisdom that he felt permeated the very walls around him. Most often, he tried to feel himself in touch with the greatest Minbari of all: Valen. Valen, the mysterious leader who simply appeared a thousand years ago, at a time when the spirits and forces of the Minbari were at their lowest ebb. It was Valen who had led his people into the light, Valen who had formed the Rangers, and Valen who had given his people prophecy that was so eerily accurate, so prescient, that one would have almost thought that Valen lived through it himself and merely reiterated what he had already seen.

Lenonn headed toward the garden, pausing momentarily to steel himself for an encounter he anticipated to be potentially the greatest battle that he had ever fought. A battle for survival, even though no weapons would be required— other than words.

His opponent waited for him, already out in the garden. Lenonn's aides had informed him that Callier had arrived, and it had been Lenonn's instruction that Callier be brought out to the garden, there to await Lenonn's coming. He did not issue the instruction out of any desire to delay, to needlessly take up Callier's time. Rather it was to give the high-ranking Minbari an opportunity to absorb the ambience that Lenonn felt the entire temple radiated. If Callier felt even a fraction of the importance of the place, and what it stood for—what those who populated it believed in—then this meeting might go far easier than anticipated.

Unfortunately, Lenonn had the uneasy feeling that he was deceiving himself. Nevertheless, he drew a deep breath and continued toward Callier. Had he chosen to, he could have made his footfalls so light that Callier—whose back was to Lenonn—would not have known he was there until Lenonn reached out and tapped him on the shoulder. But this was a time when matters must be aboveboard and honest, and so Lenonn walked with heavy footfalls so that Callier would have plenty of warning that he was not alone. Callier, for his part, did not appear to acknowledge this fact. Instead he continued staring out at the cityscape, his hands folded behind his back. For a brief time, Lenonn began to wonder if perhaps Callier hadn't gone deaf. But then Callier took a soft breath in preparation for speaking, and Lenonn knew that Callier was all too aware that Lenonn was there.

He was half a head taller than Lenonn, and quite confident in himself.

"I never tire of this view, Lenonn," Callier said in his rough voice. "It amazes me to think that Valen himself stood where I am standing so many years ago. It moves me beyond the telling."

Lenonn nodded. "Yes, I often feel his presence here." He waited for Callier to make some sort of reply, but none was forthcoming, and so he continued, "Thank you for coming, Callier. I am honored that you would travel so far."

Callier turned to face him and bowed ever so slightly. It was difficult to tell with Callier whether he was being respectful or mocking. "It is the least I can do for the honored leader of the *Anla-Shok*."

They moved slowly toward one of the benches, the better to take in the view while relaxing. "I'm not certain about the 'honored' part," Lenonn commented. "I know what they say about me."

There was, ever so slightly, a challenge at the end of the sentence, for Lenonn suspected that Callier was one of the many "they" who badmouthed in private while publicly accepting him. But Callier did not rise to the bait. Instead he replied noncommittally, "You've been listening to rumors again."

Lenonn shrugged, not denying it. In fact, he embraced it. "Rangers specialize in reports from distant places. Rumors are at the core of what we do. I've learned that the more vehemently a rumor is denied, the more often it tends to be true."

They reached the bench and seated themselves, the challenge still hanging in the air. Callier remained far too experienced a verbal warrior to do anything other than simply sit there, calmly, his eyes half-lidded, waiting for Lenonn to speak his concerns. It was, after all, Lenonn who had called the meeting, and although Callier knew perfectly well what was on Lenonn's mind, he had no problem allowing Lenonn to steer the thrust of the conversation.

"So," Lenonn finally said, "did you pass on my request for more support?"

Callier braced himself for the no doubt stormy conversation that was about to come. "I did. It was considered, and rejected."

Lenonn lost no time. "But they promised—!" he said angrily.

Callier placed a hand on Lenonn's shoulder that was both conciliatory and, at the same time, restraining. Lenonn felt the strength in Callier's fingers, and it conveyed a gentle warning that was not lost on him. "Lenonn, be sensible," said Callier. "No one questions the historical importance of the Rangers. They served their purpose and will always be remembered with honor." His gaze swept the temple.

"We set this place aside so you can continue to maintain them, as Valen said—"

Lenonn made no attempt to hide his annoyance. "He said we were to remain a fighting force, not a curiosity, a place where children come to see fossils that walk and talk and tell stories."

Now, Callier was the consummate political animal. Few understood as keenly as he the need to try and placate all sides—even those sides for which there seem to be no purpose. Why? Because no matter how certain one was that a particular body would not be required, one simply never knew for sure and so it was best not to burn bridges if one did not have to. So Callier decided that reason was the best way in which to handle the situation.

"The warrior caste objects," he pointed out. "They feel they should be solely responsible for protecting Minbar."

But Lenonn would have none of it. He shook his head impatiently and replied, "They've always objected, Callier." He began counting off all the old objections on his fingers. "They don't like our approach. They don't like that the Rangers draw from all three castes." Clearly he could have brought up any number of other complaints that had reached his ears, but it seemed a waste of time. "It's the same old story and there's no point in rehashing old arguments." Lenonn's tone changed, and he sounded as if he were giving instructions that were to be obeyed, rather than requests to be considered. "We need more resources," he said flatly. "Larger facilities. We must begin recruiting new members from among our people . . ."

Callier did nothing to hide his growing frustration. He rose and moved away from Lenonn, staring at the cityscape as if he hoped that somehow the view might provide an answer. None seemed forthcoming. "There are less than a hundred of you, Lenonn. How can I justify the expense involved?"

No single word could have so electrified and infuriated Lenonn as that one. *"Justify?"* If Callier had just confessed to murdering his children, he could not have gotten a more incredulous reaction.

But Callier would not back down. "We have carried the Rangers as part of our cultural identity, our debt to Valen, for a thousand years. How much more can you ask of us?"

Lenonn pounded his fist into his open palm for emphasis. "But now is when the prophecies said we would be most needed! We must begin to move or—"

And then he stopped. Something in Callier's face, in his posture, informed Lenonn that he was wasting his breath. This was confirmed a moment later as Callier said firmly, "I'm sorry, Lenonn. There is nothing I can do. The Caste Elders have made their decision."

Callier remained a moment longer, as if waiting for the right words to come to him, something that would assuage the anger he saw in Lenonn. But nothing came readily to mind. Deciding that remaining any longer was a waste of time for both of them, Callier steepled his fingers and bowed slightly in the traditional gesture that implied being at one's service. Then he turned to go.

Lenonn knew at that moment that he had to say something, anything. He could not let the moment end in this fashion. He knew that if Callier simply walked away the *Anla-Shok* was likely finished. The consequences of such a happenstance were too hideous to contemplate. He wasn't entirely sure what he was about to say—certainly not before he actually had said it. But once the words were out, he knew instinctively that this was the only thing he could possibly have said that would have stopped Callier in his tracks.

"Then I demand to speak with the Grey Council," Lenonn said.

It had the desired effect. Callier halted and turned to face the angry head of the Rangers. "Lenonn . . ." he said, trying to sound conciliatory, though there was no sympathy reflected in his face. Instead his expression, his eyes in particular, sent a distinct message: *Do not do this thing. You will regret it.*

But Lenonn had moved beyond regret, beyond caring about anything other than what he perceived as the survival of his race. His voice rising, he continued. "It is my right as leader of the *Anla-Shok*. I demand to see them and make my case personally."

"If you go over the heads of the Elders, you risk offending them."

The excuse seemed almost laughable to Lenonn. Here he was, concerned about the prophecy of a darkness falling upon the entirety of the galaxy. Of an enemy so formidable that it had almost obliterated the Minbari only a thousand years previously, and nothing less than the advent of the greatest Minbari in history had halted it. He was fighting for the prolongation of possibly every sentient spacegoing species . . . and he was supposed to be concerned that he would *offend the Elders*?

Causing offense did not even begin to register on his personal screens.

"Then let them be offended," Lenonn said. Then it was his turn to walk away, and Callier's turn to try to halt him.

"You operate here at our sufferance, Lenonn. If you force the issue, the Rangers may pay the price."

As an implied threat, credit Callier: It wasn't half bad. But it wasn't half enough, for Lenonn's dreams were haunted by fearsome ships that screamed through space even though there was no air to carry the sound. Beside that, everything paled. "Ignore my request, and we will *all* pay the price for their stupidity. And yours." And with that parting shot, he was into the temple and gone from Callier's sight.

Callier returned to those whom he served, and he knew even before he began discussions exactly how it would go. There would be cries of protest, there would be shouting and threats and vituperation, and even the rattling of weapons in their sheaths.

And once it was all done, once everyone had had the opportunity to show how they were not going to let themselves be pushed around by the head of the *Anla-Shok* . . . they were going to wind up giving him precisely what he demanded.

For, in truth, they had no choice.

And his meeting with the Grey Council would lead to results that no one, even with all the prophecies at their disposal, could possibly have anticipated. But in order for you to comprehend them, I must first tell you of Delenn . . .

I know, I know. You grow weary of endless dissertations on the *dramatis personae*. You want to know of the great battles, the great heroics I have promised you. Would it help to tell you that these two isolated incidents would lead to the greatest war in Human history? Yes, many Minbari died in the war, but before the end, Earth herself would stand on the edge of complete destruction. Over a quarter billion Humans would be killed.

And the irony is . . . the terrible, terrible truth that no one knows, but that I will tell you: The blood of many who died in the war is on my hands . . . my fault. My fault.

I suspect you do not believe me. You feel that, after all I have endured in the last few years, the events of history have blurred for me and I shoulder the burden of all the galaxy's sufferings. How, after all, could I—could any of the Centauri—be held responsible for a war between Humans and Minbari, considering that we did not participate?

A valid question. Trust me to know my sins, and the price I will eventually pay for them. I will make all clear to you, given time, presuming that the time is mine to take.

Now, as I was saying . . . Delenn . . .

—— chapter 3 ——

The first time I saw Delenn, back in the days of Babylon 5, she seemed on the surface to be no different than any other Minbari. Bald, with an arching bone crest and that trademark look of cold superiority and remoteness. Indeed, in those days one would have been hard-pressed to be absolutely certain as to her gender at all. She had little patience for me, nor I for her. What I should have realized at the time, but did not, was that no one on Babylon 5 was entirely what they seemed. Not Delenn, not Sinclair or Sheridan, not G'Kar . . . not even me, really. We were all mysteries wrapped within enigmas.

She was the Minbari ambassador back then. Unknown to us at the time, she was also part of the ruling group of the Minbari, called the Grey Council. Hers was a very esteemed and honored role indeed, for the Grey Council—with its nine members composed of three workers, three religious, and three warrior caste members—presides at the very center of Minbari society. The Minbari, as I have said in the past, liked things in threes.

In time, Delenn would undergo great changes, amazing

changes. She would enter a great cocoon and emerge as a being never before encountered in the history of either the Minbari or Humans. She would bear the bone crest and facial demeanor of a Minbari, but along with long, dark hair and certain other attributes that were unique to Human females. Side by side with John Sheridan, she would help form an alliance that would prove the salvation of all the races of the galaxy, including—naturally—Minbari and Humans.

Yes, the first time I saw Delenn . . .

. . . and as for the last time we met, well, that was not all that long ago. But I need not concern you with that now. I am old, my mind wanders, and it is all that I can do not to go off on too many tangents, in telling you the history of the conflict.

At the time of which I am now speaking—the time when Lenonn was to meet with the Grey Council—Delenn was not yet an ambassador to Babylon 5, obviously, since that fabled space station was not yet even a glimmer in the eye of any Human designer. Nor was Delenn yet really a member of the Grey Council.

She was, however, extremely learned in the ways of the religious caste, and the Council leader—Dukhat—had taken a personal interest in her, early in her career, guiding her learning and training. He had a feeling about her, a sense that she was destined for greatness. Indeed, it may be that his own belief in her helped impel her to her destiny, filled her with belief in herself. Made a prophecy over into a self-fulfilling prophecy. Who truly knows for certain?

At that time, the Grey Council stood at eight members. The ninth, Kadroni, had fallen grievously ill and had lapsed into a coma; consequently, she was unable to continue in her duties. After much deliberation, an offer had been extended to Delenn to take Kadroni's place. It was a heatedly debated nomination, for Delenn was still relatively young, and there were some who felt she was not ready enough, mature enough, or politic enough to become one of the ruling inner circle. But Dukhat's voice held a tremendous amount of influence, and he managed to steamroll over opposition. An amazed Delenn had accepted the offer and had engaged in the three months of concentrated meditation, learning, and sacrifice required of anyone who was to become one of the Grey Council. It was shortly before her indoctrination that the fateful meeting with Lenonn occurred.

The last time I saw Delenn, I asked her if—knowing what she knows now—she would have spoken differently. Would she have tried desperately to steer the Grey Council away from the path it eventually took?

She gazed at me with a look that was knowing and sad, and she said, "For the loss I sustained, for the deaths that resulted . . . I suppose I would, yes. But it is pointless to dwell on such things, Londo. For we are not normal beings, you and I. We are creatures of destiny. We do not have lives to lead, so much as we have parts to play. We do what we must, and second-guessing is the province of fools.

"Someone once told me that we are part of a great story. We all fulfill our roles. Even you, Londo. Even, may your gods help you . . . you."

It would be comforting to embrace that notion. Most comforting indeed. I would like nothing more than to attain absolution by simply dismissing all my actions as some sort of divine plan. How peaceful that would be.

But I do not believe that to be true. I believe that I will only earn my peace through . . . other means.

But if Delenn sees herself as part of a story, then by all means, let us continue to tell it.

A Minbari bed is a rather angular affair. It is somehow characteristic of them that they do nothing as others do.

It is little more than a simple board, which tilts at a forty-five-degree angle. In the city of Tuzanor, night had fallen and the Ranger leader known as Lenonn was asleep, no doubt dreaming dreams of past glories. Glories that would not, he supposed, ever be reflected in the mirror of the future.

Then he awoke.

Lenonn had trained himself to awaken quickly, to skip the intermediate stages and instead open his eyes, fully alert. When one is the leader of what was once the greatest fighting force in the history of Minbar, one accustoms oneself to be ready for any potential danger as quickly and efficiently as possible.

He did not know at first what it was that had roused him. The exact nature of the possible danger was not immediately evident. All he knew was that it was a sound—a sound that his sleeping mind registered as unnatural for the environment, and which quickly alerted him that he should leave his state of sleeping bliss and arm himself for a potential threat.

His eyes quickly adjusted to the darkness even as his ears identified the unexpected sound. It was the soft, gentle tinkling of bells. And then, just as quickly as they had sounded . . . they stopped.

They had seemed very distant and—in the instant analysis of full wakefulness—hardly posed a threat. But it was unlikely that Lenonn, a wily old warrior, was going to be persuaded to lower his guard simply because of the cessation of a sound. His hand softly brushed against the handle of his fighting pike, which he kept secreted in his robes. Then he closed his eyes and waited, giving the appearance of sleep but, in fact, fully alert and ready for anything. If he was to be attacked, then let his assailants think that they had come upon a sleeping foe, only to be drawn into an ambush by a wide-awake and battle-ready Minbari.

The bells began to chime again, this time more loudly and intrusively, although still with an apparent gentleness. They were also unmistakably closer. This time Lenonn tossed aside any pretense of being asleep and sat up.

Six members of the religious caste had entered the room and were lined up at the far end. They were Acolytes, trainees who had entered their holy orders at a young age and had known only study, contemplation, and obedience for the entirety of their lives. Each of them held instruments called "bell drums": triangles with small bells attached, which they shook with such an outwardly dispassionate attitude that it belied the beauty of the sound they made. Were Lenonn a more gently disposed individual, he could have simply sat there for a time, appreciating the loveliness of the moment.

Instead he was all business. "Have you come from the Grey Council?" he demanded.

The Acolytes did not respond, unless one considers another abrupt cessation of the ringing to constitute a response. They regarded him silently for a moment, then they turned away from him as if he had not spoken, moving away from him in single file, while resuming the jingle of the bells.

"Wait!" called Lenonn. "I need to speak with you! Where are you going?"

They continued to say nothing, instead simply walked out of the room. Lenonn followed them. His mind issued him a scolding warning. *Fool! They could be luring you into a trap, and you follow along obediently!* But he ignored the self-chastisement, determined to see the situation through, positive that it was guiding him toward something of far greater import than a simple trap.

He pursued them down a hallway, calling after them, "Where are you going?" They continued on their way, never slowing or wavering or even acknowledging that he had spoken. He could have stopped them easily, of course. Gotten ahead of them, blocked them, grabbed one and thrown him up against a wall, insisting that answers be forthcoming.

But he realized there was a sort of symbolism at work. If he was to be brought before the rulers of Minbar, before the Grey Council, then he was going to have to entrust himself to their methods. Trust was not something that came easily to Lenonn. It was, after all, his purpose in life to be suspicious. To trust no one. To watch the shadows . . . for sometimes, they moved when one did not watch (this, a warning passed down through the centuries, from the lips of Valen himself).

Trust, however, had to start somewhere. And now, it seemed, he was going to have to trust these silent strangers.

The Acolytes walked out of the building, never breaking their step, never slowing their measured stride. It was late, late at night, and the entire city slept. It seemed to Lenonn as if he and the Acolytes were the only ones awake, the only ones alive on the entire planet.

They moved across a high, thin footbridge that spanned the distance between two of the largest crystalline buildings, and it was at the foot of the bridge that Lenonn hesitated for a moment. But the Acolytes continued without pause across it, undaunted by the fact that the fall beneath the bridge was hundreds of feet. Wind whipped across the gap, and Lenonn felt as if his faith was being rather sorely tested. He put a foot on the bridge, tested its strength ever so slightly, and then stepped out quickly, once again moving as fast as he could to keep up with the Acolytes.

The wind whipped his clothes around and it was greatly distracting, throwing off his sense of balance. Amazingly the Acolytes didn't seem to notice. It was as if the wind were of no relevance to them.

"I asked to see the Grey Council," he called after them. "Are you taking me there? Why won't you answer me?"

When no answer came, he glanced briefly and in frustration at the stars, as if they might possess the answers that the Acolytes would not provide. He looked back at the Acolytes and continued after them . . . which was a pity, considering that if he had kept on gazing upward at the stars, he would have indeed seen the answer provided for him. Or at the very least the hint of an answer. For one of the stars had moved away from its position and was now streaking across the darkened Minbari sky.

Lenonn had never traveled this particular bridge before. By and large he disliked bridges. They left one far too vulnerable to attack. So he avoided them whenever any other means of crossing presented itself. Nor could he see too far ahead, because the Acolytes themselves were blocking his view.

Then two things happened, almost simultaneously.

Lenonn suddenly became aware that the surface beneath his feet had changed. He looked down to discover that he was standing upon a large, circular disk. It was at least ten feet across, was a dusky bronze color, and was built into the foundation of the support pillar to which this section of the bridge was attached.

The second thing to happen was that the Acolytes, having renewed the ringing of their bells, stopped, pivoted, and were now heading back toward Lenonn. For the briefest of moments he was concerned, his hand reflexively moving toward his pike. It seemed most unlikely that a group of religious-caste Acolytes would try to seize him or attempt to hurl him over the edge. Still, one never knew: there were, after all, zealots in all walks of life.

But the Acolytes never wavered. They moved around Lenonn, forming a living triangle that surrounded him. Then the bell ringing ceased, all at once and abruptly. This time he found the silence to be, surprisingly, more disconcerting than the bells had been.

He waited. He had no idea what he was waiting for, but he waited nonetheless.

Then there was a roar from overhead. Lenonn looked up in surprise and not inconsiderable annoyance. He had allowed himself to be perfectly maneuvered into a situation of extreme vulnerability. There was something over him, a vehicle of a size and shape that he couldn't immediately make out, for there was a dazzling light pulsing from the ship's underbelly. He shielded his eyes against it and wondered whether or not it was some sort of war vehicle. If the intention was to obliterate him without a trace, this was certainly an excellent way of going about it. The vehicle could simply land squarely on top of him. There would be nothing left of him but a small stain on the hull. Or one simple blast would transform him into a circle of ash.

The light became brighter, brighter still, and then focused into a beam that lanced downward from the bottom of the ship. Lenonn flinched, preparing himself for what might be the end, and then the beam seized the entire coppery disk in its power. The disk trembled for a moment, rocked. Lenonn retained his balance easily, and took some small measure of satisfaction in the fact that a couple of the Acolytes staggered. And then the entire disk was lifted into the air, higher and higher. The sleeping residents of the city may have been aware of a distant rumbling, but they were too deeply asleep to react to it on anything but the most subconscious of levels. In the morning various Minbari would likely look at each other in mild confusion and ask, "Did you feel a quake last night?" But that would be about as far as the discussion would go.

As for Lenonn, he felt relief flooding through him. He knew, beyond any question, that his demand had been met, his request answered. For as he drew closer, saw the lines and contours of the vessel, he recognized it as a Minbari transport. There was only one reason to dispatch a transport: Lenonn was to be taken somewhere. The only reasonable assumption was that he was being taken to the Grey Council.

Then relief turned to determination. For now he was to face the ruling circle of Minbar. He was taking an awful risk; were his appeal to fail, that would signal the end of the Rangers. A thousand years of tradition hung about his shoulders, and he more than felt the weight.

The Minbari cruiser, a frightening combination of elegance and predatory fierceness, moved like a leviathan through the depths of space. The transport had docked with it moments before, and Lenonn was now walking briskly down a hallway, the Acolytes on either side of him. He no longer considered them any sort of possible threat; he knew them to be what they indeed were, namely formal escorts taking him to face the Council. His mind was far ahead of the situation, anticipating his meeting. Over and over again, he had reviewed the words he intended to say, the speech he planned to make. He would only have one opportunity for this, and he prayed to the soul of Valen— wherever it might be—that he did not make a muddle of it.

He passed other Acolytes in the corridor. They would speak to each other in hurried whispers until he got within range, and then they would lapse into silence, casting wary glances at him. He wondered what was going through their minds. How did they view him? As a relic of an age long gone? As a benighted fool? As a potential hero? He couldn't entirely blame them if they were uncertain. To be honest, there were moments when he himself wasn't entirely sure of his own role. But there was one thing that he was sure of: There could be no sign of uncertainty, no hesitancy, upon facing the Council. For if he were to hesitate, then he was truly lost.

He stopped at an entrance which was protected by a huge round door. It irised open, and Lenonn was surprised to feel what seemed like a stiff breeze blowing from within. No, not a breeze, but it was definitely cooler within the chamber. The Acolytes who had escorted him thus far now halted. This was one instance where they truly needed to say nothing. The message was quite clear: From here, he was to go on alone.

He drew a deep breath, his lungs tingling ever so slightly as he inhaled the cool air from within. *In Valen's name, give me strength,* he said to himself. But judging from his outer demeanor, he appeared totally prepared to face this—the single greatest challenge of his life.

He entered the Council chamber and the door irised shut behind him.

—— chapter 4 ——

They waited for him, surrounding the circle of light. Standing at the edge, with nothing but darkness at their backs. Neither of the light nor the dark, but rather of the Between. Of the Grey.

The Grey Council. Robed figures, cloaked and hooded, waiting within for Lenonn to approach them. He did so with deliberate, measured stride, but just before he could enter the circle, he was stopped by a very distinctive voice.

"Well, Lenonn?" it asked.

He spun quickly, and his breath caught in his throat as he saw Dukhat. Dukhat, supreme leader of the Minbari, moving slowly toward him.

At first sight there was nothing especially imposing about Dukhat. He was tall and thin, in contrast to Lenonn's stockier build. Dukhat's beard was neatly trimmed, but there was nothing in particular that would seem to mark him as any sort of leader. But as he approached, he seemed to radiate an almost palpable aura. He exuded command, demanded obedience . . . and needed do nothing but smile patiently in order to receive it. When he spoke it was with the voice of a master orator, as if he were addressing the whole of Minbar with every sentence.

"You said you wished to speak with us." He made a sweeping gesture, indicating the circle of light. "Enter the circle and speak."

Lenonn did so, then he waited for Dukhat to take a position somewhere in the room. Instead Dukhat prowled the perimeter, the light reflecting off his eyes and giving him a look that seemed to lie somewhere between playful amusement and challenge.

Lenonn began to speak. As he did so, it was as if he were partly speaking to the entire Council, and partly to Dukhat alone.

"Long ago, Valen led our people to victory in the Great War against the Shadows. Before he went away, he gave us the prophecy that they would return again in a thousand years." He paused a moment to allow the full implication to sink in. "That time is nearly upon us," he continued ominously, "and the Rangers, created to be our eyes and ears on the frontier, to watch for the return of the great darkness, are not ready." It was a difficult thing for him to have to admit, but there was no avoiding it. It was, after all, the true point of the meeting.

He continued, "There are only a few of us, and most of those are old, tired from years of watching, waiting. Weary of being mocked by certain members of this council and the warrior caste, who believe we are an embarrassment. Who do not believe in the prophecy of Valen." He weighted the last comment with as much contempt and anger as he could possibly muster.

Dukhat continued to circle about, however, like a great beast playing with its prey. It was difficult for Lenonn to tell where the Minbari leader's opinions lay, which was most likely the exact state of affairs Dukhat desired. His chin outthrust, as if his trim, dark beard were leading the way, Dukhat countered, "This prophecy also said that the *Anla-Shok will* arise, they *will* be ready, and will be instrumental in the next war. So why not wait until there is proof?"

Lenonn could feel his cause already beginning to fade and had to find some way to rally to support it, especially since he was certain that he was seeing—beneath their hoods—several of the Grey Council members nodding in silent agreement.

It quickly became apparent, however, that Dukhat was just beginning to warm to his topic. "Valen created the Grey Council from members of every caste—warrior, worker, and religious—so that no one caste would have undue influence over the others." He gestured to each group, standing in threes, as he continued, "Prophecy falls under the category of religion, Lenonn. The workers need to know why they should stop building bridges and start building ships, guns, and weapons. And the warriors need to know why they may be called upon to serve . . . and to die. What do you say to them?" he demanded challengingly.

Despite the considerable force of Dukhat's personality, Lenonn did not back down. "I can only say that I believe. What more is there to say? We need support. We need money, resources, people . . . and . . ."

He knew he wasn't getting through. He knew that he had to say something that would grab their attention, seize their imagination. Something that would jolt them from their complacency, from the near-stupor that had fallen upon his race.

He had no idea where the next comment came from, but it seemed to come to him all at once. ". . . and we must attempt rapprochement with the Vorlons."

He was not entirely certain what sort of response he desired, but certainly derisive laughter was not it. That was indeed exactly what happened as several of the Grey Councilors guffawed.

But Lenonn took far more interest in who was *not* laughing. No members of the religious caste, for instance, seemed to think that the concept was at all funny. Nor did Dukhat, whose mood seemed to change the instant that the Vorlons were mentioned.

One voice, however, seemed to be laughing more loudly than the others, and Dukhat picked it out. "Morann, what does the warrior caste find so amusing?" he asked.

The laughter subsided, and the one named Morann pulled back his hood. That was part of the ritual for addressing the Council. Although he had been sniggering moments before, there was no trace of amusement now. Morann was clean shaven, and he had cold, hard eyes, the kind that one would never want to have turned upon one for fear that death was in hiding close by.

"Over the last hundred years," he said in a patronizing tone, "we have sent a dozen ships to Vorlon space. None have returned. To send more is a waste of time and effort and lives." He turned toward Lenonn and leveled that chilling gaze at him. "The Vorlons know the prophecy as well as you. But they have not come forth to contact us."

It was a valid point, but Lenonn already knew what his response had to be. He drew himself up and addressed Morann as if he were speaking from a great height. "Because they know we have fallen from grace. That we no longer believe."

Morann made no attempt to hide his disdain. "Then let them appear, and give us something to believe *in*. If they do not see the danger, then perhaps the danger does not exist."

Now . . .

I have spoken of Delenn. Delenn who, at the side of John Sheridan, had a great and amazing destiny. She enters our story at this moment, as she steps forward, pulling back her hood and saying, "Master, if I may . . . there may be a way to give the others the proof they require."

Delenn, I regret to say, does not intrude into our story in any sort of delicate manner. For, as I mentioned, she had merely been invited to join the Council, but was not yet properly initiated. The warrior-caste member named Morann did not hesitate to try to block what Delenn had to say, and though it might seem impossible, his demeanor turned even colder as he responded. "Delenn is not formally a member of this council," Morann said. "Though she stands in for Satai Kadroni, she has not yet undergone the ritual. It is inappropriate for her to speak."

Morann seemed just a bit too determined to restrain Delenn, and his anxiousness was not lost on Dukhat. "I have never yet known the truth, or Delenn, to speak only when it is appropriate. Go on, Delenn." Morann looked as if he wanted to say something in reply, but a single glance from Dukhat silenced him.

You must understand that this was, for Delenn, a pivotal moment in her life. It was the first time she was to address the Grey Council, and as the saying goes, one never gets a second chance to make a good first impression. Furthermore, Dukhat had basically dismissed Morann's valid protest in favor of allowing Delenn to speak her mind. So, in every way, Delenn had no desire to disappoint.

Delenn had an occasional tendency to rush into matters headlong, stating an opinion without allowing full time for it to coalesce in her mind. Dukhat had worked with her to rid her of this tendency, cautioning her and counseling her on the importance of taking one's time to speak. If one pauses while one speaks, for the purpose of reconfiguring one's thoughts, then one looks hesitant or uncertain. However, to pause *before* one speaks is to appear thoughtful and considerate.

Delenn paused, determining the best way to phrase what was going through her mind, and then she told them, "Valen said that the Shadows would first return to their homeworld of Z'ha'dum before moving against us. So why not send an expedition to Z'ha'dum to determine if they have, indeed, returned?"

To Delenn it seemed a sensible, straightforward solution, but it appeared to electrify the room. Instantly Morann snapped, "The warrior caste will not take part in this. Our forces are needed here to protect the homeworld. Besides," and his tone seemed to gather conviction, "the journey is long and difficult. Earlier expeditions found the area around Z'ha'dum is mined with traps and ancient defense systems. Other races have moved in, claiming it as their own."

Dukhat made a sympathetic, clucking noise, and shook his head sadly. As if concerned for the safety of the entire caste, Dukhat said, "Then you believe it is too dangerous for the warrior caste to go."

Despite Dukhat's tone, the insult was quite clear. Morann bristled as he said, "The warrior caste fears nothing. But it is a waste of our time. Further, if the Council endorses such an expedition, it would cause unnecessary panic among our people."

"I agree," Dukhat said levelly. "So they will not have to go."

Morann blinked in surprise, but recovered quickly. "Thank you," he said, and fired a smug look that somehow managed to encompass both Lenonn and Delenn.

Lenonn felt deflated. He had come so close, so *close*, particularly with Delenn's inspired notion for seeking out proof that would support Lenonn's concerns. But now it appeared as if Dukhat had abandoned the concept with barely a thought. As for Delenn, she was a study in stoicism. A considerable feat considering that her mentor and master had apparently dismissed her idea out of hand.

Then, barely a moment later, the mood of all the participants shifted one hundred and eighty degrees as Dukhat added, almost as an afterthought, "*We* will go."

Morann was stunned, and the rest of the Grey Council

members looked at each other in surprise and confusion, each of them apparently waiting for another to say something. Morann finally managed to get out, "What? But Master—"

Dukhat was still circling the perimeter, walking faster than ever, like a moving target. "We are the ones who must decide how much support to give the Rangers. We can rely on the reports of others, or see for ourselves." He paused a moment and looked both wistful and excited. "My whole life, I have heard of Z'ha'dum in whispers and legends. I think I would like to see it once, before I die. Wouldn't you, Delenn?" he asked, looking pleased with himself.

He had spoken in a coaxing way, but Delenn needed no coaxing. She too, looked pleased. "Yes, Master," she said readily.

"Then we will go,' Dukhat said firmly, forestalling any further reactions or discussion. He resumed his pacing. "We will take only a few support vessels, sworn to secrecy, to avoid the panic Morann fears." Dukhat was ever wise, ever the politician. Let everyone know that all their opinions would remain valued . . . even the opinions of those who did not carry the day. "And we will travel indirectly, stopping at various outposts until we are ready for the final jump. It is an elegant and simple solution, Morann. Thank you for giving it to me."

Lenonn watched Morann, and was amused to see Morann reflexively mouth "You're welcome." It was all he could do to contain his laughter.

Dukhat halted his circumnavigation of the circle, sending his path near Delenn. Addressing the rest in a sweeping manner, he said, "You may go now and prepare for our journey." The Council began to disperse as Lenonn approached Dukhat and Delenn.

"Thank you, Master," he said fervently. "Thank you." Not trusting himself to say anything more—for such was the intensity of his feelings in the matter—Lenonn turned and left without further word.

But Delenn's attention was not focused on Lenonn. Instead it was on Morann, who had fired her a glance sufficiently venomous to poison her back three incarnations. He turned his back to her and walked out, and doubt began to creep into Delenn's head. When she had spoken up, she had felt so positive about what she was saying, so utterly devoid of doubt. But Morann's anger seemed to speak quite loudly, and what it said was, *On your head, Delenn. On your head.*

It gave her pause, and the weight of true responsibility—the responsibility involved in participating in the Grey Council—began to fully dawn upon her.

Upon Lenonn's departure, Dukhat headed for the door, Delenn falling into step next to him. They moved out into the corridor and walked in silence for a short while. Dukhat had learned long before, however, that a "short" while was all the time that one could count on for silence from Delenn.

"You have something on your mind, Delenn," he said with an amused sigh. "I recognize that expression."

"I was only thinking," she said slowly. "I believe that Lenonn is correct, and that we must begin to prepare. But . . ." She desperately did not want to sound as if she were incapable of sticking with an opinion. Yet one aspect of Lenonn's speech truly had rung hollow to her. A thousand years ago the Minbari had been a great race, and they were still great. She could not accept Lenonn's pronouncement that they had fallen so far that the Vorlons would have nothing to do with them. "Morann is also correct. The Vorlons should have contacted us by now."

"Yes, they should," replied Dukhat, so readily that it surprised Delenn slightly. As they walked, he purposefully gazed straight ahead. "But if the legends surrounding the Vorlons are correct, remember that they do not reveal themselves quickly, and never all at once." With that, he glanced her way, and they paused.

There was something in his tone that caught her attention. She looked at him askance and asked, "What are you saying?"

"I'm not saying anything," Dukhat replied with a deliberately straight face. "I did not say anything then, and I am not saying anything now."

"But—" began Delenn.

Very abruptly, Dukhat said, "It's been a long day. I must go to my sanctum and meditate on this in private. Good day, Delenn."

She bowed to him in deference, and he seemed to acknowledge it only in the most perfunctory of manners. She watched him walk away and pondered the rather odd conversation they'd just had.

She was quite accustomed to Dukhat's habit of not providing complete responses to her questions. How often had he said to her that the best person to answer questions for Delenn was Delenn herself? But this wasn't a case of Dukhat simply being enigmatic or trying to teach her and guide her mind. She couldn't help but feel that Dukhat was actually hiding something.

It bothered her . . . even concerned her.

She continued to walk, lost in thought, and realized that her path had taken her unconsciously past Dukhat's sanctum. She would never dream of disturbing him when he had gone to meditate. Still, there was something remaining to be said, and she was beginning to wonder whether this was one of Dukhat's tests. The type that was designed to encourage her to think for herself. Perhaps he wanted her to follow, to challenge him, to question him more thoroughly. Perhaps . . .

She hesitated outside his door . . .

. . . and then she thought she heard something. Dukhat's

voice. It sounded as if he was conversing with someone. But he had told her he was going to meditate. Who was he talking to, then? Was Morann in there, trying to convince Dukhat of the error of his plan?

Glancing left and right and feeling rather guilty, Delenn sidled slightly closer to the door and listened. She was able to make out Dukhat's voice, and he had just spoken three words: "Now it starts."

What an odd thing to say. To whom could he have been addressing the comment, she wondered.

Then she heard a voice respond . . . and it was as no voice she had ever heard. It sounded as if it were many voices, synthesized as one, and surrounded by chimes.

"Yes" was all it said.

Then she heard footsteps, the sound of others approaching, and Delenn realized that it wasn't exactly the most appropriate thing to be caught standing outside the quarters of Dukhat, eavesdropping. Very quickly, Delenn backed away from the door, smoothed her robes and—looking as casual as she could—walked quickly away.

And as she did, her mind was racing. For Delenn was a very quick-witted and very intelligent female, and before she was halfway down the hallway, she was reasonably certain she knew just exactly who—or what—Dukhat had been speaking with. The knowledge filled her with excitement and a sense that she was living in what could well be a historic time.

On that score, she was correct. All too tragically correct.

— *chapter 5* —

I will speak to you now of John Sheridan.

Captain Sheridan, as I mentioned before, was the commander of Babylon 5 after the mystery-shrouded departure of Jeffrey Sinclair. They were very different men, I must say. Sinclair always seemed to me a somewhat haunted man, all too aware of the machinations of the universe that were unfolding around him and determined to overwhelm them through sheer force of will. Sheridan, on the other hand—well, it was fascinating to watch his development. While Sinclair was more the diplomat, Sheridan was more the soldier. Indeed, I believe that he was instituted at Babylon 5 precisely because he was a soldier. The Earth government felt that it could more easily control him. I believe that they also installed Sheridan in order to anger the Minbari, for Sheridan acquired quite a bit of a reputation among the Minbari in the events that were to unfold.

Some of what I will now tell you comes from Sheridan's own account that he wrote of the Great War—a lengthy work entitled *No Retreat, No Surrender*. And the rest comes from conversations I had with him during our time together on Babylon 5. There was a time when we treated each other with respect and when we actually compared notes on those early days. The days of the Great War. We would sit together over late drinks in the Zocalo to dwell on the strange circumstances that had brought us together. On the lives lost, and the lives wasted. They were times when we commiserated over how much we had been through, and we all felt very, very old.

Ironically, we had no idea how young we truly were.

Sheridan was a reasonably tall man. Clean cut and ruggedly handsome by Earth standards, so I'm told. Light hair which became progressively grayer as events spiraled out of control. He had a steely glint in his eye and the air of someone accustomed to both command and obedience. The man whom the military felt they could control went on to become a notorious rebel and the subject of intergalactic debate. In short, he developed before my eyes into one of the most innovative thinkers and dynamic leaders I have ever had the honor—and aggravation—of knowing.

But all of that happened much later. At the point where John Sheridan enters this story I tell you now, he is merely a humble commander. Young, idealistic, and determined to make his mark. He had been summoned to the office of General Lefcourt, who felt that he had the ideal assignment for young Sheridan. Sheridan entered Lefcourt's office with a combination of excitement and curiosity, but one could never have told it from his practiced military demeanor.

Nothing escaped Sheridan's notice. In one glance he took in the entirety of Lefcourt's domain: the desk and the books on the desk, which included Plato's *Republic* and the collected volumes of the military campaigns of Julius Caesar. All of it was instantly imprinted in Sheridan's mind, and could have been called up and recalled later with 100 percent accuracy if necessary. That was simply the sort of mind that Sheridan had. He missed nothing.

"You wanted to see me, sir?" asked Sheridan. Reflexively he smoothed minuscule wrinkles from his crisp new uniform jacket. The rank bars pinned to his chest gleamed so brightly that a small ball of reflected sunlight glanced off the ceiling.

"Yes." Lefcourt rose half out of his seat, returning Sheridan's salute. "Come in, Commander. Close the door and have a seat."

Sheridan did so, sitting opposite Lefcourt, his back straight, his shoulders squared. You could have balanced a glass of wine on him and the contents would remain perfectly level.

"How's your father?" Lefcourt asked.

"Fine, sir," replied Sheridan gamely. "He sends his regards and asks me to remind you—respectfully—that you still owe him forty credits from last week."

"I'll get it to him eventually." Lefcourt fixed Sheridan with a very grave look and added, "It's a sad thing, Commander: A fine diplomat has to resort to cheating at poker. Can't think of any other way the man could've beat me."

Sheridan had the sneaking suspicion that Lefcourt was only half jesting, as the general came from around his desk and sat on a couch opposite Sheridan. "I'll get right to it, Commander," he said briskly. "I have an opportunity for you and I suggest you take it."

That was all Sheridan needed to hear to get the familiar excitement stirring in his veins. Lefcourt continued, "We're sending out a mission to the border of Minbari space. The ships involved will survey the disposition of their forces and determine if the Minbari have any hostile intentions toward us. I want you on that ship as first officer."

With every word out of Lefcourt's mouth, Sheridan felt his enthusiasm withering, bit by bit. Oh, he managed to maintain a thoroughly professional demeanor. But his disappointment was overwhelming and it was all he could do not to show it. He had been under the impression that he was being promoted, given a command of his own. That the officer under whom he was serving, Captain Roger Sterns, was about to retire and he, Sheridan, was to be given command of the ship. But this . . .

Oh, of course there was the excitement of a first-contact scenario involving a potentially advanced race, but still . . .

"I'm already assigned to the *Lexington*," Sheridan pointed out.

Lefcourt shrugged. "The *Lexington*'s an old patrol ship that'll never see action again if Captain Sterns has anything to say about it. He wants to finish his tour and retire with all his parts and pieces still in working order."

Immediately Sheridan felt a quiet rage building within him. He endeavored to fight it down, because he knew that—to a degree—Lefcourt was right. But to hear it expressed in such flat terms seemed disrespectful, and Sheridan inwardly rebelled against such cavalier dismissal of an officer who wasn't even there to defend himself. Striving to keep any hint of insubordination out of his voice, Sheridan replied, "He's a good man and a fine officer. He's loyal to his crew. I feel I have an obligation to return that loyalty."

"I appreciate that," Lefcourt said in a tone that indicated that he didn't appreciate it one bit. "But career advancement depends on high-visibility assignments. This is an important mission. When it's over, you'll be that much closer to having your own command. That's what you want, isn't it?"

Lefcourt had managed to hit just the right patronizing tone with Sheridan, and it tugged at all the issues that Sheridan always carried within him. Sheridan had already progressed fairly rapidly through the ranks. He wanted to believe, with every fiber of his being, that every step up the chain of command came as a result of genuine merit. But it galled him that his father regularly played cards with all the men who wound up making the decisions, such as who got promoted versus who stayed at the same rank.

And there was just the slightest bit of nagging doubt within him that prompted him to wonder, ever so slightly, how much of his advancement was due to what he was, as opposed to who he was.

Thus, he replied, "Yes . . . but only if I deserve it. Not because I'm my father's son."

It came out with a good deal more heat than he would have liked, and he saw Lefcourt stiffen slightly. Sheridan couldn't tell whether it was because Lefcourt resented the insinuation, or because Sheridan had struck a nerve by hurling out an accusation that had more than a little truth in it. And Sheridan suddenly had the distinct feeling he didn't *want* to know which it was.

So Sheridan decided that the best thing he could do was draw the discussion away from the questions of his own relative merit, as quickly as he could. "Can I ask what ship will be leading the expedition?"

"The *Prometheus*," Lefcourt told him. "Captain Jankowski lost his XO to the *Churchill* a few weeks ago, and he's been looking for a replacement. You'd fit in perfectly."

"Captain Michael Jankowski?" asked Sheridan slowly.

"That's right. Why?"

Well, that was that, as far as Sheridan was concerned. Even had he possessed the slightest glimmer of interest . . . even if he'd toyed, however briefly, with the notion of deserting the *Lexington* for the draw of a high-profile mission . . . the news of the mission's commander was more than enough to put paid to that notion, once and for all.

Still, there wouldn't be any harm in trying to be just a bit politic. There was at least enough of the father in the son for that. Choosing his words carefully, Sheridan said, "I know some of the officers who have served under him. He doesn't handle first-contact situations as well as others. Ever since the Omega incident—"

Clearly another sore point, and this one Lefcourt made no attempt at hiding. "The military tribunal cleared him of all responsibility for what happened," he said quickly.

"I understand that, but . . ." Sheridan felt extremely uncomfortable pursuing this. For all he knew, Lefcourt and Jankowski were best friends. Hell, maybe Jankowski was engaged to Lefcourt's daughter. Who knew? Still, Sheridan decided that nothing would be served by his being reticent. "If I can speak frankly," he said, and continued, encouraged when Lefcourt nodded permission and listened attentively. "The men under his command consider him a loose cannon," he told Lefcourt. "I'd rather not walk into a situation where I might have to go up against my own CO if things got hot."

"Then you're saying no," said Lefcourt with no hint of inflection. Sheridan had heard computer voices with more animation.

"I'm afraid so," Sheridan admitted. *Be politic! Be diplomatic!* his father's voice fairly shouted in his head. Reflexively, Sheridan said, "Don't misunderstand me: I appreciate the offer, General. And you're right, this is a plum assignment and a fast track to promotion. But I can't leave Captain Sterns in the lurch, and I don't feel comfortable with the situation on the *Prometheus.*"

Lefcourt appeared to take this in. Then he sighed, nodded as if his head weighed about fifty pounds, and moved back to his desk. Sensing that the meeting was reaching a conclusion, Sheridan stood respectfully.

"Sheridan," Lefcourt informed him as he dropped back behind his desk, "you are the most stubborn man I've ever seen. And mainly at your own expense. All right." He sighed again. "If you want to shoot your career in the foot, who am I to stand in your way? Go on. Dismissed."

"Yes, sir," Sheridan said briskly, turned on his heel, and left . . .

. . . and went straight to a public call screen, so anxious

and annoyed that he didn't even want to wait until he got to his quarters. Within minutes he had his father on the line. "John!" his father said, smiling up at him from the viewscreen. Sheridan had been told any number of times that he had his father's eyes and smile. Sheridan, for his part, didn't see it. "What a pleasant surprise."

"Yes. Pleasant."

"John, what's wrong?" David said quickly.

"They offered me the post of XO on the *Prometheus*," Sheridan said.

"Congratulations!" His father was practically beaming. "She's a superb ship! This is exactly the sort of high-profile—"

"I turned them down."

David Sheridan's face fell. "Turned them . . . down? Why?"

"I had my reasons."

"What reasons could they possibly have been that surmounted such an excellent opportunity, son? The Minbari could be a more important race in Humanity's development than the Centauri! This is one for the history books, John. It—"

"How did you know that?" Sheridan immediately pounced on the opening his father had left. "How did you know that it was the *Prometheus*'s next assignment, to head to the Minbari border?"

"Well, it's not exactly classified information, John . . ."

"And do you know the assignment of every ship in the fleet?"

His father impatiently blew air between his taut lips. "Okay, Johnny, so General Lefcourt mentioned it at our poker game. So I reminded him of how perfect you would be for the job, and he ran it past Mike Jankowski, who by the way got a raw deal on that Omega business, if you ask me . . ."

"A raw deal? People *died,* Dad, and he could have prevented it! He got off and he shouldn't have, if you want my opinion."

"Your opinions, John, just cost you a high-profile assignment."

"An assignment you got for me. Damn it, Dad, we've been over this and *over* this . . ."

"Yes, we have, and I keep telling you the same thing, except you don't seem to listen, John," his father reminded him. "Your advancement is due entirely to the quality of your work. Yes, I occasionally open doors for you thanks to my contacts. But you're the one who goes through them, John. You and you alone. Now, what's wrong with that?"

"What's *wrong* with that is that I have to know that my achievements are *my* achievements. I—"

He put his hands to his temples and shook his head in exasperation, coming to the realization that nothing was going to be accomplished by going back and forth on the topic. "All right, Dad, forget it. Just . . . never mind."

"Don't get impatient with me, John," his father remonstrated him, and Sheridan saw a flash of the anger that his father customarily kept so well in check. "I'm watching out for my son. Where I come from, that's called being a good father."

"And where I come from, it's called being unable to cut the cord," Sheridan replied.

"John . . . look . . . I know you think you're unique. You always have. Certainly you are to me. And that's fine, as far as it goes. But the harsh truth is that there's hundreds of officers out there, just as good as you, just as deserving, and a lot of them with more impressive records than yours."

"You mean more politically impressive than mine. More 'high-profile.' "

"However you want to phrase it," said David Sheridan. "And those people can wind up getting preferential treatment, even though they're less deserving than you. So if I even the odds a bit . . . where's the harm in that? Hmm? You tell me: Where's the harm?"

And Sheridan tapped his chest. "In here, Dad," he said softly. "It's in here."

David Sheridan shook his head in exasperation. "I don't understand you, John. God as my witness, I don't understand you at all."

"I know, sir. And that might be the hardest thing for me to take."

They chatted a minute or so more, but really, they'd said everything they needed to say. All too quickly, they severed the connection.

Sheridan stood there, leaning against the booth, looking somewhat annoyed. He was startled when a voice—mine, to be precise—said, "You are a very foolish individual. And very lucky."

He turned and looked at me in confusion. "I beg your pardon?" he said. "With all due respect, Ambassador Mollari—"

"Ah, you know me."

"Of course. Everyone remotely connected with Earthgov knows you. The point is, with all due respect, as I said, what business is it of yours?"

"None," I said reasonably. I extended a hand and shook his firmly. "None at all, Commander—?"

"Sheridan," he answered, eyeing me with more than a little suspicion.

"Sheridan." I said the name, rolling it around in my head to try to remember it. There was something about the deep intensity of this young man that I found intriguing. "I could not help but overhear your discussion."

"Why couldn't you help it?"

"Because I was eavesdropping," I said, surprised that I had to explain that which should have been so self-evident. "I am rather bored, you see, waiting for what I believe to be the impending and inevitable disaster that is about to befall your race. Am I to understand that you turned down a position on a ship that will go into Minbari space?"

"That's correct, yes."

I eyed him curiously. "Tell me, Commander: Do you understand the difference between doing that which is correct and that which is right?"

Sheridan made no pretense of comprehending even in the slightest what I was talking about. He shook his head.

"To do what is correct is to take an action that—from all present information—seems to be the proper way to proceed. On that basis, what you have done is woefully incorrect."

"Now, look," said Sheridan.

I put up a hand, indicating to him that I had more to say. "However, the subjectiveness of 'right' depends entirely on what history decrees to have been the proper course of action. And I have a very distinct feeling that history will judge your actions in this matter to be very right, indeed. If nothing else, you can have a clear conscience in that you were not present on the *Prometheus*."

"Why?" Sheridan suddenly asked with urgency. "Why, what's going to happen? What do you know?"

"Know? For certain? Nothing." I shrugged. "I do not expect trouble. However . . . I anticipate trouble. And if I were you, Commander . . ."

"Yes?" He folded his arms, looking a bit impatient. "If you were me, you'd what?"

Many answers occurred to me. Ultimately, however, I realized they were all pointless, and instead simply said, "I would likely let foolish pride overwhelm me, just as you have. Good day to you, Commander." And I left him standing there, filled with questions and no answers.

A fairly common state of mind for all concerned, as it later turned out.

* * *

Sheridan's future ally, Delenn, likewise found herself faced with questions, although she already suspected that she knew the answers.

The mighty Minbari cruiser that served the Grey Council had taken up a stationary position in hyperspace . . . that physics-defying realm that provides shortcuts through space and cuts down tremendously on the amount of time required to traverse the huge distances between our various worlds. Just think: If it were not for hyperspace, we would never be able to wage war with quite the same degree of efficiency. Generations would actually go by, living in relative peace. It could even be a trend.

Ah well. To have a galaxy free of strife, I suppose we must dwell in a fantasy world where hyperspace does not exist. But in our war-torn universe, it is all too real. And at this particular time in our narrative, a Minbari transport was in the process of approaching the Minbari cruiser. From her vantage point within the cruiser, Delenn watched with great interest and anticipation.

She headed quickly down to the cargo bay, just in time to watch several crates being wheeled past. Out of the corner of her eye, she spotted the pilot, a young Minbari named Eisonn, and she immediately walked over to him. He saw her coming and, for just a moment, he looked as if he were tempted to quickly bolt. But he was of the religious caste, as was she, and he was all too aware of her rank and station. Clearly she desired to speak to him, and to run from her presence would be a rather formidable insult. It simply was not an option.

"Excuse me," said Delenn. "Did you just pilot in that transport?"

"Yes," Eisonn replied.

"It is dangerous to deliver cargo while in hyperspace. Why did your crew take such an unusual risk?"

"I do not ask questions. I only follow orders."

Feeling that honor and proper decorum had been satisfied, Eisonn then endeavored to beat a hasty and diplomatic retreat. But Delenn would have none of it, walking quickly beside him as he headed down the hallway. "Whose orders?" she inquired.

"I am told they came from Dukhat himself," Eisonn told her with sufficient gravity that he hoped it would deter any further questions. "The deliveries must not attract undue attention from outsiders."

"But why the secrecy?"

Eisonn was beginning to become a bit frustrated. The female clearly did not take a hint, would not back off in the face of resistance. *Ironic, I suppose. He didn't know the half of what she was capable of. At the time, I suppose, neither did she.*

"I don't know," he said in an angrier voice than he would have liked. "Once each week we are given a different rendezvous point. We wait, and a ship arrives. They transfer cargo to our ship, and we bring it here. That's all I know."

He hoped that would be the end of it. He should have known better.

"You must have *some* information about your cargo," she persisted.

"Something to do with life-support systems, alternate atmospheres. That's all I know."

He'd picked up speed, his stride roughly twice as fast as hers and increasing exponentially. She called after him "What kind of alternate atmospheres?" but he was too far ahead. He didn't consider himself safe just yet; for all he knew, Delenn was so relentless that she might leap the intervening span and tackle him around the knees.

Fortunately enough for him, the voice of Dukhat called to her. Eisonn had never been so happy to hear the Minbari leader in his life, and mercifully darted around a corner as Delenn was distracted.

"Delenn!" called Dukhat.

She stopped in her tracks, the voice of her master freezing her in place. She turned toward him as he approached. There was a look of gentle remonstration on his face.

"It is almost time for the ceremony. You are not prepared. Are you reconsidering the invitation to join the Grey Council?" he asked.

She made no effort to hide her surprise at the question. "No, of course not. Why would you even ask such a—?"

"Because," Dukhat told her archly, "a member of the Grey Council would not bother herself with such trivial details as cargo shipments and transports. Would she?"

Delenn began to get the same feeling from Dukhat that she'd gotten from Morann at the Council meeting. The notion that he was so concerned over subjects that Delenn might broach that he was standing on protocol for the simple purpose of shutting her down.

"No, Master, of course not," she said slowly, "except where it may involve larger issues. You see, only an alien life-form would require an alternate atmosphere."

He couldn't quite look her in the eyes, although he was far too dignified to appear disconcerted. "What of it?" he asked.

"I was only thinking of what you said earlier, and remembering that—from time to time—aliens have come to us pretending to be Vorlons. Since no one alive has ever seen them, it's easy to be deceived."

Give Delenn credit: She played Dukhat perfectly. By tweaking his pride, she took for granted that which he would not have readily admitted, and so made that assumption part of the conversation. A given, if you will. "Are you saying I'm being deceived?" he demanded, and then it dawned upon him what he'd said. A quick look of chagrin crossed his face.

Delenn merely smiled. They both knew that she had already won this little encounter, this verbal fencing match. No need to press the issue. Delenn, in a silky tone, said, "I'm not saying anything. I didn't say anything then, and I'm not saying anything now. Unless you are saying you've seen a Vorlon . . .?"

Dukhat could not help himself. He returned the smile, partly because he'd just had his own words thrown back in a display of ingenious irony, and partly because of her deftness in maneuvering him—Dukhat, mind you!—into such a disadvantageous position. Not for the first time, he found himself breathing a small prayer of thanks that she was on his side.

"I am saying . . . even less than you," he countered. But then, after a moment's thought, he added, "Except for this: When the darkness comes, if you ever have doubt about your actions, all you need do is look into the face of a Vorlon. Once you see that, all doubt is erased forever."

Something had crept into his voice that Delenn had never heard before. It was a sense . . . of wonder.

Perhaps aware of how he sounded, Dukhat quickly changed the subject. "Now we must hurry," he told her. "Or you will be late for your own ceremony."

And, draping his arm around her shoulders, he headed off with her down the corridor.

It would be the last moment alone they would ever have.

chapter 6

The *Prometheus* was a very impressive vessel, that I will admit. The pride of the Earth fleet. And, as we have discussed, pride goes before a great fall.

Indeed, it is ironic that the vessel bore that name. For Prometheus, in Human mythology, was a titanic individual who brought knowledge to Humanity in the form of fire. In doing so, he handed the Humans a double-edged sword, for it granted them both the potential for great advancement, and the capacity to obliterate themselves with greater efficiency than ever before. Because of his crime, Prometheus was chained to a rock, and mighty birds would sweep down and consume his body for all time.

And the *Prometheus* was to follow in this grand tradition. On the one hand, it represented the pinnacle of Human progress, a shining symbol of what mankind could accomplish. And on the other hand, its presence was about to levy a terrible, terrible cost against Humanity. One that would make the fate of the mythic Prometheus seem merciful by comparison.

The Humans had no idea what sort of fall awaited them,

however. Instead the *Prometheus* was busy performing its duty, moving through hyperspace with an almost reckless abandon. The way that a child, having just learned to walk, will dash without fear or concept of personal consequence across a room, heedless of what can happen when an obstacle presents itself.

The *Prometheus* was a zero-g vessel, for the Humans did not then have a means of creating an artificial gravity field. Indeed, the gravity on the Babylon 5 space station was achieved entirely through a steady rotation, the same as that on any planet. When it comes to their spacefaring vessels, however, the Humans have a variety of ingenious means of coping with lack of gravity. In the case of the *Prometheus*'s bridge, the Humans belted themselves into their stations so as not to be floating off all over the place at inopportune moments. Earthforce officers who had a problem with spitting when they spoke generally tended to have somewhat truncated career paths. Who needs globules of Human saliva floating about in front of them? Feh. They are a disgusting race sometimes.

At the helm sat Captain Michael Jankowski, of whom Sheridan had spoken with such less-than-glowing terms. Jankowski was a slim man with black hair, a weak chin, and the air of an ambitious ferret. He wore a headset so that he could keep in instantaneous communication with all departments of the mighty ship.

When Sheridan had turned down Jankowski's offer, Jankowski had chosen a solid first officer named Alan Chafin. Chafin had many of the same reservations Sheridan had, but his ambition was more driving than Sheridan's. Chafin was monitoring the instrumentation, and he announced, "Approaching the next rendezvous point." On the screen in front of him, the glow from which provided most of the light at his station, he checked the location of the *Prometheus*'s escort ships. All were close enough to provide protection, but far enough away that they did not present a threat of collision when the vessels leaped back into normal space.

"Very good," Jankowski said briskly. "Prepare to jump to normal space."

"Navigation, prepare to jump," said Chafin.

"Jump," ordered Captain Jankowski.

The jump point formed directly ahead of them, the technology working perfectly as the diamond-shaped gate activated and a tube of coruscating energy burst from nowhere. Why should it not, after all? It came from the Centauri. One would expect no less. Within seconds, the vessels emerged into open space, a mere hour's journey away from the border of Minbari space. The final hour of the age of innocence of mankind. The child, charging across the room, was about to skin his knee very, very badly.

Delenn, dressed in her robes of the Grey Council, walked slowly down the corridor of the Minbari cruiser . . . the corridor that led to the chambers of the Grey Council. Members of both the religious caste and the warrior caste lined either side of the hallway, standing tall and proud, honored to be part of a tradition that stretched back centuries. At the far end of the corridor stood Dukhat, and in his hands was the staff of the Grey Council. He held it horizontally, blocking Delenn's way. Every step that was about to be taken, every word about to be spoken, was carefully determined through generations of repetition and custom. They were the words first spoken by Valen when he originally called the Grey Council together, one thousand years before.

"Why do you come here, Delenn?" Dukhat intoned.

It was everything that Delenn could do to keep her voice even, prevent the excitement and anticipation of this moment from making her sound nervous or unsteady. "I come to serve," she replied.

"Whom do you serve?" he asked.

"I serve the truth."

"What is the truth?"

It was a deceptively simple question, and yet one that had not been immediately evident for so many years . . . years that had nearly driven her people apart before the simple truth, as presented to them by Valen, was made clear.

"That we are one people, one voice," she said.

As Dukhat continued, Delenn felt as if her soul were being lifted up, buoyantly, on great wings. She felt as if the stars themselves were calling to her, summoning her, beckoning the spirits of all her kin from the past and from all of her future—drawing upon everything she had been and would ever be, elevating her to this moment.

For a thousand years ago, you see, the Minbari were engaged in a great war against a great enemy. And a great man came to them. His name was Valen, and he was a Minbari who was born not of Minbari, or at least so it was said, armed with mighty weapons from another time. He marshaled the forces of the Minbari and their allies, helped them to drive back the darkness. But before he did so, he asked the Minbari three questions—unsurprising since, as I mentioned, the Minbari seem positively obsessed with the number three. And those three questions were the same ones now posed to Delenn by Dukhat:

"Will you follow me into fire?" asked Dukhat. "Will you follow me into darkness? Will you follow me into death?"

Such was the power and charisma of Valen that the answer given him, long ago, was that of unswerving affirmation. One would have to think that, in these more cynical times, there would have been a good deal more hesitation. Ask it of most Humans, I should think, and the questions would likely end up in committee, to be pondered by politicians and bureaucrats, the answers never to be forthcoming.

But the Grey Council, Valen, and Minbari pride stem from a different era. With excitement in her eyes, Delenn answered unhesitatingly, "I will."

"Then follow," Dukhat instructed her.

He raised the staff vertically, turned, and entered the chamber of the Grey Council. The rest of Delenn's . . . peers, for that was what they were now . . . were waiting for her. Their hoods were drawn, but she felt as if she could sense Morann's gaze harshly upon her. She suspected that they were never going to get on particularly well, the two of them.

She refused to dwell on it. Refused to let it ruin such an important moment for her.

She stepped into the middle of the circle, the light shining down upon her. Slowly, an Acolyte approached her with the most sacred relic of Minbar: the triluminary. To you or me, it would appear to be little more than a glowing triangle, not much larger than your two palms put together. But to the Minbari, it was a direct connection to the time of Valen himself, a perfect link. Past, present, and future, the three sides of time, coming together in perfect symmetry.

Delenn raised her hand to the triluminary and to her surprise it glowed in response. Her voice sounded deep and husky to her, and very loud within her own head. "I am gray," she intoned. "I stand between the darkness and the light. Between the candle and the star."

The only thing in the room that glowed brighter than the triluminary was the smile on Dukhat's face. He could not have been more proud had Delenn been his daughter, as he watched her fulfill one part of her amazing destiny.

Unfortunately, at that moment, a more violent aspect of her destiny was bearing down upon her with frightening speed . . .

Chafin felt cold.

It wasn't from the atmosphere of the bridge; that was

carefully maintained and was quite comfortable. No, it was the information that his scanner was delivering to him. Chafin had known going in that this was a potential first-contact scenario, and had further known that Jankowski was not necessarily the best man to have in such a situation. But he had told himself that he would be able to deal with it should the eventuality present itself.

What he had been unprepared for, he realized, was what he was feeling as he reverified what his scanners were telling him. There was a gnawing in the pit of his stomach. It wasn't fear, for Chafin was no coward. No . . . it was dread.

"Sir," Chafin said, his voice maintaining a professional, even keel, "we're picking up a silhouette at the edge of scanner range."

Jankowski frowned. "I thought this area was supposed to be well outside the Minbari transfer points."

"Aye, sir, it is," Chafin confirmed. "There's no reason they should be here."

"Unless," Jankowski said, his eyes narrowing in suspicion, "they're looking for us."

Chafin definitely did not like the sound of Jankowski's tone. It carried a potentially dangerous combination of paranoia and eagerness. Chafin had no idea why the Minbari would possibly be looking for the Humans. It made absolutely no sense. There'd been no contact, no messages back and forth. No challenge, no gauntlet thrown down. This was, more than likely, merely coincidence. But if Jankowski already was seeing it as more than that, and the Minbari were not, then the possibilities for miscommunication—and perhaps even disaster—were abundant.

Exuding caution from every pore, Chafin suggested, "Should we jump back to hyperspace?" That would have been the wisest maneuver.

"Negative," Jankowski said immediately. "We just jumped in, and I don't want to put any more strain on the engines than we have to. Besides," and he shifted in his chair, "if it is them, I want to see if we can get a look at them."

Alarms were now screaming in Chafin's head. "Captain, our orders were to avoid a first-contact situation unless authorized to—"

"I know our orders, Commander," Jankowski said sharply. There was the sound of rebuke in his voice. Perhaps he thought Chafin was challenging his authority. As events would shortly prove, Commander Chafin was not challenging enough. "Now take us in at an oblique angle, and keep the scanners at maximum. If we do this right, they won't even know we're here."

The response was written all over Chafin's face. *We're already doing it wrong*. But he said nothing other than, "Aye, sir," and followed his captain's orders.

Within a few minutes, he nodded. "Scanners confirm target is unknown vessel. We read two primary vessels and several support ships."

"Let me see," Jankowski ordered.

Chafin punched up the schematic on a monitor, and a spiked, sketchy wire-frame image of the ships appeared on it. Even that flickered and jumped nervously. Jankowski looked none too pleased. "Is that all we've got so far? Just the silhouette?"

"Scanners are having a hard time locking on," Chafin replied. "They may be using some kind of stealth technology."

Jankowski stroked his chin thoughtfully. "Any hostile action yet?"

"Negative, sir," Chafin said, not entirely able to keep the relief out of his voice. "They may not have noticed us yet."

"Bring us in closer," Jankowski ordered. "I want as much information as we can get."

Chafin couldn't believe it. He turned in his chair, and his tone and demeanor hovered just shy of insubordination. "Sir, our orders—!"

But Jankowski didn't let Chafin get beyond those first three words. He was the sort of captain who was convinced that he knew all there was to know, and that suggestions from his officers were threats to his authority. A very sad state of mind, that. Only someone utterly lacking in confidence is so driven to try to prove that they possess it in abundance.

"Our orders are to get information on the Minbari. If we can come back with a profile of their warships, they'll be handing out medals by the bucket. We handled the Dilgar. We can handle a few stray ships. Now bring us closer."

Chafin couldn't believe it. Medals? The *Dilgar*? What in the name of God had possessed Jankowski? What the hell kind of priorities were these? One wrong move could launch an interstellar incident. Was Jankowski aware of that at all, or was he so obsessed with his own self-confidence and swagger that he simply didn't understand it?

For a moment, just one moment, Chafin considered disobeying the order, telling Jankowski flat out that he was acting precipitously and refusing to carry out what he was being told. But he knew exactly what would happen. Jankowski would simply relieve him of command, stick him in the brig, and replace him with the next man in line.

No. No, if there were going to be any problems, then Chafin at least wanted to be there on the bridge and to have a fighting chance of retaining command of his own fate.

"Aye, sir," Chafin said.

In a corridor of the Minbari cruiser, Dukhat stopped a passing crew member. Delenn and the other members of the Grey Council were standing nearby as Dukhat said, "Ah, Enfili, tell the captain that we have concluded the ceremony and we can begin the final leg of our journey. Tell him to set course," and he paused, displaying the noted Dukhat flair for the dramatic, before he concluded, "for Z'ha'dum."

Delenn smiled inwardly as the Minbari crewman moved away. In some ways, Dukhat—who bore an awesome responsibility for the Minbari race upon his shoulders—had never really grown up. He displayed an almost childlike glee over the mere mention of their destination. Perhaps it was his ability to keep such close touch with that youthful enthusiasm that enabled him to handle his responsibilities so adroitly.

Then Delenn noticed that Morann was engaged in a whispered conversation with another Minbari crewman. She could instantly discern from his demeanor that they were discussing something of great concern. And Morann looked genuinely worried. Anything that could worry Morann was definitely alarming, for Morann's infernal self-confidence did not allow him to routinely display apprehension. A moment more, and then Morann walked back to the Grey Council, pausing just long enough to allow Dukhat to walk on ahead.

But the moment Dukhat was out of earshot, he wasted no time in saying, "The sensors have detected an echo that seems to be following our course. They may be alien ships on approach. I've told them to go to maximum power on the scanners so we can verify." He lowered his voice even more as he added, "No reason to concern Dukhat with it until we know more."

This brought concurring nods from the other members of the Council.

Poor fools.

If they only knew . . .

Chafin felt his heart begin to race as his readings gave him precisely the information that he was dreading. "Sir," he said, "alien ships are changing course, moving in our direction." A warning signal blinked at him. "Picking up scanners. Extremely powerful . . . I've never seen anything like them . . ." Then he swung about in his chair, and this time there was no hint of challenge or defiance, but merely alarmed information being provided. "They've seen us!"

And Captain Jankowski, the medal seeker, Captain Jankowski, dreaded enemy of the Dilgar, suddenly felt the same chill that Chafin had experienced minutes earlier. The first stirrings that he might very well have thrust himself into something for which neither he, nor his crew, nor perhaps even the Human race, was prepared. "All right, get us out of here," Jankowski said quickly, making the first good decision of the past half hour. "Prepare to—"

Chafin was already ahead of him. He'd been prepared to fire up the jump engines and send the *Prometheus* hurtling back into hyperspace from the moment they'd first picked up the Minbari on their scanners. But he was thoroughly alarmed to discover that all of the comforting readings that moments before had assured him escape was available at the touch of a control had abruptly vanished. "Jump engines not responding," Chafin announced.

The only thing that kept Jankowski from leaping out of his chair in alarm was the strap. Had it not been there, the motion would have carried him halfway across the room and likely knocked him cold. Which, considering what was to happen next, could only have been an improvement. *"What?!"* he spat out.

Shaking his head in exasperation, Chafin was desperately trying to find a means of bypassing the problem and was having no luck at all. "Alien scanner arrays are interfering with the electrical systems. Tremendous EMP output. Trying to reroute . . ."

Jankowski thudded an angry fist on his armrest. "They drew us in deliberately," he barked in an accusatory voice. "Wanted to get us within range of their scanners so they could shut us down!"

There was something about the moment that seemed to call for Chafin hauling off and belting his superior officer, but that hardly seemed as if it would be especially productive. "Sir," he pointed out, trying to keep the sarcasm from his voice, "you said you wanted to get as much information on the enemy ships as possible. What if they want to capture our ships for the exact same reason?"

Thoughts of medals flitted away. Jankowski—always most concerned about his image—was now contemplating what it would be like to go from hero to fool. To being responsible for the Minbari garnering all the information about Humans that they desired, while the Humans came away with nothing except humiliation. "Then we have to make sure that doesn't happen, Commander," he said flatly. "Go to red alert. Try to open up a channel. Tell them . . . we mean them no harm."

He prayed that the Minbari could be reasoned with. That they would see the Humans posed no threat.

As it so happened, his prayer was answered. But in a perverse twist that would indicate that the Human God has a sick sense of humor, Jankowski was unaware that he'd been granted his request. Indeed, one can almost picture the Human God throwing up His hands and saying, "I tried! But they wouldn't even listen to *me*!"

Not surprising. No, not surprising at all.

Never had the Grey Council so quickly reassembled after having disbanded mere moments before. They were within the Council chamber, and the walls had transformed into screens with assorted images of the intruders portrayed upon them. They were on all the walls around them, and Delenn couldn't help but feel as if she were surrounded. Then Dukhat entered, moving quickly, his attention obviously being required. She was struck by the complete change in his demeanor. The playfulness, the amusement, was gone. Instead he was all business. "What is it?" he asked.

"We detected these alien ships approaching our space," Morann told him.

Dukhat frowned, staring at the vessels whose images adorned the upper reaches of the Council chamber. "I've never seen those markings before. Who are they?"

"I believe they are the Humans," Delenn theorized. "I have investigated them on my own."

The mere mention of the word seemed to galvanize Dukhat. Delenn was surprised. Though word of the elusive Humans had reached some in the Grey Council in the past, she had never mentioned her studies to Dukhat before, since she did not consider the subject to be of overwhelming importance. The Humans were merely one of any number of such races that Delenn had investigated, since her thirst for knowledge was virtually unquenchable and she found all manner of things to be of interest. So the startled reaction from Dukhat caught her off-guard, as Morann stepped in. "They have tried to contact us, but we do not understand their language. As is our custom, we are approaching with the gunports open."

Dukhat stiffened. "By whose order?"

Morann appeared surprised that Dukhat had any question in his voice. "Master, that is the tradition of the warrior caste, a gesture of respect and strength. They can see our weapons; they can see we approach them openhanded."

Dukhat started to reply, but he was never heard, as a sudden explosion rocked the Minbari cruiser. And just like that, with one shot . . . the Humans signed their death warrant.

The movement in the surface of the lead cruiser caught Chafin's attention immediately. Something began to protrude from the craft, leading Chafin to make a snap, and quite accurate, assessment. "Sir! Alien ships have opened gunports!"

Jankowski visibly paled. "Are they preparing to fire?"

Chafin shook his head in frustration. His readings were all over the place. It was like trying to pick out the words to a song while the broadcast was enveloped in static. He wanted to slam the console with his fists. "I don't know! I can't tell—!"

"Talk to me," Jankowski ordered with rising concern. "Is there a lock-on?"

"The scanner's too powerful! I couldn't tell even if they were . . ." And then he saw similar movement on the other vessels as well. "They've *all* opened gunports! Enemy presumed hostile! Weapons hot!"

He could have waited. Jankowski, in order to avoid starting a war, could have gambled with his ship, his life, and the life of his crew. He could have waited until he was fired upon in order to make certain that the threat was genuine. That it wasn't a bluff, or saber rattling, or—indeed—what it truly was, namely a sign of respect.

But he did not. He would not take that risk. He placed his own survival above all the potential ramifications, and shouted, "Hell . . . all batteries, all forward guns . . . fire at will! I repeat, *fire at will!*"

The *Prometheus* unleashed its firepower on the unprepared Minbari cruisers. Taking their cue from Jankowski, the other Earth destroyers ripped into the cruisers as well. Within the Minbari vessels, entire bulkheads were blown apart, girders ripped from their moorings and sent smashing down on the fleeing Minbari crewmen. Religious-caste members, untrained for war, prayed . . . and died. Warrior-caste members, prepared for battle all their lives, fared little better. They had been caught completely unprepared, and the Earth destroyers pressed their advantage.

Credit the Minbari that they did their best to recover. Within moments of the unprovoked attack, steely blue-gray fighters swarmed from the nose of one of the cruisers, hurtling toward the Earth vessels like infuriated, tri-winged insects. Return fire pummeled one of the Earth destroyers, which had moved to intercept the attack as the *Prometheus* concentrated its fire on the lead Minbari cruiser.

Debris had fallen all around Delenn, and it was nothing short of miraculous that her skull was not caved in. She staggered to her feet in the corridor, looked around in confusion. And then, to her horror, she saw Dukhat, half buried in rubble that had plummeted from overhead.

There was no way that Delenn should have been able to haul Dukhat out of his entombment, but she did. Drawing strength from who-knows-where, she shoved aside girders and metal, dragged Dukhat out from under. She refused to even entertain the notion that he might be fatally injured. Her mind was still having trouble coping with the reality of the situation. It was all a dream, yes, that had to be it. A bad dream, a nightmare, one in which the most joyous and honored day of her life was to be forever joined with one of the greatest tragedies ever to be inflicted upon the Minbari.

Her mind knew, beyond all doubt, that yes, it was a nightmare. But her heart knew better. She heard a voice cry out *"Help me! Somebody, help me!"* and there was such terror in it that it didn't even fully register on her that it was, in fact, her own voice.

From all around her there were explosions, alarms screeching, the sounds of running feet and orders being barked. Over all of that, the last words of Dukhat could not be heard. He whispered to her and she tried to hear him. She drew close to him, put her ear to his lips, but all she managed to detect was a single, unsteady death rattle.

And she howled in a voice that she not only didn't recognize as her own, but this time didn't even seem vaguely Minbari. It was the cry of a lost soul.

***

Jankowski was not out to destroy the Minbari. He merely wanted to save his own neck. And the opportunity shortly presented itself as Chafin saw the electronic systems on his board suddenly snap to normal. He now had full access to the jump engines, and there could only be one reason for it. He shouted, "We hit the scanner array! We can jump now!"

"Then get us the hell out of here!" Jankowski ordered.

Seconds later a jump point opened, providing salvation there in the depths of space. The Earth fleet leapt into hyperspace and, seconds later, vanished.

Delenn clutched Dukhat's body to her, sobbing hysterically, and then Copelann, one of the Grey Councilors, stumbled toward her through the debris and confusion. He gasped upon seeing Dukhat lying in Delenn's arms. It took only the merest glance to confirm that Dukhat was already gone. Copelann was filled with rage, but he fought to steady himself and deliver the message as quickly as possible.

"Delenn, we need to strike back, but the Council is divided. Do we follow them back to their base and take revenge? Or wait and find out what happened? Yours is the deciding vote, Delenn."

His words registered deep in the roiling cauldron that had become her soul. To a degree, she blamed herself. She had researched the Humans, studied them. If she had been more thorough, somehow she might have anticipated this. She had underestimated them, dismissed them. She should have shouted a warning to fire upon them before they were given the opportunity to attack, for clearly such barbarians were not entitled to the courtesies accorded civilized races.

"He was the best of us," she said, her hand running along the unmoving brow of Dukhat. "They struck without provocation. There was no reason . . . animals . . . brutal, unthinking . . ."

The rage flooded through her, and her body uncoiled like a spring. Her fists balled, her arms stiff, she allowed the fury to take her as she snarled, "They deserve no mercy! Strike them down! Follow them back to their base and kill them! Destroy them! All of them! Do you understand me? No mercy! *No mercy!*"

Copelann ran off down the hallway, and suddenly Delenn was aware of other Minbari—Grey Council members, caste members, anyone and everyone within proximity—charging toward the fallen Dukhat. But none of them was carrying medical equipment, as if this were a last-ditch effort to try to save him. Instead they were carrying hand weapons of all sorts.

Delenn looked around in newborn confusion as they formed a wall around the fallen body of their leader. Directly in front of her was Morann, and next to him, Lenonn. What sort of danger could be so overwhelming that—?

And then it hit her. Then she realized.

She saw him approaching, a bizarre and terrifying individual.

A Soul Hunter.

The Minbari had formed a solid wall of bodies around Dukhat, and Delenn shoved her way up to the front line and linked her elbows with the others. They radiated defiance, and the Soul Hunter was momentarily taken aback. "You would not let me perform the function for which I have been prepared all my life? You are a most cruel people, you Minbari."

"Get away from him," Delenn said tightly.

"You are making a terrible mistake," the Soul Hunter told them. "If the soul is not carefully preserved, it will be forever lost."

"If the soul is carefully preserved, it will be forever trapped and unable to move to its next incarnation," Delenn shot back. "You shall not have him."

"Consider carefully the gamble you are making with—"

"You shall not have him!"

Her response was so infuriated, so intense, that the Soul Hunter disappeared without raising any further issues.

—— chapter 7 ——

Oh, the champagne was flowing at Earthdome.

A gathering was being held in the main reception hall to celebrate the great victory which had been achieved by the *Prometheus*. I remember the room as clearly as if it were yesterday. There was General Lefcourt, moving from one dignitary to the next, nodding, smiling, accepting congratulations. Never far behind him was Captain Jankowski, likewise accepting all the praise that was being offered him.

Several times throughout the course of the evening, the visual log from the *Prometheus* was run on a large screen. Every moment, from the move out of hyperspace, to the first contact with the Minbari cruiser, to the open assault, hurried battle, and escape, was played out in loving detail. There was even applause as the weapons of Earthforce ripped into the cruisers, ships belonging to an unseen, unknown enemy who had been about to fire, without provocation, on the exploratory Earth vessels.

"Hell of a job, Captain," Hastur, the presidential aide, was telling him. He clapped Jankowski on the back and winked approvingly at Lefcourt. "Clearly, General, you picked the right man for the job. You're to be commended."

Jankowski spotted someone across the room, and turned to Lefcourt. "General, I see someone I should really say hello to." The general nodded, indicating that Jankowski was free to go, and quickly Jankowski crossed the room, zeroing in on his intended victim.

For standing off to one side, taking in the celebration but not truly seeming a part of it, were Captain Roger Sterns and his second-in-command, John Sheridan. Sterns was dark-skinned with hair graying at the temples, hardened eyes, and an air about him that indicated he did not suffer fools gladly. Sterns was holding a drink. Sheridan's hand was empty. Sterns and Sheridan noticed that Jankowski had zeroed in on them, but made no move as Jankowski—with his accustomed swagger—strode up to them.

"Well," he said confidently. "Well, well, Commander Sheridan. And what do you think now?"

Sheridan looked politely confused. "I beg your pardon, Captain Jankowski?"

"Could have been you out there, Commander." He gestured toward the monitor which was, at that moment, replaying the encounter. "Could have been you striking a blow for the safety of the Earth alliance."

"Could have been me on the ship that fired first," Sheridan said evenly.

"And you consider that a bad thing?" Jankowski looked astounded. "You know, Sheridan, word got back to me regarding your comments. It must be galling you to have been so completely wrong. You could have been part of the winning team, Sheridan. But perhaps it was lucky that you turned me down after all. I suspect that if it was up to you, the *Prometheus* would be scrap metal by now and the security of the Earth severely compromised."

"If it were up to me, you'd be court-martialed," Sheridan said, bristling, but Sterns put a cautioning hand against Sheridan's chest to calm him.

Jankowski looked at Sterns with a cold eye. "Keep your officers in check, Captain, if you would be so kind. I do not appreciate hearing such commentary delivered by an officer who is so jealous of the achievements of others that he has to try to denigrate a heroic event in order to quell his own envy."

"Rather taken with ourselves tonight, Mike," Sterns said coolly. "If you ask me, you look rather like a trapped deer in that playback. I'm somewhat surprised that you take pride in it."

"We attacked and demolished an enemy whom the Centauri claimed was vastly superior" was Jankowski's arch reply. "We brought back telemetry and information on the Minbari vessels, albeit—I admit—limited. And we let yet another race know that Humanity is not to be taken for granted."

"Oh, you've sent that message quite loudly, I assure you."

Jankowski looked surprised, for neither Sheridan nor Sterns had spoken. He turned and I emerged from the shadows of the nearby corner, a drink in my hand and a sense of doom in my heart.

"Ambassador," Jankowski said in a most condescending tone. "I'm surprised you would actually show up here."

"I live for surprises," I told him. "But may I ask why you are, in fact, surprised?"

"Because General Lefcourt told me that you advised against any encounter with the Minbari."

"I did, yes," I agreed.

"You said," and Jankowski was swaggering with confidence, "that even the Centauri at their height never went head-to-head with the Minbari."

"That is also correct."

"You said that we might—what was your phrasing?— wake up the dragon."

"Right a third time," I said with every appearance of extreme joviality. "And you have."

"You know what I think?" Jankowski said.

"I would be fairly ecstatic to know your opinion," I told him. Sheridan and Sterns were looking from Jankowski to me and back again, uncertain of why I had inserted myself into their conversation.

"I think that the Centauri are stinking, worthless cowards."

Lefcourt had drawn within range of the conversation, and there was now a distinct expression of alarm on his face. "Captain!" he said, catching Jankowski's attention. It was more than likely that Lefcourt shared his opinion, but he was far too politic—or simply in too good a mood—to say so.

And I laughed. I think my laughter made them nervous. "No, no . . . it's quite all right," I said. "You're certainly entitled to think that. And now I will tell you what *I* think . . . no. Actually, I will tell you what I *know*."

"Please do." Jankowski gestured expansively.

"I come here," I said, "because I make it a point never to miss a send-off."

Jankowski looked to Lefcourt, who in turn looked at Sheridan and Sterns. Both shrugged, not pretending to understand. "Send-off—?" asked Lefcourt at length.

"Why yes. A send-off party for the Human race. You see . . . you are dead, and simply do not know it yet. All of you. Everyone in this room, more than likely. Everyone in your system, everyone on this planet. And you, my dear captain"—and I pointed at Jankowski—"will go from being the hero of the hour to the demon of the century. For you have, as you say, sown the wind, and the whirlwind you will reap will be as nothing that you've ever known."

"Ambassador, such gloom and doom," Lefcourt chided, trying to achieve some degree of joviality. "This is a party, after all."

And I raised my voice far more loudly than I had intended, so that it carried even over the noise of the other guests. It was the drink in me, I suppose, or maybe just the desire to let the arrogant fools know just what they had done to themselves. *"This is not a party, this is a wake!"* I roared.

Enough people heard my ire that conversation momentarily subsided. Then there were subdued conversations, confused whisperings, pointed fingers, and even more pointed glances. Jankowski and Lefcourt shook their heads and moved away from me. Sheridan studied me thoughtfully. "You really think the Minbari will strike back?"

"I know they will," I said.

"You have inside information?" Sterns asked.

"I have my contacts, but not in this instance. My usual contact has been incommunicado. Indeed, that alone is enough to alert me. If he's that busy, then he's busy as part of preparations for a counterattack. But since I am unable to give specifics as to what a Minbari strike might be, your superiors assume that I am simply refusing to admit what they desire to hear. You see, they think that the Minbari are afraid of Humans." And I proceeded to laugh again, for truly it was a rather amusing thought. "The Minbari . . . afraid of Humans!" I guffawed once more.

"Ambassador—" Sheridan began.

"Tell me, Commander . . . Captain . . . do you have family? Loved ones? Yes, of course you do," I said as they nodded, uncomprehending. "Might I suggest that you spend some time with them. Take vacation time if you have any coming to you. Sick days as well. Trust me on this: Saving it for future use will prove to be an exercise in futility."

And before either Sheridan or Sterns could reply, we began to notice something. From the far ends of the great hall, assorted military aides were moving quickly through the crowd, whispering to officers in hurried conference. As that happened, in each instance, the officers blanched or gasped or in some way or other made clear that they were stunned by what they were hearing.

Jankowski was sipping a drink at the time and he actually choked on it, which made for a most impressive spew. Lefcourt likewise appeared shocked, and someone was approaching Captain Sterns when the news suddenly became common knowledge, courtesy of the large monitor which had been set up in the upper portion of the room.

The monitor was now carrying an Interstellar News Network broadcast, and there was an INN newscaster who looked as stunned as the various officers had been. She was saying, "And this footage, just broadcast to INN, has been confirmed as genuine. We repeat, it is genuine . . . and shocking."

The screen rippled for just a moment, and then we were seeing a broadcast of an Earth fleet located in the depths of space. The broadcast was transmitted from within one ship, and we were seeing what the ship itself was seeing on one of its screens: a cluster of Minbari cruisers, advancing quickly. Other Earth vessels were in evidence, and they were being cut to pieces. A hail of beams tore out of the cruisers, smashing through one Earth ship after another. Ships either erupted quickly in fireballs, or else blasted apart to leave bodies floating in the coldness of space . . . bodies which were promptly incinerated by additional bolts from the Minbari weapons.

We heard a frantic voice, presumably the voice of the captain whose ship was providing us the view of the ghastly tragedy. "This is the *Euripides*, we surrender," he begged— *begged*—them. "For the love of God, we surren—"

He did not manage to get out the rest of the sentence, for we saw a coruscating beam of energy angle toward our view, and then the *Euripides* was promptly blasted out of existence.

We returned to the shaken newscaster, who said, "We repeat: A war fleet believed to belong to the mysterious

Minbari has struck at a core Earthforce base, destroying every single vehicle that—"

Then she stopped, clearly reacting to something off-screen. She mouthed a word . . . the word "no" . . . and then managed to say, "Ladies and gentlemen . . . we have . . . we are going live to Jericho Three . . . a station, a colony with nine hundred residents. It is . . . it is presently under attack by the Minbari . . . repeat, we go live . . ."

"Live" may have been too generous a term. Jericho 3 was the base for the fleet Captain Jankowski had led into Minbari space.

Several Minbari cruisers were clustered around the colony, and they were ripping into it with the same ruthless efficiency that they had used upon the hapless *Euripides*. While two of the vessels were busy slicing through the colony's defenses as if they were not even there, a third targeted the reactor and blew the place to bits. At least those living there did not suffer for a particularly long time.

"A wake," I said once more, for emphasis, as the stunned assemblage watched the drama being played out before their eyes. And then I turned and walked out as the confused clamor began to grow behind me.

Over the next days and weeks, the video log of the *Prometheus* would be transformed from Jankowski's greatest moment to his greatest debacle. Those who had sung his praises would go back, review the material with a jaded eye, and find the captain's performance extremely wanting. His actions would be analyzed, second-guessed, reviewed and re-reviewed. A sequence of events that at one point had been viewed as a great military victory for Earth would come to be seen as the death knell of the Human race, sounded by a captain driven by ego and false pride. The name of Michael Jankowski would come to be synonymous with arrogance run amok.

Given time, they would crucify him.

***

The message went out to the Minbari, and was presented to the Grey Council. They were assembled there, in the blue-gray light of their inner sanctum, as Delenn faced them and announced, "The Humans have offered us a sacrifice. They would send us the one directly responsible for the death of Dukhat . . . a man named Jankowski. He has been tried by the Humans in their military court, been stripped of rank and title. They offer this to us as a means of making amends."

"They are afraid," Morann replied, voice dripping with contempt. "They would shrink from the consequences of their actions. They are terrified of our power, of our might. They would toss one of their own to us in hopes of appeasing us, as if we were some sort of ancient gods to be bought off with a token."

"Perhaps they feel that we seek justice, and hope to provide it for us through the condemnation of the Human who slew Dukhat," Delenn said slowly.

"Justice?" Copelann drew back his hood and addressed the Council. "This isn't about justice. There is no reason to assume that this Earth captain is in any way unique or an aberration, and there is every reason to assume just the opposite! Furthermore, the Humans only offer us this accommodation because of fear. If we were a race weaker than they, or, for that matter, were they to encounter any new races who could not stand up to them, they would continue their barbaric ways unabated!" He slammed a fist into his palm. "Would you negotiate with a hive of stinging creatures if they offered to expel one of their company? No! You would burn the hive away, remove it as the danger that it is! And so must it be with Humanity!"

"Copelann is right!" Morann snarled. "We must stay our course! We must not turn away! In the name of Dukhat, we will ignore this latest plea from the Humans. Besides, it has gone beyond the mandates of the Grey Council. Our people thirst for revenge. They know the Humans for the murderous creatures that they are, and desire nothing more than their obliteration. Were we to turn away from the course we have set, it would tear our population apart."

There were nods from all around.

The question was never even put to a vote. There seemed no need. And Delenn, the death of Dukhat still freshly seared into her mind, said nothing. Gave no voice to her most intimate thoughts. Indeed, there was no reason to, for the inner uncertainties she carried were not yet sufficiently great to vent them to the Council.

For you, Dukhat, went through her mind. And she was vaguely disturbed to find that the thought gave her no satisfaction whatsoever.

—— *chapter 8* ——

The briefing room on Earthdome was packed with Earthforce officers. On a large screen, they were watching what amounted to a visual catalogue of military atrocities. Colony after colony, and ship after ship attempting to defend them, all destroyed. Blasted to scrap metal, blackened and burned, and more lives snuffed out with each passing moment.

On a raised platform, General Lefcourt and an associate of his—an older, thinner, gray-haired general named Fontaine—watched in silence. There were no murmurs passing through the crowd as they witnessed the destruction, no whispered conferences. There was just respectful silence, both for the loss of life that they were witnessing, and for the awareness that they were confronted with power beyond any that they had come to know, expect, or understand.

The screen switched from footage of the Minbari slaughter to a schematic that showed the progress of the fleet. This finally drew a verbal response: startled gasps mostly, followed by a low level of urgent muttering.

Lefcourt's voice cut through the buzzing of voices. "The incidents you have just seen have been repeated at half a dozen bases in just the last few days. Where the Minbari strike, nothing is left alive. Even ships no longer capable of fighting are targeted and destroyed. So surrender on any scale is not an option. Every attempt we've made to communicate with them has been . . . rebuffed."

He did not need to spell it out. Everyone in the room knew what had gone on with Jankowski, knew that his actions had been publicly discredited and he himself offered up as a bargaining chip. The Humans knew nothing of Dukhat, of course. They knew only that Jankowski had fired precipitously, and first, and they were willing to discuss that criminal act with the Minbari, especially if it meant opening a line of communication. But that attempt, along with all the others, had been met with only stony silence.

"They are moving methodically through the outer colonies," Fontaine continued, "wiping out our defense structures, leaving the colonies vulnerable. Civilian structures are being left alone for now. We know the Minbari have a caste system, including a warrior caste, so they may be fighting in a way consistent with that structure, taking out our warriors first, then going after the rest later."

"They intend to eliminate our defensive capability all the way to Earth," Lefcourt predicted ominously. "Then, with no one to stop them, they'll head back out again and finish the job of wiping out every last man, woman, and child of the Human race."

There was a long moment of silence. What was basically a death sentence for Humanity had just been read. They looked at one another, trying to draw upon some ray of hope, unable to find any.

Nor was General Fontaine able to provide any of his own. "Since the first engagement," he told them, "we have not won a single battle against the enemy. Their ships are immensely superior to our own and use some kind of stealth technology we haven't been able to beat yet.

"We called you here because we wanted you to see the situation for yourselves. We want you to go back to your units and make them understand two things: one, that we need a victory against these forces . . . any victory . . . to increase morale; and two, that unless we find some way to defeat the Minbari, the Human race ends with the current generation.

"Dismissed."

It was a curt and abrupt way to address the troops, but Lefcourt saw no other way to handle it. This was not intended to be a session which coddled them or gave them a false sense of security. This was a reality check, designed to put an awareness of imminent annihilation into what were, ideally, the best military minds in the field. This was more extreme than instilling the fear of God into them. After all, the Human God—even on His worst day—had left a handful of Humans in existence for the purpose of perpetuating the species. The Minbari had no such mandate.

In the crowd were Captain Sterns and Commander Sheridan. As the others filed out around them, Sterns looked to Sheridan with something that Sheridan had never seen in the man's eyes before: hopelessness.

"How do we beat them, John?" Sterns asked. "You saw those records. Any ship that goes up against them loses."

Sheridan shook his head vigorously. "I've never believed in the idea of an undefeatable enemy, Captain. Any ship can be destroyed."

"I hope to hell you're right," Sterns said. He paused a moment, considering the situation, and then said, "It'll be a few more days before the *Lexington* is fully outfitted, engines recharged. You could see your folks."

"You're going to need me here, Captain. They'll understand," Sheridan replied briskly.

"You're sure?"

Sheridan was surprised at the lack of certainty in Sterns's voice. "If you were in my position, would you go?"

"Under normal conditions, no. After what I just saw—" He hesitated, then said, "Yeah. I'd go."

The military base was massive. Hundreds of soldiers headed into cargo bays and transports prepared to take off into a starry sky that suddenly seemed far more threatening than it ever had before.

A wavy-haired, rugged young pilot named Ganya Ivanov was in the pilot ready room, pulling together the last of his personal effects, when he heard his name being paged over the public-address system. "You've got a visitor," his sergeant's voice announced. "Room seven! You've got five minutes! Get to it, we've got to launch!"

Ganya looked at his peers in confusion and even with slight suspicion. His last "visitor" had been a rather scantily clad young woman whose presence had been arranged by his cohorts on his birthday the previous month. But no one seemed to be paying him any attention. Instead their thoughts seemed a million miles away. Which they undoubtedly were. So, with a mental shrug, Ganya headed off toward the specified room.

The interview room was very spartan, with white walls, a desk, and two chairs. When he entered he saw that there was a young woman waiting for him, her back to the door, staring thoughtfully at a starmap that was hanging on the wall.

"Susan . . ." he said, "what are you doing here? You were supposed to be at university."

His Russian accent was a bit more pronounced than Susan's. It had to do with the company they had kept growing up, really. Ganya had remained with a fairly small circle of local associates, while Susan had always been far more aggressively "continental" in her tastes. Educated at a number of boarding schools outside the Russian Consortium, she seemed to take a zealous joy in keeping the company of virtually anyone *except* the fairly conservative Russians that her father would have preferred. "You know me," Susan countered. "Never where I'm supposed to be. I wanted to see you before you left."

From outside the room there was the sound of transports taking off, of marching feet. Susan and Ganya had to raise their voices just to be heard. Teasingly, he said, "I thought big brothers were supposed to look after their little sisters, not the other way around."

She shrugged. "So sue me."

"I will," he told her with exaggerated graveness. "Later. After I get back."

There. He had said it. They both knew the subtext of her visit. The words she dared not speak, but which he read in her deep blue eyes. The worry that her brother would go off to fight and die, and she would never see him again. Susan had already suffered terrible losses in her life. She felt as if, were she to sustain one more, she would crack completely. In order to bolster her, Ganya smiled for the first time, and then moved to embrace her. She held him so tightly that he felt his ribs buckling against each other. "I'm just worried, that's all," she admitted. "I keep hearing these terrible stories about what's going on out there."

He shook his head. "It's not as bad as everyone says. We've won several major victories against them already."

She sighed and stepped back. "You always were a terrible liar, Ganya."

His instinct was to try to defend the lie, to say that she had misread him. But he didn't even bother. Susan had indeed somehow always known when he was lying. It was a mystery to him how she was able to tell, but she was. "The important thing," he said confidently, "is that you shouldn't worry. I can't do what I have to if you're going to be worried about me." He patted her on the shoulder. "I'll be fine. The military takes care of its own."

"Good," she said. "Then you'll back me up when I sign up in a few months."

He looked as if she'd just slapped him. "Susan Ivanova, you can't—!"

Whenever Susan Ivanova had decided that a subject was effectively closed, she folded her arms tightly. She did so now. "I'll be old enough then. On the news they say they need everyone who can fight."

In his heart, Ganya knew the truth—that it was slim odds of the Human race even surviving those few months until Susan's enrollment and training would prepare her for combat. But he wasn't about to tell her that. Approaching from a different direction, he said, "Father won't stand for it."

"It's my choice, not his."

"You don't need to do this . . ."

Then the sergeant's voice sounded once more over the public-address system. "Ivanov, Ganya . . . report to Bay Nine for immediate launch."

Ganya felt a flash of regret. She'd come all this way, gone to so much effort to see him, and they'd wound up spending what might be their last moments together arguing over a matter that would very likely be moot. "I have to go," Ganya said tonelessly. He paused uneasily for a moment, wanting to be strong for her and finding it difficult. "Take care of Father while I'm gone. And . . ."

She always knew he was lying. She always knew. And so, with every fiber of his being, he had to believe what he was about to say so that she, too, would believe it. With 100 percent conviction he said, "And I'll see you soon. I love you, little sister."

She smiled. She believed. Or at least she wanted to. "I love you, too."

He started to turn away, to head out the door, and then she called, "Wait! Remember . . ." She fished for words, and then hauled them in. "Remember when we got lost when we were camping, and then I lost my earring and we got found and you made me feel better by telling me it was lucky? And then we played on the same team, and I had only the one earring and we won—"

Her words had come out all in a rush, and it had been difficult for Ganya to follow all that she said, but he nodded gamely. "Of course I remember, but—"

She removed one of her earrings and handed it to him. "Take it, for good luck. I won't wear it again until you come back. Until you give it back to me. That way we know you'll come back."

He hesitated a moment. Her small hand was folded into his, and they remained that way for a moment. He smiled and nodded, took the earring, and slid it into his pocket. Then he took her head between his hands, and kissed her on the forehead.

"I'll see you soon," Ganya said, and he was gone.

Many years later, Susan Ivanova would tell me of that moment. As was so often the case with these revelations, it would occur in the Zocalo, the "watering hole" of Babylon 5, and she would be quietly drinking herself into a stupor as she memorialized the anniversary of that day. She would sit there, speaking of Ganya, and the entire time she was gently pulling at her earlobe. The one that was devoid of an earring. I stayed there with her, probably the only one on the station who could match her drink for drink.

She told me of how she maintained herself and her steadiness until after Ganya left the room. Then she watched him go, peering through the window in the room, and it was only at that point that she allowed the emotion to overwhelm her and the tears to pour down her face.

Curiously, she shed no tears in the Zocalo when she related it to me.

I think she was out of them.

***

At a transfer point of the transport station, John Sheridan waited for the next westbound transport. He paced, annoyed with himself that he was taking the time away. But Sterns's words had haunted him, and he had finally decided to take the time to go and visit his parents. For the future appeared bleak, and if worse came to worst, well, he would very likely have enough regrets in his life without having to dwell on one more.

There was another member of the fleet at the same station. He was on the eastbound side, waiting for the ground transportation that would take him to the central staging point where pilots were assembling . . . which only made sense, since, from his uniform markings, it was clear that he was a pilot.

Sheridan looked the other man up and down. He was of fairly serious demeanor, with dark hair and heavy eyebrows. There seemed to be an almost piercing intelligence in his eyes, and when he spoke it was in a deep voice that seemed to originate from somewhere around his ankles. "Where you heading?" he said conversationally.

"Colorado," Sheridan said.

"Good." The pilot nodded approvingly. "If the Minbari attack Boulder, it'll be nice to know we have a line of defense there."

He said it so seriously, with such a straight face, that it took Sheridan a moment to digest that the pilot was making a joke. "I have family there," Sheridan explained.

"I figured as much," the pilot said amiably. "Wife? Kids?"

"Parents," Sheridan said. "And my sister, if she makes it in. But no wife or kids, no."

"Any prospects?"

Sheridan shrugged. "Well, my sister keeps trying to set me up with her best friend." He paused. "You?"

"Just coming back from visiting my . . . significant other," the pilot said.

"Fiancée?"

"Catherine and I decided to leave it open, at the moment."

"Open." Sheridan laughed softly and sadly. "Very optimistic, making long-term plans that way."

"I have no choice," the pilot said. "I have to believe we can win. I have to believe I'm coming back. If I didn't—if I didn't have an intrinsic lack of belief in my own mortality—I couldn't climb into the cockpit of my Starfury."

"Understood." Sheridan nodded.

"Humanity will survive, you know."

There was something in the pilot's voice that, for the first time, fully engaged Sheridan's attention. "How are you so sure? Lack of belief in *everyone's* mortality?"

"Instinct," the pilot said confidently. "I do not . . . cannot . . . believe that everything that Humanity has accomplished, that everything we've aspired to, will simply come to an end. To be obliterated by a superior race, just because they can. There has to be more to them, and more to us, than that." He shifted his weight to one foot and stood with his hip slightly outthrust. "I've studied other races, you know. Charted their progress. For every single one, their development has been far, far slower than ours. It's as if we're rushing, or even being rushed. As if we're intended for some great purpose that's coming upon us sooner than we think."

"You're saying we have a destiny." Sheridan smiled. Had to admire the man for his zeal if nothing else.

"Yes," the pilot said with complete sincerity. "A destiny. A destiny that has to involve more than being the victims of genocide. I feel it. I feel it in my soul."

Sheridan wanted to say, *Good place*, but it sounded too flip. Then he felt a rush of air as the maglev ground transport heading westbound glided into the station. Sheridan gripped his overnight bag firmly and then held out a hand to the pilot. "John Sheridan," he said. "Best of luck to you . . . and your soul."

The pilot shook the proffered hand and replied, "Jeffrey Sinclair. The same to you."

His last view of Sinclair as the transport pulled away was of the solitary pilot, waiting on the station platform and being surrounded by other passengers. In a crowd and yet, somehow . . . alone.

He promptly gave the meeting no further thought and, indeed, within a week or so had more or less forgotten about it. Just another chance chat with a fellow member of Earthforce.

It would not be until the Mars Riots some time later that they would encounter each other again, their chance meeting upon a transit station a long-faded memory.

How fortunate for some that memories can fade.

Would that I could forget.

My presence, meantime, was required most urgently at Earthdome. This did not come as a tremendous surprise to me. Just as Jankowski's stock had plummeted with the advent of the war, mine had risen. I had warned them not to confront the Minbari. I had presented myself at their victory celebration and told them precisely the consequences of their rash actions. They had not believed . . . but now, now they believed. And the presidential aide, Hastur, was quite convinced that simply admitting that belief would assuage my ego and bring me solidly into the Earth camp.

We walked slowly down a hallway that was lined with various documents and memorabilia celebrating Earth's incursions and expeditions into space. Hastur was, by turns, cajoling, flattering, wheedling. But I knew what it was he wanted, and I simply kept shaking my head and saying, "I'm sorry, but there is nothing I can do."

Hastur kept his hands pressed together, constantly flexing

his fingers as if he were molding clay, or perhaps trying to shape a situation to his liking. "We're not asking the Centauri government to intervene militarily. We know that won't happen." He made it sound as if it were the most obvious thing in the world, when the fact was that they had already approached us, repeatedly, on that very topic, and been unhesitatingly turned away. "We're talking here tactical and strategic support."

"And weapons," I added in a "but of course" manner.

"You and the Minbari are two of the older races. Your technology is far above our own. If we had access to some of your weapons we'd at least have a fighting chance."

He was, of course, welcome to think that. It was not exactly an opinion that I, or anyone in my government, shared. Had it been, we might have taken the chance if there was sufficient gain to be had. As it was, it would have been madness. But I had no desire to get into a debate over what chances the Humans might or might not have if we merely gave them combat technology. Opting to bypass the entire discussion, I simply said, "It is not our policy to supply advanced weapons to developing worlds."

"We'll pay any price," Hastur said quickly.

"Yes, and then we will pay the price when the Minbari come after *us* for helping *you*. No, there is not enough money in your entire planet to justify that risk."

"Londo, if you'd just listen . . ."

At which point I had had enough. If *I* would listen? I had tried to caution them, to tell them what it was they were getting themselves into. They had not listened to me. Now I was supposed to heed their words?

"Listen?" I demanded. "To what? The voice of a race that is about to become extinct?"

My pronouncement of the fate of Hastur's kind was, I admit, somewhat harsh, and the look on his face certainly reflected that. But I was not feeling particularly genteel that day, or receptive to being made to feel guilty over a situation that I had tried to warn them away from. I shook my head and said, "No, I'm sorry. I've always been very fond of Humans, but we cannot risk angering the Minbari. There is nothing I can do. I'm sorry," I said again, and then walked away.

Hastur stayed there until I was gone, undoubtedly thinking that I was unaware of what he was going to do next. No greater fool was there than Hastur, I can tell you. My spies informed me of his every intention before it even was acted upon.

Why?

Because the individual he was to meet with had a very big mouth.

His name was G'Kar, and in later years he would develop into perhaps the most canny, most implacable, and most formidable individual I had ever met. But at that point in time he was young and foolish, and did not hesitate to spout his plans to assorted lieutenants. Lieutenants who were, in turn, all too eager to supply information to me in exchange for certain perks and privileges that I accorded them under the table. That was always the Narns' problem, you see. Insufficient unity. Even though, at that point, the Narns had freed themselves of Centauri rule, there were still those who were all too eager to keep on the good side of the Centauri in the event of a—shall we say, regression in relations?

Through them, I learned of the meeting between G'Kar and Hastur which took place mere moments after the Human and I had parted company.

G'Kar was a powerfully built Narn, with the blazing red eyes typical of that race; the brown, spotted, and hairless skin; and an outthrust jaw that only added to his general air of pugnaciousness and arrogance. He was also a member of the Kha'Ri, the central governors of the Narn regime.

He was seated in a chair in Hastur's darkened office, waiting patiently for what he was certain Hastur would say. When Hastur entered, G'Kar wasted no time on small talk. "Well?" he said.

Hastur sighed. "He refused to help . . . as you said he would."

G'Kar leaned forward and smiled with satisfaction, his red eyes glowing with excitement. "The Centauri care for no one but themselves. They would sooner see your world in flames than lift a finger to help."

Harsh words, considering that when I had proffered a finger earlier, it had been to point the Humans away from a path of self-destruction. But it is always far more convenient for the aggrieved party to feel that their difficulties are the result of someone other than themselves. Hastur nodded, appreciative to hear something akin to consoling words from another race. "So it would seem," he admitted. Then he clapped his hands together briskly. "All right then, G'Kar. What help can we expect from the Narns?"

G'Kar again leaned forward, eagerly, into a stark beam of light that accentuated the coarseness of his spotted skin. "When we drove the Centauri from our world after a hundred years of occupation, we seized many of their weapons. We took them apart, studied them, learned to turn their own weapons against them. And we are willing to sell them to you."

Hastur could already feel butterflies of hope flitting about in his stomach. "Aren't you worried about the Minbari?" he asked.

G'Kar shook his head. "If they capture any of the equipment, they will assume it came from the Centauri, attack them . . . and we win by default. And if they should learn that the weapons came from us . . ." He shrugged. "We endured slavery for a hundred years. A slave is immune to the fear of dying, because to die is simply to end the cycle of pain."

Hastur could not have been less interested in Narn slavery, history, or cycles of pain. "How much can you sell us?" he asked eagerly.

"As much as you can afford. But the price will be high," G'Kar cautioned him. "Human currency has been devalued on the interstellar market, so it will take a great deal to convince the Kha'Ri to sell you arms and provide support. But I believe it can be done. Assuming we have a deal."

The aide stuck out a hand and said, "We have a deal, G'Kar."

Within half an hour of the deal being struck, I knew of it.

And within twenty-four Earth hours of my awareness, I had managed to finally get word through to my contacts with the Minbari. I admit, I did hesitate over it slightly. The providing of weapons was a straw at which the Humans were clutching, and my decision to endeavor to deprive them of it was not one lightly made.

Then again, the Narns were endeavoring to get us into trouble with the Minbari. That was the deciding element, really. One bad turn, after all, deserves another.

Even though Jankowski had been busted in rank, it was decided that day that he was to be brought in for further debriefing. For that matter, there were some who were advocating that he should be brought in in some sort of advisory capacity, for there was no denying one simple fact: He was the only captain to survive a direct conflict with the Minbari. General Lefcourt sent word to Jankowski's apartment that he was to report immediately.

There was no response.

A military attaché was sent there to retrieve him, and knocked on the door authoritatively. Still, there was no response from within. The attaché gained entrance to the apartment and the stench hit him immediately. Before his eyes adjusted to the flickering darkness, his nose had already told him what had happened.

Jankowski, or what was left of him, was seated in front of a screen. Playing across the screen was a series of scenes strung together, clearly recorded by Jankowski and edited together as some sort of private collection. It was scene after scene of Minbari destruction, blasting apart ships, slaughtering thousands of innocent people, intercut with the video log of the *Prometheus* and Jankowski giving the order to open fire, thereby starting the war.

There was a note next to Jankowski's body. There was also a Phased Plaser Gun which had slipped from Jankowski's lifeless hand. The note simply had three words: "On my head." Blackly ironic, one supposes, considering that the remains of Jankowski's head were rather difficult to come by after the PPG had blown off the top of it.

And the number of captains who had truly survived an encounter with the Minbari had, just that quickly, dropped to zero.

Sheridan's parents, David and Nancy, and his sister, Elizabeth, had made quite the fuss over his homecoming. It was as if there was an unspoken dedication toward trying to avoid dwelling on the trip's purpose. Instead they spoke of trivialities, of family plans. They laughed over incidents from the past, chatted about routine gossip. On the surface, it was no different from any other family reunion.

Around eight in the evening, there was a knock at the door. Sheridan remained in the comfortably furnished living room, discussing the outlook for next year's baseball season as if it were a given that there was going to be one. He heard Elizabeth talking to someone and then, moments later, Elizabeth walked in with a slim, brown-haired woman at her side. Sheridan reflexively rose, and somehow immediately knew who it was even before Elizabeth said a word.

"Mom, Dad, you remember Anna," she said, then turned to John and said, with a mischievous expression, "John, this is Anna Keller. Anna, my brother, John."

She extended a hand. He took it firmly, and looked deep into her eyes . . .

. . . and felt nothing.

This was her? This was the girl that Elizabeth had spoken of so often as being the ideal match for her brother? She seemed pleasant enough, certainly. Exceedingly attractive, in fact. And Sheridan studied her the rest of the evening, as she remained and joined in with the Sheridan family conversation. She was most certainly bright. A pleasant conversationalist, a charming raconteur, and—as it turned out—a horrible singer when she jumped into an off-key rendition of an old show tune. But she was enthusiastic, John had to give her that.

That was all, though.

The evening ended on a pleasant enough note, and after Anna had left, Elizabeth turned eagerly to her brother and said, "What did you think?"

"Could you be any more obvious?" John asked her sarcastically.

"Probably not. So what did you think?" she repeated.

"She seemed nice, Elizabeth."

"And . . . ?"

"And . . ." He shrugged. "And that's all. What do you want me to say, that there were wild sparks? That I was half tempted to sling her over my shoulder, take her out, and ravish her? She's a nice woman, sis, and that's it. Period. I didn't feel any chemistry, any spark, anything that I know you want me to say I feel. I'm sorry. Should I lie to you?"

"Of course not," she said, but she made no effort to hide her disappointment.

Sheridan spent the night fitfully, lying on his bed and staring up at the stars through the skylight. He had always used to enjoy this view. Not anymore. Now all he could do was picture others like him up there, fighting, dying, while the enemy relentlessly sliced through them as if they meant nothing.

Word had reached him about Jankowski, and it had saddened him. Heaven knows he had no love for the man, but he wouldn't have wished such a pointless death on anyone. Then again, was it any more pointless than the deaths of those who were flying valiantly into battle with the Minbari, to fight and die against overwhelming odds?

There has to be a way to beat them. There has to be. The thought consumed Sheridan and he did not sleep much that night. The next morning he decided there was no point in waiting around any longer, and so he quickly packed his change of clothes and headed for the front door while everyone in the house was still sleeping.

Or, at least, he thought that was the case.

But when he emerged into the living room, he was surprised to see his father, David, sitting there. He looked for all the world as if he'd been expecting his son to come tiptoeing through.

"Going somewhere, John?" he asked.

"I . . . really have to get back. Captain's expecting me."

David nodded understandingly. Then, surprisingly, he said, "What did you think of Anna? Nice girl."

"Very nice girl," Sheridan said, a bit impatiently.

"But no spark."

"No, no spark," he said to his father, looking rather uncomfortable with the discussion. "Why does everyone have a problem with that?"

"No problem with it, son. Except it seems from where I sit that you just sort of figure, well, hell, why bother getting attached? No point. We're all dead soon anyway."

"I don't think that," Sheridan said, a bit more sharply than he would have liked. He looked down at his feet and then said, "Good-bye, Dad."

David sighed and shook his head. "Shame for you to come all this way and not say what you came here to say."

Sheridan dropped his overnight bag to the floor with barely concealed exasperation. "Well, why don't you tell me what that is? I mean, you seem to know everything I'm thinking. So save me the time of having to say it."

"All right," David said, sounding disgustingly reasonable about it all. "You want to tell me how angry you are that I inserted myself into your career. That no matter how great your accomplishments, no matter what you achieve in your career, you're always going to wonder whether or not you would have managed anything of true importance without me. Here's the answer: No."

Sheridan felt his jaw tighten at his father's apparent smugness, but David continued unhesitatingly, "And that's only fair. Because, you see, I could never have accomplished anything of importance without you."

He gaped at his father. "What are you talking about? You have your career, your achievements . . ."

But David Sheridan waved them off dismissively. "I'm a diplomat, John. That's all. A successful one, but a diplomat nonetheless, and diplomats are a credit a dozen. It took me a large portion of my life to realize that the truly important things in my life are right here, in this house, at this moment. My God, John . . . you're about to go out and try to contribute whatever you can to saving this planet. I have never been prouder of anything in my life. But in the final analysis, all I did was put you here. You did the rest. Yet I'd like to think that you wouldn't deny me taking some personal pride in that, would you?"

Sheridan half smiled. "No, sir."

With an amused chuckle, Sheridan admitted, "Not off the top of my head, no."

"Good."

They stood there for a time, the distance between them seeming to shrink ever so slightly. Nonetheless, there seemed to be something more. Something that Sheridan needed . . . and he had no idea what it was.

And his father asked him a deceptively simple four-word question:

"What do you want?"

"What do I want?" Sheridan asked. His father nodded. And Sheridan, without hesitation, said, "I want to know how to defeat the Minbari. I want to see my people take pride in themselves and live without the fear of possible obliteration. I want . . ."

And he thought of the man from the transport junction. He thought of Sinclair.

"I want to know that there was some point to it all. Some greater purpose, some meaning to existence, rather than that we simply came this far so we could all go to hell in one great flaming ruin. That's what I want."

"Then you'll have it," his father said with confidence.

"How do you know, Dad?"

"Because," his father replied, "I have never, in my life, known you not to get something that you wanted if you really, truly put your mind to achieving it. And with so much at stake, I don't expect this to be the first time you fail." He paused, then added with conviction, "You won't let us down, John. You won't let yourself down. Not the John Sheridan *I* know. The man I'm proud to call my son."

He wasn't much of a hugger, David Sheridan wasn't. So when he tried to do it with his son, it was an awkward and unaccustomed movement. But his son took it for what it was: a valiant effort. And he returned the embrace.

"You're a hell of a diplomat, Dad," John said.

"Got no choice. I have to live up to the standard of excellence set by my son." He patted him on the shoulder. "Come back safely, John."

"It's the only way *to* come back, Dad. And I know I will. After all," and he smiled, "it's what I want."

—— chapter 9 ——

Delenn did not know what she wanted.

She looked out of the window of her quarters within the Minbari cruiser. Delenn had been doing more and more investigation into the Humans, now that they were the enemy. Specifically, she had researched their history of warfare, and quite a formidable history it was. She had gone as far back as she could, and had been intrigued by Human wars which had a scope that bordered on the mythic.

There was one in particular, the Trojan War, that interested her for three reasons (of course).

First, because the Trojan War had involved an individual who predicted disaster and foresaw a great enemy . . . and would not be believed. Much like Lenonn, who had arrived but moments before, and who even now was seated near her, lost in his own thoughts.

Second, because there was a large vehicle involved, a Trojan "horse"—an Earth animal—which appeared to be nonthreatening, but in fact contained a hidden enemy . . . much like the *Prometheus*.

And third . . . there was a woman. A woman named Helen, the cause of the war. Hers was said to be the face that launched a thousand ships.

Helen.

Delenn.

Similarity in names, to be sure. And as she imagined her reflection superimposed over the ships of the fleet—her face upon the vessels—she saw irony that was impossible to ignore.

There was another Earth saying she had stumbled upon: Those who do not listen to the lessons of history are doomed to repeat it. So many people died in the Trojan War . . . in all the wars thereafter . . . and for what? For what? Border disputes that could have, should have, been resolved in some other way. Incidents that seemed to demand bloody retribution and became bloodbaths in which millions of innocent lives were lost.

And, unlike Minbari, who believed that their souls went on to new incarnations, Humans were not uniform in their beliefs as to what happened after they died. Which meant that they risked their lives, were willing to throw them away, with no consensus as to whether that sacrifice would have any long-term meaning. They hurled themselves into the void and, for all some of them knew, they were never coming back, nor were they likely heading toward anything except eternal oblivion.

The face that launched a thousand ships was stony and silent, and could not help but feel that, from somewhere near, Dukhat was watching.

And frowning.

She heard the door open behind her, but gave no indication to that effect. Instead she continued to stare out the window, as if hypnotized by the view. When the new arrival spoke, she immediately knew the voice as Morann's. For some reason, she was not surprised.

In recent days, Morann's attitude toward her had seemed to shift. Whereas originally he'd had little patience for her, somehow the crucible of war had forged—if not a full alliance—at least a grudging respect for her.

"Good evening, Delenn," he said. When she made no reply, he held up a data crystal. "The latest reports from the front. Three more of the Humans' deep-range colonies have fallen."

Speaking so softly that he had to strain to hear her, she told him, "Leave it on the table."

He did so, but did not immediately depart. Instead he eyed her with curiosity. "I should think you would be pleased by the progress of the war."

She turned to face him. "What pleasure can be found in beating an enemy that never had the slightest chance of defeating us?"

He sounded mildly scolding as he said, "Is that sympathy I hear in your voice, Delenn? I'm surprised. You were the chosen of Dukhat, after all. You were his favorite. Does his death mean so little to you?"

She gestured toward space as if she could encompass the whole of the Minbari fleet with one wave of her arm. "Dukhat would never have approved of this slaughter!"

"Perhaps." Morann agreed so readily that it quickly became clear to Delenn that Morann might well have struggled with that very thought. But if he had done so, he was not about to admit it. Either that, or he had dismissed it as not worth considering. "We will never know, because the Humans murdered him. This is simple retribution."

She shook her head. "This has gone beyond retribution, Morann. This is madness. It is genocide."

Lenonn finally broke his silence. "Yes, it is. And you're right, Delenn. The Humans cannot oppose us. So one can only wonder why the warrior caste has embraced this war so enthusiastically. Would you like to know what I suspect?"

"I'm breathless with anticipation," Morann said sarcastically.

Rising from his place, Lenonn speculated, "The warrior caste loves to win and hates to lose. It's easier to fight a weaker opponent and be guaranteed victory than to oppose a far more dangerous enemy."

The insinuation was that the warrior caste was composed of cowards, but Morann ignored it, since it was literally beneath commenting upon. Instead he focused on Lenonn's now almost mythic paranoia. "Are we back on the Shadows again?"

"They will come," Lenonn said. "Soon."

"Legends," Morann said dismissively. "Nothing more. The Humans are a real enemy. An enemy I can touch, see . . . and kill." He drew himself up proudly. "This we have done, and this we will continue to do, with no help from your so-called Rangers."

"They continue to watch for the true danger," Lenonn warned.

"Do they?" Morann asked sarcastically. "How ambitious." He circled Lenonn, voice dripping with contempt. "Watch the frontier and report back. Better than engaging the enemy. Better than risking their lives. And considerably better than dying, is it not, Lenonn? Sometimes I wonder where your loyalty really is."

Lenonn trembled with barely contained rage. "You dare?" he whispered.

Driving home the point, Morann sneered, "Or is it simpler just to be a coward?"

Morann never even saw Lenonn's hand move. But in the next instant, the denn-bok, the fighting pike that was the preferred weapon of every Ranger, was extended. Morann took a cautious step back, suddenly realizing that he might have gone too far. For all his years, for all his obsessions, Lenonn was not a threat to be dismissed. Indeed, at that moment all of his anger was singularly focused on Morann, and it seemed as if he were angry enough to smash Morann back into another incarnation.

Then Delenn stepped in between the two of them, her hands outstretched, forming a barrier. "Stop this!" she said angrily. "Stop it, both of you! Morann . . . get out."

Sounding not unlike a recalcitrant child, Morann started to say, "I was simply—"

But Delenn would hear none of it. "I said *get out*!"

Morann paused for a moment, just long enough that it didn't seem as if he were hopping to instantly obey Delenn's command. At his own pace, he slowly headed for the door. But he paused at the exit, to throw back over his shoulder, "You're too old to command the *Anla-Shok*, Lenonn. You would do well to give it to those young enough to fight. Then you can go off to the sea, and join your beloved Valen."

It was easy enough for him to be confident at that point, of course, now that the immediate threat from Lenonn was past. With his customary swagger, he strode out of the room, leaving a very quiet Delenn and an extremely chagrined Lenonn, who retracted his fighting pike and turned to face Delenn.

He bowed slightly in deference. "I'm sorry, Delenn. I was your guest, and I acted poorly."

She shook her head. "You only did what I would have done if I had a pike in my hands. No apologies are required." She turned back to the window, dwelling on Lenonn's warnings, and thinking of Troy, and the unbelieved predictions of Cassandra. For one moment she envisioned the majestic crystal towers of Minbar, with flames licking the skies, while powerful and frightening black vessels hovered overhead. And screams . . . there were screams, and whether they came from within her, from the ships, or from the withering soul of Minbar itself, she couldn't begin to tell.

Endeavoring to dispel the dark mood that had fallen upon her, she said, "When you arrived, you said you had some information for me?"

"I have arranged for the transfer of all Dukhat's belongings to this ship," Lenonn told her. "I have brought everything that was his, Delenn. Even re-created his sanctum. Only you and I have access for now."

His tone was very peculiar, but Delenn—wrapped up in her thoughts—didn't notice at first. She nodded absently, appreciative in a distant manner of Lenonn's dedication to the memory of Dukhat. But she didn't take it beyond that.

Lenonn realized that he wasn't quite getting through to her. He was silent for a moment to provide a contrast, and then he cleared his throat extremely loudly. It was such an odd sound for him to make that it caught Delenn's attention. That was when he said, with as much unspoken meaning as possible, "I think you should go there, Delenn. I think you should go as soon as possible."

She looked at him quizzically, but he said nothing more. Merely bowed and exited.

Delenn waited there another moment, glanced one more time at the formidable fleet arrayed around them, and then headed out after Lenonn. But when she stepped into the hallway, there was no sign of him. She stopped a passing crewman and asked him where Dukhat's possessions had been transferred to, and was given directions to a previously empty quarters two decks up.

Delenn quickly made her way there. She paused when she saw a pair of Minbari religious-caste guards standing outside the doors. But when she drew within range, they quickly stepped out of her way, as if intuiting that she wished to enter.

Lenonn had been right. She had been in Dukhat's quarters any number of times, and the reconstruction was amazing. It was virtually a shrine to the great, fallen leader. But it was . . . it was different, somehow. Darker, more foreboding. As she entered, and stopped in front of a wall hanging that resembled the triluminary itself, shadows seemed to move almost with a life of their own. Suddenly everything that Lenonn had been warning about seemed to vibrate with new resonance within her.

It wasn't her imagination, she realized. The shadows *were* moving, coming toward her, and . . .

She stepped back, gasped in surprise, her hand fluttering to her mouth as a form separated itself from a corner of the room. And there was a sound accompanying the movement, a sound that seemed like rippling musical notes.

The being who had emerged was like none that she had ever seen. He (she? it?) was garbed inside a massive, fairly shapeless encounter suit—an immense, deep red, heavily robed garment that served as a sort of movable and protective atmosphere-containment unit. Its cloak looked like great folds of chain mail. There was a huge, angular, cyclopean helmet upon its head (or at least what she presumed to be its head), and the projections on what approximated the shoulders bore a faint resemblance—if one were given to flights of fancy—to wings.

The musicality, like the sighing of stringed instruments, sounded all around her, and she wasn't sure how much was actually in the room and how much was in her own head. The alien being simply stood there, apparently waiting to see what she would say, what she would do.

"What . . . who are you?" Delenn managed to get out, but by the time she had spoken the words she already knew the answer. This must have been the individual whom she had overheard Dukhat talking to when she had inadvertently eavesdropped outside his quarters. The chime, the tonality of the sounds accompanying it, was unmistakable. "You're . . . are you a Vorlon?" she asked slowly.

It/he/whatever nodded. With a being so slow and ponderous, even the most minute and casual action seemed filled with portent. And this time a word—the same word she'd heard uttered all that time before—floated out of whatever and wherever the being's mouth might be.

"Yes."

"Yes."

She had not expected the second response, for she had not seen the second Vorlon. She couldn't quite understand how in the world she had missed it. For that matter, how had they moved about on the cruiser undetected? The religious-caste guards had not looked particularly perturbed, didn't act as if there were extraordinary, legendary beings in the room that they were guarding. How had they gotten in there? In crates, perhaps. That was the most logical notion. Lenonn had had them transported in crates and left in the room. They would not have needed air to survive within the confinement of the crate, since the encounter suit would give them all the atmosphere support they required.

Or perhaps they simply willed themselves from one place to the next. With Vorlons, anything was presumed possible.

The second was costumed similarly to the first one, though its helmet was dark blue, and possessed a glowing red eye in its center. The edges of the encounter suit seemed sharper somehow, more curved and even a bit more (and here her imagination might have gone a bit overboard) threatening.

"What . . . is your name?" she asked the first Vorlon.

"Kosh," it replied.

She turned, waited for the second Vorlon to respond. But no reply was forthcoming, and she had the sneaking suspicion that she could have stood there from that moment until Doomsday and the imposing being would not answer. "What do you want?" she continued. "What are you doing here?"

"Creating the future."

In the frontpiece of the helmet belonging to the one called Kosh, a small green "eye" irised open. The air shimmered in front of it, and Delenn was stunned to see a holographic image of Dukhat.

She was horrified to realize that, in her mental picture of him, she had already—*already*—begun to lose small details from her recollection of him. The details of his posture, the exact timbre of his voice, she wasn't sure exactly how she remembered them, until she saw them in the image.

When Dukhat spoke it was in a fairly straightforward, matter-of-fact manner, as if he were not delivering information that could and would have serious ramifications for all the Minbari, past, present, and future.

"If you are seeing this message, it is because I am dead," Dukhat said. He did not seem daunted by the prospect of his own demise. Indeed, he appeared slightly amused at the prospect. "I leave this in trust of the Vorlons to give it to the right person, at the right time. I ask you to trust them as I have."

He was not necessarily speaking to Delenn, or anticipating doing so. He was trusting in the judgment of the Vorlons. She couldn't help but hope that, wherever Dukhat was at that point in time, he would be pleased that the Vorlons had selected her for . . .

For . . .

For what?

Unaware of the inner turmoil that was racing through Delenn's thoughts, the holographic image continued unwaveringly. "They have come to us in secret, to prepare for the coming war. They say we will need allies . . . in particular a race that is, so far, unknown to us, called Humans."

Upon her hearing that, it was as if someone had connected a wire to her spine and sent a powerful jolt through her. It took her a moment or two to fully refocus on what Dukhat was saying. "If we have not already done so by now, it is my hope that you will work with the Vorlons to find these . . . Humans . . . and bring them into the battle on our side."

On our side? she wanted to scream at the projection. *On our side? We are in the process of systematically exterminating them to avenge* your *death and you tell us now they're supposed to be on* our *side?* She was shaking her head in slow disbelief as Dukhat continued, "The allies of the Shadows are gathering at Z'ha'dum. Their masters cannot be far behind. They must be stopped. Finish the work I began. Finish it . . ." Then he vanished.

Why did you not bring them before the Grey Council? Delenn's mind demanded irrationally of the projection, for naturally it could neither hear nor respond, and the originator was gone. It was terribly frustrating, for she had no idea why. No idea at all . . .

Yes. Yes, she did.

Valen had told them. Prophecy had told them. Lenonn had told them. Even Dukhat had once asked about a rumored race called Humans, an inquiry lost in the squabbles of the Grey Council. Everything that they needed in order to do the right thing had been shown to them.

Lenonn had been right after all . . . right about the Minbari falling from the light, right about their not being worthy. They had no faith. That was the problem. They should have taken their predicted future on faith. The Vorlons wanted them to have that faith, for that would have made them worthy. But they did not, and so the Vorlons had only appeared to their greatest leader. To Dukhat, and now to her.

To *her*. Which made her part in all of this . . . what, exactly? She did not know for sure, but a part of it she most definitely was, whatever "it" turned out to be.

It was only then that the full, true horror of their situation dawned on her, with such fearsome magnitude that she was completely appalled. "The Humans," she whispered, as if admitting some deep-down, horrific secret.

"Yes. They are the key," Kosh intoned with that haunting musicality.

She looked at the empty air where the holographic image had floated only moments before. "He . . . didn't know. Couldn't know that . . . we are at war with them." She could only imagine the awfulness of Dukhat's dying moments. She realized now, beyond any question, that with his last words he must have been trying to tell her that. To force the words from the depths of his dying body, because he would have known the horrible consequences the Humans were about to face because of their actions.

In response to Delenn's observation, Lenonn's voice suddenly spoke. "And that is why it must be stopped."

He moved toward her, and she had no idea whether he had been present in the room all along, or had just entered now. But how long he had been there was secondary to her attempting to fully comprehend the information she had been given.

"You knew?" she asked in surprise.

He nodded. "I found out when I arrived, when Dukhat and I worked out our strategy for involving the Grey Council and the warrior caste."

Strategy? The entire meeting had been orchestrated? She wasn't entirely certain how to feel about that. It meant that Dukhat had been less than candid with them, had endeavored to manipulate them, and had indeed succeeded. He'd worked in tandem with Lenonn, giving the Grey Council the impression that they were operating under free will, when the fact was that they were being maneuvered through a carefully choreographed bit of politicking. Delenn wasn't certain whether to be amused, angry, or somewhere in between.

As if sensing her momentary confusion and borderline

anger, Lenonn made an impatient gesture as if to indicate that the time for such indecision was past. "We have lost valuable time already due to this . . . distraction. If we do not end this soon, more time will be lost. We must stop the Great War before it starts . . . or millions of lives will be lost."

—— chapter 10 ——

Let me tell you about Dr. Stephen Franklin.

A more dedicated, hardworking, and occasionally sancti-
monious Human I cannot recall meeting. He was in charge
of the medical facilities on Babylon 5. He was so driven that
he almost drove himself crazy there for a while. Then again,
we all have our temporary insanities, I suppose . . . some
of us less temporary than others, when you think about it.

Franklin was a solidly built, square-jawed man with a
deceptively gentle face that went a long way toward hiding an utterly uncompromising personality. He also had
somewhat darker skin than most Humans I encountered.
Apparently on Earth entire wars have been fought over
the subject of skin pigmentation. In all my reading about
Humans, I was never able to determine precisely why that
was. Then again, Humans excel at needing no reasons to
do whatever it is they wish. A very, very odd race.

Prior to the Earth/Minbari War, Dr. Franklin had ended
his association with Earthforce. He had some—shall we say
unresolved?—difficulties with his father, a general in that
branch of the service, and as a result had left Earthforce—

and Earth, for that matter—to carve a career for himself that had no military attachments. However, when the war broke out Franklin's conscience got the better of him and he returned to Earth and volunteered to help in whatever way he could. He was immediately pressed into service to prepare for the inevitable flood of wounded.

When he had first been introduced to the facilities in Earthdome that were intended to act as an infirmary designed to cater to the needs of Earthforce personnel, he had been appalled. Then he had been angry. And then he had put his foot down. As a consequence, he'd gotten his foot stepped on.

At which point, with great reluctance, he had brought his father into the picture.

His rationalization for involving General Richard Franklin was that Franklin-the-elder had just as much interest in quality facilities as did his son. It was up to Stephen to be able to stitch injured men back together again, and it was incumbent upon Richard to make certain that the care being offered was the best care anywhere.

So when Stephen came to the conclusion that the facility being offered to him was substandard—there were very few returning survivors, after all—he felt he must let the appropriate authorities know. He could think of no one more appropriate than General Franklin, and no one more capable of getting things done, as well. On that, Stephen had been absolutely correct. The Earthdome facilities were, indeed, brought up to snuff.

The bottom line, of course, was that Stephen had had to swallow some pride. But when it came to the needs of men and women who were risking their lives, then Dr. Franklin would gladly take a large heaping helping of pride stacked three meters high.

Franklin was, at that moment, in the process of taking several doctors on a guided tour of the infirmary.

Before the tour, they had expressed a great many concerns, and that was understandable. None of them had any idea exactly what they'd be facing. All they knew was that they'd be dealing with patients who might be wounded in ways that were completely unknown to Earth medical science. So it was understood that they were going to need topflight equipment to deal with it. Seeing their growing sense of relief, as he spoke with confidence and assurance about what they could expect in terms of medical support, Franklin once again congratulated himself on doing whatever was necessary.

"And the worst cases of radiation poisoning will come here for treatment," Franklin was saying. "When this goes online, it'll be the best facility of its kind anywhere. We don't know what kind of enhanced energy weapons the Minbari are using, but—"

He was about to continue with a show of utter confidence that the facility would be capable of handling whatever was tossed at it. It was precisely this sort of measured, reasoned assurance that the new doctors needed to hear.

Unfortunately, what they heard next was an outraged bellow of *"What the hell is* wrong *with you, Franklin?"*

Franklin couldn't quite believe it. Stalking toward him, arms moving like pistons, was General Fontaine.

General Fontaine, by the way, was my source for learning of the following encounter. You see, Earthforce made several more attempts to try to earn my interest and support and, through me, that of the Centauri empire. Fontaine took it upon himself to become a "confidant" of mine, describing the war effort in nauseating detail. Perhaps he thought I would be impressed with the way in which the Humans were handling themselves. I admit I was not particularly interested. However, he usually chose to share these discussions over drinks, for which he invariably paid. Far be it from me to reject the hospitality of anyone, much less someone who wishes to join me in imbibing and will pay for the privilege.

Fontaine was not predisposed to flying off the handle or to sudden bursts of rage, so whatever it was that had him upset, it had to be fairly formidable. How in the world it could possibly involve Franklin, the young doctor clearly had no idea. "Sir?"

Turning to face the other doctors, Fontaine said brusquely, "Out! This is private!" Taking him at his word, the doctors fled the confines of the infirmary, and Franklin stared at Fontaine in obvious confusion.

Fontaine was waving a folder about so aggressively that he nearly hit Franklin with it. "I just got this report about your activities before you rejoined Earthforce," he snapped. Franklin glanced at the folder but didn't appear to attach much importance to it. Perhaps he was under the impression that he simply had nothing to hide or be ashamed of. Fontaine waved the folder about for emphasis as he bellowed, "It says you spent three years hitchhiking on starships, trading your services as ship's doctor for free passage."

The sun evidently had not yet risen on the horizon of Dr. Franklin's comprehension. "That's correct, but I don't see—"

Fontaine flipped open the file, as if he didn't already have the offending documents memorized. "And during that time you had contact with a group of Minbari off Beta Durani."

"Yeah." To Fontaine, it seemed as if Franklin's continued indifference was at this point beginning to take on an air of being forced. "One of their ships had gone down, there was no one else around, and I did all I could to save them. But we didn't know what we were dealing with, and they all died." He shrugged, not out of a sense of callousness, but more from the point of view of a man who had tried to do his best and it simply hadn't been enough. It happens, even to the best of men.

He tapped the folder. "It's all in the report—"

"The hell it is!" The general's lack of diminishing rage clearly surprised Franklin, who was apparently under the impression that simply pointing out the facts would be enough to assuage Fontaine. "I see statements about their language, their general physiology, a little about their culture." He shook his head fiercely, clearly considering what he had before him inadequate. "I know you, Franklin. You weren't out there sight-seeing. You were gathering medical data. Was there an autopsy?"

Franklin seemed to shift uncomfortably in place. "Yes."

As if cross-examining a witness in a court of law, Fontaine continued, "And did you or did you not collect detailed information about their biology, their DNA, and other areas that just might be considered vital to the biogenetic warfare division?"

"I did."

For the first time, there was a trace of anger in Franklin's eyes. Fontaine believed it was because Franklin knew that he had been found out, and was furious over the general's cleverness. As for me, in retrospect, I think it more likely that Franklin was angry over what he knew the general was about to say.

"And where are those notes?" Fontaine asked. He reined in his ire just for a moment. If Franklin had, at that point, said something to the effect of, "Sorry, sir, it's an oversight. Here they are," and produced them on the spot, a smile would likely have blossomed on Fontaine's face and he would have called Franklin heroic, patting him on the shoulder like a long-lost son.

Instead Franklin seemed to brace himself, like a person squaring their shoulders and hurling themselves into a fierce rainstorm. "Sir, I'm a doctor," he said slowly. "My job is to save lives. In my opinion—"

"I don't give a rat's ass about your opinion, mister!" Fontaine bellowed, a fact that was already reasonably clear even without discussions of the proffering of a rodent's hindquarters. "I want those notes."

"I can't do that."

Franklin seemed so matter-of-fact that it stopped Fontaine cold. One did not lightly tread into the area of insubordination. In fact, Fontaine could not recall the last time that it had happened. "Excuse me? I . . . don't think I heard that."

"I can't allow my notes to be used in creating a biogenetic plague that could, conceivably, wipe out an entire race."

Fontaine was absolutely staggered. He could not believe what Franklin was telling him. At that moment, as far as Fontaine was concerned, Franklin was a traitor. Not simply to the Earth government, but to the entire Human race.

He had difficulty believing that the son of General Richard Franklin would behave in such a manner. He decided, just for a moment, to think that perhaps the good doctor simply didn't realize the gravity of the situation. That perhaps it had not been explained to him in sufficient words of one syllable. As if speaking to someone who was mentally defective, he said, "That's what they're trying to do to us, son, or have you not been following the news lately?"

"I know," Franklin said, as reasonably as if he were discussing scores in a sporting event. "And if we do the same, how are we any different?"

And Fontaine erupted with fury. "Damn it, mister—!" he shouted.

But Franklin would not be intimidated, and he raised his voice to the general, shouting back, "I'm sorry, General, but as a doctor, I cannot allow my notes to be used in the production of weapons of war. Under the military code of justice you cannot ask me to go against my conscience!"

Fontaine tried to make himself heard above Franklin, bellowing "You can't talk to me like that!" but it became apparent to him that Franklin was not listening. Then he spun on his heel and for just a moment, Franklin likely thought that he'd managed to turn away Fontaine's wrath somehow. But Fontaine instead shouted *"Security!"* and that was when Franklin knew he was in major, major trouble.

Several security guards appeared at the door, and it looked as though they were even less inclined to be reasonable than the general. Fontaine stabbed a quivering finger in Franklin's direction and snarled, "Dr. Franklin is under arrest. He will be held until he provides the information I have requested." He began ticking off instructions on his fingers. "I want his office searched. I want his house searched. I want every data crystal, every record, every report confiscated by sixteen hundred hours." He turned back to Franklin, who was completely stone-faced. "God help you, son, because from here on out, the blood of every soldier that dies in this war is on your hands."

Franklin looked as if he wanted to reply to that, to deny it, but before he could get a word out, Fontaine snapped, "Get him out of here." The guards lost no time in grabbing Franklin by either arm and "escorting" him out of the infirmary.

They hauled Franklin down the corridor, past the doctors who had been evicted so unceremoniously from the room. They gaped at Franklin as he was brought past them, and he paused only long enough to say to them, "We have met the enemy . . . and he is us." And then he was dragged away.

—— *chapter 11* ——

There were many things John Sheridan was convinced that he would become in his lifetime, and many things that he was certain he would never become. Of the latter, "discouraged" was quite high on the list. Particularly when it came to the subject of dealing with an enemy.

He had never stopped believing that any enemy could be defeated, that it was just a matter of figuring out how. And he very much wanted to continue to believe that in regards to the Minbari. In fact, the two ideas were far from mutually exclusive. He still believed the Minbari could be defeated, but he was beginning to wonder if Humanity would last long enough to find the way. Perhaps the Minbari would sail through the Human race, slaughtering every last one of them, and move away into the depths of space with their mysterious weakness—whatever that might be—a tight little secret.

He lay in his bunkroom aboard the *Lexington*, a battle cruiser belonging to what they referred to as the *Hyperion* class. Since there continued to be zero gravity throughout the vessel, he was held in place via straps. He pondered the situation and desperately searched for some sort of positive aspect he could seize upon. None presented itself.

They had lost two more ships to Minbari hit-and-run attacks in that day alone, and it was Sheridan's guess that the enemy was softening up the Humans for a major offensive. The *Lexington*'s commander, Captain Sterns, to whom Sheridan had remained loyal, had not slept in two days. There were rumors throughout Earthforce that the Minbari had some sort of "ace" cruiser that alone was responsible for the destruction of two dozen Earth ships in the previous three weeks. However, no one had survived any attacks to confirm that.

And as he lay there, a worse thing was gnawing away at Sheridan, the true guilt that he had found he could not voice to anyone.

It plagued Sheridan that he had turned down the post of second-in-command aboard the *Prometheus*, the ship which had fired the shots heard around the galaxy. Sheridan, the conscientious man that he was, had begun to second-guess his decision. If he had been aboard the bridge at the time of the attack, might it somehow have turned out differently? Might he have managed to turn Captain Jankowski away from what ultimately proved to be a course that was destructive to all of Humanity? In short, might Sheridan's presence have avoided the Minbari's stampede of extermination?

It was still unknown to the Humans just what exactly had set the Minbari off. They did not know of Dukhat. They did not know of the Minbari tradition of displaying weapons as a sign of respect. For all they knew, the Minbari were simply mad-dog killers who had decided to wipe out Humanity because . . .

Because why?

It made no sense to him. This was a race that was clearly advanced. They had more than proven the point that, in any sort of true battle situation, Humanity posed no threat.

Why was such a truly superior race bent upon obliterating a lesser one?

There had to be a reason, and it all came back to the *Prometheus* firing the first shots. They had not been fired upon. Everyone, in reviewing the video logs, had come to that realization. And Sheridan had started thinking that, had he been there, perhaps he would have been able to head off the chain of events that had led to the war. Because Sheridan knew, beyond any question, that had he been in Jankowski's position, he never would have fired the first shot in a first-contact situation. Even if it meant leaving oneself open to a hit. He simply never would have done it.

Understand, the odds are that—had Sheridan been on the *Prometheus*—the exact same series of events would have transpired. Had Sheridan refused the direct order, Jankowski would likely have relieved him of command, just as he would have done with Chafin had Chafin declined to fire upon the Minbari. Deep down, Sheridan knew that. But Sheridan was, and is, a man of conscience. A man fully capable of second-guessing himself to death.

Perhaps that was what helped him to keep going when others had already surrendered to despair. The feeling that, in some way, he bore a degree of responsibility for the situation, and it was up to him, personally, to deal with it. To make amends.

But how?

He had no time to dwell on it, however, for—as exhausted as he was—his rest was suddenly disrupted when a klaxon sounded through the ship, and an urgent voice called, "All hands, battle stations, repeat, all hands, battle stations."

Sheridan was far too much the professional to hesitate even a moment. It was as if the exhaustion fell away in a heartbeat as he quickly undid the straps, to make his way to the bridge of the *Lexington*.

But as he rose from his bunk, his elbow bumped something that had been affixed to the wall, and it floated free. He snatched it from midair and looked at it.

It was a picture of Anna.

His sister, Elizabeth, had sent it to him just before he had left Earth. On the back she'd scribbled, "She thinks you're gorgeous." Sheridan's first instinct had been to simply toss the photo away, but something—he had no idea what—had prompted him to take it with him. He rationalized that he was doing so because he knew it would please his sister.

He had no rationalization as to why he slid the picture into the inside of his jacket . . . nor any further clue as to why he stuck it onto the board of his station when he arrived on the bridge moments later.

It was not as if the *Lexington* was alone. There were half a dozen destroyers and support vessels accompanying it. It was an array of power that would have proven daunting to virtually any other race that the Humans might have encountered. Unfortunately for them, the Minbari continued to be less than impressed by even their best efforts.

As Sheridan strapped himself into his post on the bridge, snapping in the final buckle of his five-point harness, he came to the dismaying realization that he wasn't thinking about beating the Minbari during this engagement—presuming it was the Minbari they were about to face. Instead his primary consideration was how they would survive at all.

Any enemy can be beaten echoed in his head. Now all he had to do was get himself to believe it.

The initial alert had been sounded by long-range sensors automatically maintained by the ship's computers. Sheridan switched over to manual control and skimmed the array. He felt his heart beginning to speed up as he announced, "Computer alert confirmed. Picking up Minbari-style transmissions. Target bearing mark nine nine seven two one. Should be in visual range."

"Let me see," Sterns ordered.

The screen on the *Lexington*'s bridge flickered and the silhouette of a small ship moved through it. Sheridan set about confirming the sightings with the other ships, which had likewise picked up the intruder on their own sensor arrays. Everyone was coordinating with the *Lexington*, which was the point ship.

"Silhouette confirmed," Sheridan informed his captain. "Looks like a short-range transport. Could be a scout, or a straggler that got separated from a larger fleet."

He was about to add a third possibility, but Sterns beat him to it. "And it could be a decoy, drawing us into an ambush."

Sheridan nodded slowly. "Should we pursue?" he asked.

If there was any moment that underscored the difference between captains Sterns and Jankowski, it was this one. Whereas Jankowski, with dreams of the medals awaiting him, might very well have gone after the transport with eager carelessness, Sterns stroked his chin thoughtfully before replying, exercising extraordinary caution, "Negative. I won't risk the fleet until we know exactly what we're getting into."

Sheridan couldn't help but dwell on the fact that it was that very caution which had prompted some people to consider Sterns with scorn. But while Sheridan was relieved over his captain's judicious handling of the situation, he felt constrained to point out, "She'll be leaving visual range any moment, and the scanners can't lock on."

Sterns thought for a moment and then touched the communications console. "Launch bay, this is the captain. Launch solo fighter, I want that transport followed."

At the first sound of a red alert, the fighter pilots had run down to the launch bay with attitudes ranging from eagerness to dread. Sitting in the cockpit of his Starfury, Ganya

Ivanov's mood was somewhere in the middle. He felt no driving desire to get out there and prove himself. On the other hand, he was not particularly daunted by the thought of facing off against the Minbari. He had that same comfortable limited sense of his own mortality that Jeffrey Sinclair carried with him.

It was that ideal combination of personality traits which prompted the launch bay watch commander, in glancing over the duty roster when the captain's order came down, to zero in on Ivanov's name. So it was that mere seconds after the order was issued, Ganya received the command to pursue the Minbari transport.

Even though he had already run a systems check, Ganya nonetheless glanced over his array before he launched. Then he glanced, ever so briefly, at the earring Susan had given him, dutifully attached to the side of the control console. He touched it briefly, for luck, and then he sent his Starfury hurtling into the void, flames spurting from the engines located on the tips of its four wings.

He had once told Susan that the first moments when one is in space were the most exhilarating that one could hope for. The stars shone all around him as he sat in the vivid crimson glow of the cockpit. He still remembered the first time he had been in space and wondering why the stars looked odd to him. It had been a second's realization, of course, that seeing stars twinkling was so ingrained—thanks to atmospheric distortion—that any other way looked unnatural. He had laughed over it, and since then had come to take it for granted.

I wonder if the stars looked different to him this time. If he had any . . . inkling of what was to happen.

His sister, Susan, came to believe that he did. For even as Ganya went in pursuit of the transport, Susan Ivanova was in the dorm room at university, sleeping, and her dreaming mind turned to Ganya. This was not unusual. Invariably, she imagined him in pitched battle, Starfuries exploding all around him, but Ganya safe and sound, protected by the earring, protected by her love for him, battling the Minbari and laughing at adversity.

But this time, in this dream, she felt no such things. Instead she simply felt . . . cold.

As for what Ganya felt, well, we have no true, subjective record. We do have logs of the conversations, the "chatter." We have the watch commander advising Ivanov, "She's got a big head start on you, Eagle Seven."

"Roger that," Ivanov said. "Hitting afterburners, maximum thrust."

An asteroid field, albeit it a not particularly hazardous one, lay in the transport's path. Or perhaps the transport was seeking shelter there, Ivanov reasoned. The engines roared around him as the Starfury pursued the vessel.

"She's accelerating," Ivanov informed the bridge of the *Lexington* as he prepared himself to avoid any collision. "Taking evasive action to stay with her."

On the bridge of the *Lexington*, Sterns instructed Sheridan, "Move us out slowly but keep up with them." With a small, lopsided grin, he added, "Maybe we've actually caught a break this time."

Sheridan hoped to his God that Sterns was right as he relayed the order to the rest of the fleet. The fleet, as one, moved to pursue the Starfury, which was, in turn, pursuing the Minbari transport.

Sterns was already one step ahead of the situation. He had no intention of destroying the Minbari transport if it could be at all avoided, and said as much to Sheridan. Sheridan looked a bit surprised as he said, "After all the ships of ours they've destroyed, you're not interested in returning the favor, sir?"

"We have to send a message, Commander," Sterns said reasonably. "We've shown the Minbari that we're capable

of striking first. And we've shown them that we're capable
of being destroyed. We've shown we can be merciless . . .
there are rumors, I've heard, rumors of captured Minbari
being tortured and killed. Now what we have to show
them . . . is that we can be compassionate. It is my intention to capture the transport, with all hands alive, if possible.
With any luck, it leads to face-to-face discussions with the
Minbari involving the return of prisoners. It's easy to destroy an enemy who has no face, no personality. To obliterate those you have demonized. If we can make the Minbari
think of us as something other than simple targets . . . we
might be able to put an end to this madness."

"In your opinion," Sheridan noted with just a touch of
irony. From what he had seen of the Minbari, he wasn't
holding out much hope that any sort of olive branch extended to them would be greeted with anything other than
pruning shears.

But Sterns merely tapped his armrest. "Granted, my opinion. But it's my chair. That means my opinion counts more
than most."

Now it was Sheridan's turn to grin slightly, but then they
heard the voice of Ganya Ivanov over the open channel.
"Eagle Seven to *Lexington*, she's flamed out. Lying dead in
space."

It appeared that Ganya was quite correct. The forward
thrusters of the Minbari transport had fired once, as if the
vessel were aware that it was being pursued, and then
flamed out. The transport was tumbling end over end, out of
control.

"Stand by, Eagle Seven, we're moving in," Sterns said.
He turned to Sheridan. "Any further radio chatter?"

"Negative. She's running silent."

"Keep moving us in," Sterns said, with a trace of eagerness in his voice.

It was clear to Sheridan that Sterns's enthusiasm was

growing. How much more merciful could one be than to spare a helpless foe? Indeed, how many helpless Earth ships had been wiped out by the Minbari when their pleas for mercy were ignored?

Nevertheless . . .

"Sir, I don't like it," Sheridan said, double-checking his readouts. "Just before the transport flamed out, it fired its forward thrusters, cutting acceleration down to almost nothing. If I were running from the enemy, engines failing, I'd try to keep my inertia going on the off chance I could get away instead of just lying there, waiting to be caught."

"Maybe he wants to be captured alive, rather than take his chances getting killed in that asteroid field."

Thinking out loud, Sheridan countered, "And maybe they want us at a precise, predetermined location." And then a terrible thought struck him. "Their jump engines are a lot more precise than ours, Captain. They can target an area of less than a hundred yards. If they jumped into the middle of us—"

Sterns's eyes went wide. "Holy . . ." he whispered. Snapping on the communications console, he barked, "This is fleet command, all ships, break off, I repeat, break—"

And suddenly the entire vessel lurched from an energy wave of tremendous proportions.

Dead center of the fleet, right in the middle, a jump point formed. The jump point itself released so much energy that it demolished two of the Earthforce destroyers immediately. Sheridan looked away as the vessels became nothing more than two massive fireballs, quickly snuffed out in the vacuum of space. A third destroyer was severely damaged by the impact, and then a massive Minbari war cruiser roared out of hyperspace, blasting away.

What emerged looked like a gigantic, ribbed whale with long, sweeping fins. This was, indeed, the war cruiser that had been rumored to exist. Its name was the *Drala Fi*, translated as the *Black Star*, and it was the pride of the Minbari fleet. The Minbari were quite certain that, against the *Black Star*, no vessel stood a chance. Based on the *Black Star*'s record up to that time—and considering the immediate progress of the newly joined battle—there was no reason to think otherwise.

The initial fire struck the *Lexington* amidships, blasting out a chunk of the vessel, rocking it once more. Bulkheads caved inward, barely holding together. Launch bays one through eight erupted in flame as the Starfury fighters—prepped to fly into battle—never had a chance. The ships exploded, transforming the interior of the bays into an inferno, and it was all that the emergency crews could do to prevent the disaster from encompassing the whole of the cruiser.

Not that the rest of the *Lexington* was trouble-free. Systems went down all over, and mere seconds after the engagement had begun, the *Lexington*—the fleet leader—was hanging dead in space while other ships erupted in mushrooms of flame all around it.

It had all happened so quickly that it had barely had time to register on Ganya Ivanov. Part of him was still waiting for the rest of the Starfuries to come barreling out of the *Lexington*, to leap into pitched battle against the Minbari cruiser that had appeared from nowhere, dropped into their midst, and proceeded to tear the fleet to pieces. And just as his mind was beginning to accept the full horror of the situation, the engines on the Minbari transport flared to life. The decoy whipped around with speed that Ivanov would never have credited, and opened fire on the Starfury.

Many, many light-years away, Susan Ivanova awoke from her dream, sat upright drenched in sweat and screaming a single word. That word was *"No!"* and we can only assume that it was the final word uttered by her brother as his Starfury was blown to pieces by the Minbari transport.

Two of the Humans' remaining mobile destroyers tried to break and run, any stomach for combat having been completely lost. The *Black Star*'s weaponry lashed out, cutting one of the destroyers to ribbons and zeroing in on the second. In the meantime the *Lexington* simply hung there, apparently—and effectively—helpless.

On the now darkened bridge, Sheridan coughed violently, trying to wipe his eyes clear and see through the smoke. Flickering consoles sent bizarre colors and shapes dancing across his face. His instinct was to try to get over to the captain, but if he unstrapped from his station, all he would wind up doing would be floating helpless in zero gravity. So he shouted into what was essentially blindness, "Primary systems hit! Weapons and jump engines are down! Only navigational thrusters still functioning! Orders?" Nothing but silence, a silence as dead as space, came back to him. He called again, "Captain? Or—"

But he never got out the remainder of the word. For after a few moments, the smoke had cleared ever so slightly, and what he saw stunned him to the pit of his stomach.

A support beam had been ripped free from the ceiling over and had plowed through where Sterns had been sitting. And make no mistake, Sterns was still there . . . but only in spirit, not in body. In terms of body, there was not much of anything left. All Sheridan was able to make out was a trickle of blood flowing from beneath the fallen pylon, turning to red globules that began to float around the bridge. The falling debris had more or less obliterated the ship's captain.

John Sheridan finally had a command of his own. If he was looking for orders, he had to look nowhere but to himself. Unfortunately, all he could muster for the first few moments of his command was a shocked silence and a feeling of overwhelming helplessness.

He stopped thinking. Instead he began to proceed entirely on instinct. There were rules, procedures to handle virtually any situation, even one as calamitous as this. Sheridan ran through them in his mind.

A ship needs two things to win a battle: movement and weapons. One can be the most masterly tactician in the universe, but if one is stationary and has no offensive capability, one will not survive. It is that simple.

Movement. Weapons. Both of those requirements echoed in Sheridan's mind as he tapped his console and prayed that the communications links were still functioning . . . and that there was anyone still alive belowdecks to respond to him. "Bridge to engine room . . . do we have power yet?"

"Negative, sir," came a voice from the engine room. Sheridan immediately knew it was not the voice of the engineer. If he remembered correctly, it was the voice of Second Assistant Engineer Staite. He didn't even want to think about what the current status of everyone above Staite might be.

Suddenly the bridge was rocked by a small asteroid. The *Lexington* at that point had no maneuverability at all with which to deal with the asteroids, and the current situation of helplessness was not conducive to prolonged life. "Engine room, if we're hit by many more of those asteroids, we'll breach the hull and we'll all die. Is anyone there unclear on that particular concept?"

"No, sir," Staite said.

"Then keep working." In the meantime, his thoughts were racing. *If one can't move, find someone who can.* "Communications," he said briskly.

"Online," came Heuser over the comm channel.

"Can you contact Earth, send a distress signal?"

"It's possible," Heuser said, not sounding particularly enthusiastic about the likelihood. "But sir, that Minbari cruiser only left because it figured we were dead. If we send out a distress signal, it'll come back and finish the job."

"And if we sit here and do nothing, we're just as dead."

"Roger that, sir," Heuser said with what sounded like a sigh.

Slowly Sheridan turned to face the soot-covered faces of the crew—no, *his* crew now. They looked battered. Defeated. Frightened.

And something within Sheridan refused to break, refused to give in. This was the single greatest test of his life, and his spirit seemed to rise above it. To have no doubt that somehow, *somehow*, they would triumph.

Any enemy can be defeated. Find the way. Find the way . . . now. **Now, damn it, now.**

He spoke before he had fully formed his plan . . . before he even really knew what he was going to say. "Firing control, do we have any tactical nukes left?"

The voice of Azizi in firing control came back almost immediately. "Yes, sir. Three two-megaton warheads, with proximity fuses."

"All right," Sheridan said. His impulse was to rush, but something made him speak slowly, calmly, as if time were entirely on their side. "All right. I'm authorizing use of the tactical nukes. Firing control, remove the warheads and get them down to . . ." He glanced at the consoles to see what was left. "Launch bay nine, ASAP. Communications, stand by to broadcast distress signal, but not until I give the order."

"Aye, sir."

He took a breath. Everything was in place, the plan that he had cobbled together ready to be initiated. He paused a moment, and then said to the bridge crew, "I would be less than honest if I said I was sure this was going to work. It might. And it might not. We might very well get blown up right alongside the enemy. But at least we'll have a fighting chance of taking them with us. Unless anyone has a better idea...?"

That last comment was said with a sense of hopefulness. But no response, no suggestion came. Instead there was an almost uniform shaking of heads.

"Nuts," Sheridan said, clearly disappointed. He sighed. "All right, then we'll stick with my plan." Sounding surprisingly jaunty, he added, "Hell, I didn't want to live forever anyway."

The next minutes were the most tense of Sheridan's life. Every passing second he expected the Minbari war cruiser to turn its attention back to the *Lexington*. But the Minbari did not seem to notice the EVA-suited figures who had dropped out of launch bay nine, proceeding to the nearby asteroids. Whether it was because the asteroids were interfering with the Minbari sensors, or whether the vast war cruiser was simply interested in pursuing those few members of the fleet who had any apparent fight left in them, it was impossible to know for sure. All Sheridan knew was that he felt as if he were chewing his fingernails down to nothing, figuratively speaking, feeling horribly exposed until he finally heard the EVA team leader make an announcement.

"Nukes in place. Heading back for the barn."

Sheridan could barely contain the relief in his voice as he said, "Roger that." This time when another asteroid struck the *Lexington*, he didn't curse it as he had the others. The asteroids, at least for the moment, were no longer the enemy. Instead they were the only ally that the beleaguered destroyer had. "All right, send the distress signal. Just hope we don't have to wait too long. I don't know how much more of this we can take."

There was a brief moment of silence, and then Lieutenant Heuser announced from his station, "Looks like you're going to get your wish. We've got an echo on approach vector. Might be them. Coming into range now."

The screen flickered, the transmission extremely unsteady and filled with static. Nonetheless, Sheridan was able to make out the slow, ominous approach of the Minbari cruiser. The *Black Star* moved toward the *Lexington* with utter confidence. After all, an Earth ship at peak condition posed no threat to the *Black Star*. So what possible problem could so damaged a vessel as the *Lexington* give them?

Sheridan did not like the way the approach was going as he noticed the vulnerability of his ship. He tapped his comm channel and said, "Bridge to navigation. The enemy has a clear shot. Fire docking thrusters, get us behind one of those asteroids. Let 'em think we're trying to evade." As much to himself as to the nav station, he continued, "They want to finish the job, let them come to us. If we don't get them into the right position, we're dead."

The *Lexington* did as its new captain ordered, maneuvering with what little ability it had left and putting an asteroid between itself and the *Black Star*. Seeing it as the last, desperate act of a soon-to-be-dead Earth ship, the *Black Star* casually adjusted its source to angle around. Sheridan came to the realization that he wasn't breathing as his finger hovered above the firing button. "Here we go. A little closer . . ." he said softly, and took a brief moment to glance at the picture of Anna.

"Sir, she's locking on!"

Too soon, a voice screamed in Sheridan's head. "A little more," he said with growing urgency, as if ordering the Minbari vessel to stop targeting the *Lexington*.

"Confirmed weapons lock! Energy spike! She's ready to fire!"

He'd run out of time, and the Minbari cruiser was still not in perfect position, but he had no choice. "Now!" he shouted, and stabbed down on the control.

The nuke nearest the enemy detonated just as the Minbari cruiser was about to fire on them. It shredded a section of the *Black Star,* completely shocking those within who had felt, until that moment, impervious to harm from the Humans. The *Black Star* quickly angled off, either to try to get a shot from a distance, or perhaps simply deciding that one more destroyer was not worth the risk.

"She's out of range of nuke two," Sheridan was informed. "Only one left."

But Sheridan was tracking the direction of the Minbari cruiser, saw where it was heading, and smiled grimly to himself. "That's all we need," he murmured as he saw the cruiser's position intersect perfectly with the third nuke's hidden position. "See you in hell."

He slammed down on the button.

The nuclear warhead is one of the Humans' more efficient weapons. They first tested it on themselves, obliterating several entire cities. The intervening centuries since the weapon's first use had not dimmed its effectiveness, as the *Black Star* proved when it blew apart. It was, from all accounts, a most impressive display and took—by the standards of such things—quite some time as one section after another after another of the ship erupted.

The shock waves smashed asteroids together, and the asteroids in turn pounded against the *Lexington.* This might have served to destroy the ship, but instead it provided the *Lexington*'s salvation as the impact sent the vessel spiraling away from the progressive, explosive death of the Minbari cruiser.

When the *Black Star*'s mighty engines went up, the annihilation of the vessel accelerated, and within a few minutes there was nothing left to mark that the *Black Star* had ever been there except for a few dying embers trailing off into the darkness.

It was the single greatest—actually, the only—victory that the Humans had had against the Minbari. And the Minbari, for their part, gave a name to Sheridan. A name they spoke privately in angry whispers and infuriated bellowing, as howls went out for blood in revenge for all those lost upon the former pride of the Minbari fleet.

And that name was . . . "Starkiller."

—— *chapter 12* ——

Delenn was conversant in many areas and had many impressive abilities. But never before had she displayed quite such a dazzling mastery of the verbal technique known as "understatement."

"The situation is getting out of control, Lenonn," she said.

What is most striking about this particular bit of understatement is that she made it when the *Black Star*'s fate was not yet generally known, the vessel's destruction having occurred only moments earlier. Had she known about it, the comment might have seemed a bit more self-serving, as if she were sanguine about the situation until it actually had a negative impact on the Minbari themselves.

As it was, the pronouncement was based on cool, clinical observation of the war's progress and what seemed, to her, to be a slow, steady march toward an inevitable and genocidal conclusion.

She again stood in her quarters in the Minbari cruiser that served the needs of the Grey Council, facing a most concerned Ranger leader. "So far, we have hit only the outer colonies," she continued. "They are sparsely populated, with minimal defenses. Soon we will begin to hit colonies and stations closer to the homeworld of the Humans." She shook her head, unable to keep the worry from her voice. "Every day that passes sees more death, and every death will make it that much harder to intervene."

Lenonn had come to the same conclusion, but he had no recommendation to offer. "Then what do you suggest?" he asked.

"A peace offering." Delenn was beginning to pace, as if the motion might stimulate thought. "Anything that can open the way for negotiations."

"An apology?" he suggested, but immediately shook his head. "The others will say that's a very little payment for the murder of Dukhat."

He was surprised, however, to see that Delenn did not necessarily dismiss the idea out of hand. "But it is a start, Lenonn. Enough, perhaps, to call for a cease-fire. Give us time to find a solution." She put a hand on his shoulder. "That's why I need you, Lenonn. I cannot contact the Humans directly, or ask any other member of the Grey Council to do so. We cannot act alone. But someone else might be able to contact them unofficially. Someone the others would respect, with a history of service and unchallenged loyalty. Someone like you, Lenonn."

Again Lenonn was shaking his head. He hated to feel as if he were the voice of doom, but Delenn was suggesting things that simply did not seem feasible to him. "I appreciate the compliment you pay me, Delenn, but . . ." He gestured helplessly. "But how do I do this? If I contact them directly, the Grey Council will hear of it and interfere. The Humans will almost certainly consider it a trap."

Delenn, however, was ahead of him. And for that, as it turned out, she had me to thank. She did not know about, or even care about, the source of the information in her possession. It only mattered to her that she knew. You will remember that I had gotten word to the Minbari of the Narn intention to sell arms to the Humans. Well, this information had made its way to Delenn, and she intended to put it to use in a most unexpected manner. "There is a way," she said slowly. "Our intelligence reports indicate that the Humans have made a deal with the Narns to buy weapons. Through the Narns, we can arrange a meeting in neutral territory. But the danger is great," she warned. "The Humans may attempt to capture you. And the Narns cannot be trusted on the best of days."

Lenonn shrugged expressively. "To live is to risk." He considered it a moment more, and then nodded in brisk acceptance. "I will have my Rangers contact the Narn government and set things in motion. With luck the meeting could take place in . . . three weeks. Perhaps four. No sooner."

Delenn was not particularly happy about that. Every passing day was that many more lives lost, that many more souls crying for vengeance. It seemed to her that the more time that went by the more difficult it was going to be to have some sort of peaceful end to this business. But she had to acknowledge the realities of the situation, and so she said, "It will have to do." Almost as an afterthought, she added, "I've been gathering information on their language, culture. I'll make a copy for you this afternoon. It may prove . . . useful. And thank you, Lenonn."

"No, thank *you*," he replied. "The Rangers have asked only one thing: to serve, to have the opportunity to lay down their lives in a righteous cause. At my age, I feared I would never again have the chance to serve my people as one of my order should. Thank you for giving me this opportunity. Whatever comes, I will meet it with joy."

And with that, he bowed to Delenn and left her presence, leaving Delenn to worry. For all she knew, she was sending Lenonn to his death. It was not a decision she made easily or happily, and it was almost as if his happiness in having the opportunity made it more, not less, difficult for her.

She wondered how many more difficult decisions lay ahead for her, and wondered—not for the first time—whether Dukhat's support of her ascension to the Grey Council was a blessing or a curse.

For Stephen Franklin, time did not quite have the importance that it once had.

If there is one thing in this universe that a doctor is aware of, it's that the time that each and every one of us has allotted to him is special, precious, and all too fleeting. It is never to be wasted, but always to be valued. Franklin had vowed never to waste a minute of the time that had been given him. Indeed, I must admit to you that, in later years, that attitude would come back to haunt him. His compulsion to maximize every minute of every day would drive him to a stimulant addiction that would nearly cost him everything.

But that was to be many years in the future, as part of a destiny that would await him on Babylon 5. At this particular point in our story, however, Dr. Franklin did not see himself as having a destiny outside the four walls of his cell.

He had half expected regular visits from General Fontaine, eager to shout over his refusal to cooperate, but he had been surprised when that joyful happenstance did not occur. Instead he was simply left there, day after unending day. He wondered if they were trying to wear him down. Or perhaps Fontaine was so angry with his insubordination that he intended to leave him there, with no hearing, no due process, no nothing, until he rotted.

There was even the worst-case scenario he had developed for himself, which was that they had forgotten all about him. They were busy fighting a war, after all, and perhaps everyone involved had simply moved on to other things and his arrest had slipped their minds. He had fallen through the cracks, as Humans like to say.

He did anything he could to keep his mind active. He would study his body and name every bone, every muscle, every organ within it. He would run through assorted diagnoses in his head, or take names of various complexly named diseases and see if he could form other words from them.

And after what seemed to him to be an eternity of time, there was the turning of a latch in his door. When food was brought to him, it was slid through a small chute in the door. This time, someone was actually opening it, preparing to . . . what? Come in? Bring him out?

He blinked against the light that came filtering in from the outside corridor as someone stepped into view in the doorway. Franklin was sitting on the floor, and did not feel any overwhelming compulsion to scramble to his feet. Consequently, the new arrival seemed almost gigantic in stature. The figure stood ramrod straight, hands draped behind the small of his back, and his head was shaking slowly in what appeared to be a most disapproving manner.

It was an attitude with which Franklin was all too familiar.

"Hello, Father," he said dryly. And I mean "dryly" in the most literal fashion. He was surprised to realize that his voice was little more than a croak. He'd fallen out of practice speaking.

"Well, well," General Franklin said, in a voice that was mocking and—as per its custom—quite low. "Look where you've landed yourself." He stepped in, coming more clearly into view and making no effort to hide his disgust over his son's present situation. "What the hell did you think you were doing?"

"It's good to see you too, Father."

"Don't get flip with me, Stephen. You have absolutely no idea how much trouble you're in."

"Oh, I think I can take an educated guess."

" 'Educated,' yes. You know, Stephen," General Franklin said ruefully, "sometimes I think that's entirely your problem. Education, or too much thereof. You overthink things, overanalyze them."

"An analytical mind is generally considered an asset in a doctor," Stephen replied as he slowly pushed himself up to stand. His legs were a bit cramped from sitting for so long, and he tried to shake them out, restore circulation to them. He was only partly successful, his knees still exhibiting the urge to buckle under him. He leaned against a wall to help support himself.

"Yes, but it's a drawback when it comes to soldiers," the general shot back. "And like it or not, if you're serving in Earthforce, that's what you are, first and foremost. A soldier. And a soldier follows orders."

"I'm sorry, Dad, but first and foremost, I'm a doctor. I follow my Hippocratic oath, and one of the main parts of that oath is to promise that I will do no harm. Handing the army a recipe to mix up a genocide cocktail strikes me as doing one hell of a lot of harm."

"This is a war, son." His father thumped a fist into his palm for emphasis. "It's a different set of rules. You're a healer, granted, but you're a Human first, aren't you? Humanity stands a good possibility of being wiped out, and if you had information in your possession that can avoid that, don't you see that General Fontaine had a right to ask you to give it to him?"

"Absolutely I acknowledge that," Franklin said evenly, as he took a seat on his bunk. "But what I had was a right to tell him 'no.' "

"It's war," General Franklin repeated. "All the niceties, the theories, the polite mind-set, all of that goes right out the tubes when you're facing down an enemy that wants to wipe you out—obliterate you from the memory of the galaxy. Don't you see that they view you as a traitor, Stephen? As someone who is withholding valuable information, and disobeying a direct order to make that information available? My God, son, in the old days, they could have marched you out in front of a firing squad and had you shot!"

"So instead they're going to leave me here to rot. Thank heavens for modern-day sensibilities."

But General Franklin was shaking his head. "No . . . they're not going to do that, either."

There was something about his tone of voice that immediately caught Stephen Franklin's attention. "What do you mean? Dad . . . what are—"

"I've spoken to some people, Franklin," said his father. Franklin moaned audibly, but General Franklin ignored the noise and continued, "There are . . . possibilities to be explored."

"Do they involve the Minbari?"

"Yes."

"Not interested."

"Stephen!" protested his father.

But Stephen was vehemently shaking his head. "I'm not going to do anything that would risk the obliteration of an entire race."

"Do you think I don't know that?"

"You probably know it, but I don't think you respect it," Franklin said, a bit more sharply than he would have liked.

The general took a step forward and towered over his son. "Now you listen to me," he said in a low, angry voice. "If it were up to General Fontaine, he'd leave you here until the second coming of the Dilgar. Whatever else you may think of him, he is a superior officer and deserving of the same respect that you would have others give to you. Now, I've spent a good deal of time talking to him on your behalf—"

"I didn't ask you to intercede for me," Franklin told him.

"True enough. And if you had, that would likely have been more than enough to make me refuse. But I feel some degree of obligation to do what I can for you, whether you want me to or not. I'm here with an offer, Stephen. An offer for you to put your knowledge of the Minbari to use in a way other than that of germ warfare."

"Oh really?" Stephen said doubtfully, with undisguised sarcasm.

It almost seemed as if electricity filled the cell as his father said, in a tone so frigid that it seemed to be icing up the walls, "I have never lied to you, Stephen."

And Franklin knew that this was true. Feeling chagrined, he looked down. "No. You haven't. I didn't mean to imply that you ever had."

The general looked as if he was ready to argue the point, but let it pass. Instead he said, "Stephen . . . let me be utterly candid. This offer that I'm coming to you with is the best you can hope for. You may wind up spending the rest of your natural life in the stockade. The only upside to this is that, if the Minbari have their way, then that will not be a particularly long period of time. On the other hand, if you agree to the terms I'm about to set forth, you have an outside chance to not only get out of here, but maybe— just maybe, if everything goes right—aid in resolving this ghastly Minbari situation."

"And if everything goes wrong?"

"Then you'll very likely be killed."

"And it doesn't bother you? The notion that you might be sending your son off to die?"

"Obviously," the general said with a grim smile, "I'd like to see you come back in one piece. But if I'm to have a choice between my son dying on his feet, in service of his race . . . or dying alone and sitting on his butt in a cell . . . I know which I'd choose."

And to his surprise, Stephen laughed softly. "They should put you in charge of army recruitment, Dad. The way you present options, who could possibly turn you down? So . . . tell me what I have to do to get out of this rat trap."

He told him.

And for Stephen Franklin, suddenly the prospect of dying on his butt in a cell didn't seem entirely unattractive.

There were two massive explosions in the briefing room.

The first was that of the Minbari warship—or at least footage of it—being blasted apart by the nuclear warheads that Sheridan had seeded in the asteroids. The second was the explosion of cheers, shouts, and applause that came from the Earthforce officers, soldiers, and assorted civilians who were crammed into the two-story briefing room, watching the replay of Sheridan's triumph.

On the upper-level briefing room platform, General Lefcourt stood above them all, looking down like a god from on high. Next to him was Sheridan, elevated to almost divine stature simply by his proximity to Lefcourt and the magnitude of his accomplishment.

Humans have a charming phrase, which is as follows: "Needless to say." I'm not entirely sure why they employ it; if one doesn't need to say it, then why make a point of how one is not going to bring it up? Followed, invariably, by a discussion of the very topic that had been deemed unnecessary to broach. What a curious race they are.

"Needless to say," General Lefcourt declared, "we plan to broadcast this on every major planetary network for the next three days." Lefcourt had come to me shortly after the triumph to boast of it, and perhaps to swagger a bit. I allowed him to. What harm was there, after all? I also supplied him with the name and status of the destroyed vessel, which I in turn had garnered from my Minbari contacts. I had also been informed of their ire over the destruction of the vessel, and knew that there were factions who were advocating a very profound and comprehensive retaliation.

That bit of information, however, I did not share with Lefcourt. Why ruin his good time, after all?

"The *Black Star* was their flagship," he continued. "We've shown that we can take on their best, outthink and outfight it. Commander, anything you'd like to add?"

It was Sheridan's moment of glory, the spotlight squarely on him. He did not shrink from the challenge or responsibility at all. "Yes, General," he said gamely. "I've had the chance to study their style of combat. The Minbari are very meticulous, and that makes them inflexible. They don't improvise well, so when something unexpected happens, they retreat rather than adjust. Anything you can do to confuse the enemy will give you a superior position during the engagement. They have more firepower, but if you can get them to respond to you, then you have an advantage."

There was a broad-based bobbing of heads, and General Lefcourt said, "Thank you, Commander." He paused a moment to let Sheridan's words sink in, and then said, "And if any member in the press corps asks about the morality of sending out a distress signal and hitting the enemy, remind them that the Minbari do not take survivors. They were on a mission to murder the *Lexington*. They paid the price.

"Dismissed."

The room began to empty out amid excited pockets of conversation. Sheridan could pick out snatches of it here and there as officers discussed possibilities with each other. It gave rise to new hope and excitement for him. If pressed, he would have been forced to admit that he wasn't sure just what tactics might be employed to "confuse the enemy." Then again, he didn't have to be. He had given them hope, and it was fully possible that others—now that it had been revealed that the Minbari vessels could be blown up as readily as anyone else's—would rise to the challenge.

Lefcourt drew closer to Sheridan, speaking in low tones. "That was quick thinking on your part, Commander. You're to be commended."

Sheridan wasn't entirely certain what Lefcourt was referring to: his actions in the field, or his impromptu speech in telling the troops how to respond to the Minbari.

"You were right to stay where you were," Lefcourt continued. "Thanks for arguing with me. Now . . . I have another job for you."

He might have tried to argue the point with Lefcourt—point out that, had he been there on the *Prometheus*, they might not have been in this fix in the first place. But he'd learned a long time ago that, when someone hands you a compliment, it's advisable to nod and smile. Sheridan nodded and smiled, and only then did Lefcourt's comment about another job penetrate. "But . . . my ship—" he began.

Lefcourt shook his head. "Is going to be in spacedock for some time being repaired. I need you for this immediately."

Sheridan had no basis upon which to protest. No one knew better than he, after all, the extent of the damage that the *Lexington* had sustained. It was rather unreasonable, to say nothing of a waste of manpower, to keep Sheridan tucked away while the ship underwent repairs.

The trip to Lefcourt's office was very quick, and also somewhat strained. Lefcourt did not wish to discuss the nature of the mission until they got to his sanctum, but naturally they did not want to travel in dead silence. So Lefcourt made what amounted to odd chitchat, which made Sheridan feel a bit uncomfortable. He quickly learned that there was nothing stranger than a superior officer pointedly trying to talk about nothing. Thus, when they arrived at Lefcourt's office, both Sheridan and Lefcourt let out a small sigh of relief.

Sheridan had not had a great deal of interaction with Narns in his career, but naturally he was able to recognize one on sight. This is what occurred when he strode into Lefcourt's office and a Narn who had been seated in a chair opposite Lefcourt's desk rose to greet him. "Commander Sheridan, this is G'Kar," Lefcourt informed him. "He's here on behalf of the Narn regime, which has agreed to sell us weapons to help equalize the battle."

"Commander," G'Kar said, bowing slightly, and Sheridan matched the gesture.

"He's here to make arrangements for a covert mission," Lefcourt continued. "A Narn cruiser will transport you to one of our abandoned listening posts in Sector 919 where, in theory, you will rendezvous with a representative of the Minbari."

Sheridan had not been entirely sure of what to expect of this mysterious mission, but *that* was most certainly not among his guesses. In point of fact, he could not quite believe what had been said, and his incredulous look wasn't lost on Lefcourt. You see, the "Starkiller" was just paranoid enough to wonder if this peace mission might have been put into motion in order to give up the destroyer of the *Black Star*, as a means of placating the infuriated Minbari. Still, he knew he had to put that thought out of his head.

As if reading his mind, Lefcourt amended, "Note that I said 'in theory.' We've heard that certain elements of their government want a meeting, to discuss finding a way out of this war that doesn't involve the annihilation of Earth."

"Most progressive of them," G'Kar commented. It seemed to Sheridan that G'Kar was none too thrilled about the proposition, and he realized that G'Kar was in no better a situation than his own. If a peace were made, then the Narns would lose out on a potentially large sale, to say nothing of having missed the opportunity to make it look as if the Centauri had been dealing weapons to an enemy of the Minbari. And not to mention the fact that he was putting his own neck on the line, for if this were, in fact, a trap, then the Minbari might very well be laying it for the Narn who arranged to sell the weapons.

If Sheridan had to guess, he would have said that, whatever arrangements G'Kar was making, he was likely going to keep himself as far in the background as possible and nowhere near the actual site of the meet.

"It could also be a trick," Lefcourt acknowledged. "We want you to make contact because you've shown you can handle yourself against them if things get hot. Your record on first-contact protocol is outstanding."

"And I'm expendable," Sheridan added ruefully.

Lefcourt opened his mouth a moment as if prepared to debate the notion, but then closed it again. He realized it was pointless to discuss that aspect because, in point of fact, Sheridan was right, and all the discussion in the galaxy wasn't going to change it. "Once we know it's safe and they're serious, we'll send in the negotiators."

"Anyone else on my team?" asked Sheridan.

"Just one."

He went to the door of his office and opened it. Security guards escorted in a somewhat irritated-looking young man who was introduced to Sheridan as Dr. Stephen Franklin. It was painfully obvious to Sheridan that neither Lefcourt nor Franklin seemed particularly enthused about seeing each other. "Dr. Franklin," Lefcourt said slowly, with what sounded like irony in his voice, "had a fair amount of physical contact with the Minbari before the war. He can verify that these individuals are who they say they are, and be on hand in case things go badly."

"You volunteered?" Sheridan asked, glancing at the security guards and knowing the answer to the question before he asked it.

"I didn't have that much of a choice," Franklin replied. "It's the only way they'll let me out of the stockade." He sighed and shook his head. "It's a long story."

They had a lengthy trip ahead of them, and Sheridan reasoned that—were Franklin interested in telling that story—there would be plenty of time to hear it. "What about a translator?" he asked.

"We've been told that your contact has studied your language," G'Kar interjected. "Just in case, I will go along, since I am fluent in Minbari and English."

So G'Kar *was* going to accompany them. This surprised Sheridan to no end. "It's going to be dangerous," Sheridan pointed out.

G'Kar shrugged. "Perhaps. But if all goes well, you will owe us a great debt. And debts can be very profitable."

"I don't have to tell you how important this mission is, Commander," Lefcourt said, making no attempt to keep the gravity from his voice. "We're still only a few months into the war. There are millions of lives at risk in the inner colonies, then here in the home system. This has to go well, John. There's no other choice."

"And if the only way out is for Earth to surrender?"

Lefcourt's back straightened as he said, "Officially, that's up to the negotiators. Those are my orders. Unofficially . . ." He paused, and when he spoke next, it was without the usual air of bombast that accompanied his pronouncements. "We're losing this war, John. And if the only way the Human race can survive is to surrender . . . then we'll surrender."

It was a pronouncement that was staggering to Sheridan. Keep in mind that this was a Human who had just been feted with a hero's welcome after providing what was considered to be the great triumph of the war. To follow up such a victory with talk of surrender, well, it was very difficult for him.

But in his heart, he knew that Lefcourt was speaking truly. And he further knew that he was, at that particular point in time, quite possibly the last, best hope for peace.

* * *

I mentioned to you earlier one of G'Kar's eager lieutenants. I will now provide you his name, which was G'Mak. G'Mak was a crafty and quick-thinking individual, hovering just inside G'Kar's inner circle of confidants.

It was not long after the meeting between G'Kar and Sheridan that G'Mak returned to his quarters, his thoughts in a turmoil. G'Kar's plan to aid the Humans in a meeting with the Minbari left him with a throbbing feeling of dull anger. G'Mak played a pivotal role in arranging the acquisition of weapons and the clandestine payment for same. Everything had been in place, when G'Kar had abruptly informed G'Mak that the deal was on hold. That, indeed, matters seemed to be going in another direction. When G'Mak complained of the lost revenue, G'Kar spoke of debts to be called upon down the line.

G'Mak and G'Kar had always nicely complemented each other, for G'Kar always strove (with varying degrees of success) to plan for the grand scheme of things, while G'Mak concentrated instead on smaller matters. There were times when those different visions conflicted with each other, and now was definitely one of those times.

So frustrated was the normally alert G'Mak that he did not even realize he had someone waiting for him in his quarters, at least until I cleared my throat. Then he jumped, startled, and said, "Mollari! What . . . what are you—!"

"Relax," I said calmly, rising from my seat. "No one saw me come here."

"If they did . . ." He tried to find the words to describe what an awful eventuality that would be.

"No . . . one . . . did." Though supremely calm, I had an air of joviality about me, which very likely put him on his guard. That was most wise of him. "So, G'Mak, is there anything you wish to tell me about?"

His eyes narrowed as he said, "Not at the moment, Mollari, no. Matters are . . . proceeding as we discussed."

"Is that a fact?"

He nodded.

"How very interesting," I commented. "You see, that is not what I hear. What I hear, through my own resources, is that there is a meeting planned between the Humans and the Narn. That the final arrangements are being made for an arms shipment. I would like to know the when and the where."

My resources, of course, were the words of Sonovar of the Minbari. Now word was filtering through the various castes of some sort of meeting with the Humans and the Narn, and there were even whispers that a Minbari was involved. Possibly a traitor to the Great Cause.

This was as close as the rumors could come to pinpoint Lenonn's involvement, for he had been very thorough in maintaining the cap of secrecy. That there was a peace initiative involved was unknown, even to Sonovar . . . and even to me.

"Look, Mollari," G'Mak began to say.

But I waved off his words as if they were of only the mildest interest to me. "I know what you are going to say," I said, interrupting him. "It is one thing to provide me with information as to your government's activities, in hopes of building your own power base and an alliance with the Centauri. You are most wise, G'Mak. At the moment, Narn has its freedom. But the future may bring any number of possibilities, eh?"

Frankly, I had no real belief that G'Mak's concerns would ever amount to anything. Even at that time, the "great Centauri empire" was a joke, a . . . a shadow . . . of its former self. G'Mak's reasons for his actions seemed to me needlessly involved. But under circumstances like those, one learns not to question someone who is making himself useful.

"But it is quite another thing," I continued, "to provide me with information that may very well lead to the certain death of one of your own—what's his name again? G'Gar?"

"G'Kar," he corrected.

"Ah, yes," I said, nodding. I had never met G'Kar before. That delightful moment was to occur at a later time.

I took a step closer and said, "G'Mak, you owe him *nothing*. In matters such as these, it is survival of the fittest. G'Kar's masterminding a weapons sale to the Humans— a race that is surely doomed—and that can only bode ill for the Narn. You know this, for you know that I have informed the Minbari that the Centauri have nothing to do with the transaction. So G'Kar's little attempt at misdirection is doomed to failure, and only the Narn will be left to answer for the actions of a handful of individuals. And if you think the Minbari will be any more merciful to your people than they have been to the Humans, then you are sadly mistaken."

Slowly G'Mak nodded, clearly considering my words. But then he asked a question in such an idle, casual manner that I did not at all perceive the truth behind the words. "Tell me," he asked. "What if the Minbari were interested in a peace initiative?"

"What?" I said, making no attempt to hide my disbelief that the question could even be posed.

"What if it were not a weapons negotiation? If, instead, it were a peace negotiation—?"

I did not realize it at the time, you understand, but it was the single most important question that had ever been posed to me. And I, fool that I was, did not recognize it.

"A peace negotiation is an impossibility," I said flatly. "You do not speak directly to the Minbari, G'Mak. I do. I have my contacts, my sources, and believe me when I tell you, G'Mak, there is no mercy in them. No compassion. The Humans committed a dreadful transgression. I have not gone into detail with the Humans, describing their crimes to them, for I have no desire to let them know the depth of my connections with the Minbari. If I did, then for all I know, they would toss me into one of their delightful little holding cells until such time that I opt to tell them everything I know.

"I have no desire to spend any part of my life in such inhospitable surroundings if it can be at all avoided, and I assure you, G'Mak, avoid it I will. But I will tell *you*, my dear G'Mak, that my contacts have been very specific on this point. Peace is an impossibility. G'Kar is either being misled, in which case he is too stupid to be allowed to live. Or else he is lying to you, which means he does not trust you . . . which further means that he suspects you to be a traitor to him."

G'Mak looked rather shaken at this. I cannot say that I blame him. Narns are, by and large, a rather barbaric and savage race. One does not wish to have a Narn angry at one, if one can help it.

I know that I didn't.

For I shall tell you something that I have only told a handful of people: I had, by that time, had a dream. A premonition, if you will. I had dreamt that I was an old man, very old . . . much as I am now. And I was struggling with a Narn, who stared down at me with a single gleaming red eye and a snarl of pure animal fury upon his spotted face. He had his hands upon my throat and he . . . he . . .

Ah. I have upset you. Pardon. Please excuse an old man and his insensitivity. I have lived with this vision for so long that it no longer has any impact on me, and so I neglect the effect that it might have on others.

The dream does have a relation to the rest of the story, but I shall not discuss it now. Let us minimize it, move on so that we do not dwell upon it excessively, and so make matters overly morbid.

So . . .

G'Mak looked none too happy over the two possibilities that I had suggested to him. Pressing my advantage, I leaned forward and told him, "You will be doing yourself a favor, G'Mak. Indeed, you may well be doing the entire Narn homeworld a favor. You do not need either a liar or a fool in a position of power, and I regret to say that in G'Kar you apparently have both. It is tragic, but there it is. Now, you have the option of being a hero, G'Mak. Will you take that option? Will you be the hero that Narn needs and that I know you can be?"

Very, very slowly, G'Mak nodded again.

And he told me exactly what I wanted to know.

Understand, my friends, the concept of "orders." That is something you do not yet understand. You children, you think to go to bed early is an order. To clean up your room is an order. The hard orders . . . those are the ones you discover later. The order to leave your friends on the battle-field. The order to fire on the weak and the powerless. My orders . . .

I'm sorry. What? Did I . . . nod off in midsentence? My apologies. That has been happening more and more frequently of late. Sooner or later it will stop happening. Sooner rather than later, I think.

Yes, my orders were to prevent the Narns from using the war to establish closer ties to the Humans. In retrospect, these instructions were samples of the pure mindlessness inherent in the mandates handed me from above. The Humans were doomed to extinction in any event. What matter if the Narns had close ties or distant ties? Either way Earth was destined to be but a pile of ash. Let the Narns become friends with the Humans. In the long run, the only advantage such an alliance seemed capable of producing was that the gray-white remains of Humanity might make convenient fertilizer and actually encourage the growth of greenery upon the rather bleak Narn homeworld.

Look at me, my friends. I am old and fragile. Put aside my title for a moment, my symbols of office. I am just a man: no more, no less. Hearts pumping, albeit with some artificial aid. Flesh and blood. Given to as much mortal fallibility as anyone else. I can issue the pronouncements I wish, and people can and will obey them. But that doesn't necessarily make them, or me, right. I am simply in charge. And the greatest asset that someone in my position can have is someone at his right hand to tell him that he is wrong.

I have one such. Or at least . . . I had. But I have not seen him for some time.

My orders regarding the Narns and the Humans were wrong. But there was no one to let my superiors know that . . . including me, for my antipathy toward the Narns was second to none. Perhaps that antipathy colored my view of the Narn aid in the peace initiative. I rejected the notion that the Narn were involved in anything other than weapons trade because I was too accustomed to thinking of the Narn in a warlike manner.

What I did not know or understand is that G'Kar was a man of peace.

I would like to think that I could be forgiven this. You see, G'Kar did not know it at the time himself. He felt the need to rationalize his involvement by putting it in terms of potential long-term gain. The time that he spent on Babylon 5 became a great spiritual journey and awakening for him. I envy him that.

Damn him . . . I envy him.

As I said, I would like to think that I could be forgiven this misunderstanding on my part. But that is wishful thinking. I cannot expect anyone to forgive me when I cannot forgive myself.

I did not know that it was to be an attempt to end the war. Didn't know because of the limits of my orders, the limits of my own worldview, and the limits that I had placed upon the Narns, which were a dark reflection of my own limitations.

And so I gave the order to intercept them. To stop their mission from succeeding. Great Maker forgive me . . .

. . . for I doubt I will ever forgive myself.

—— chapter 13 ——

The world did not even have a real name.

It was that much of a backwater, out-of-the-way planet. The Minbari, the Centauri, the Humans, and the Narns all had mentions of the planet on their starcharts, but each called it something different, each employing only a designation to identify the planet's location in space. No one thought anything of it, which is what made it the ideal place for a quiet little meeting that no one was supposed to know about.

Someone had attempted to colonize it at some point . . . the Drazi, I believe. But a meteor strike had completely disrupted the world's ecosystem, turning it from a reasonably inhospitable world to a place that you would not send your most hated ex-wife to. And I would be familiar with this concept, having more than my share of hated ex-wives.

To this world came Sheridan, Franklin, and G'Kar.

Their destination was a small, stark bunker, one of the few remaining structures from the abortive Drazi colonization. Small whirlwinds kicked up the ground around them as they made their way to the structure. Sheridan squinted against the intensity of the wind and, one or two times, felt as if the gale was going to lift him up and carry him away. He placed his hand on his jacket and felt the slight crispness of a picture against his chest. It was the picture of Anna, which he now carried with him at all times. He drew comfort from it for no reason that he could readily discern.

They reached the bunker and Sheridan tried the door. He couldn't budge it. This was just wonderful; a peace initiative upon which the existence of an entire race would hinge, and they couldn't even get into the designated meeting place.

G'Kar came up from behind, touched Sheridan on the shoulder, and gestured for him to step aside. Sheridan did so and G'Kar put his fairly impressive muscle into it, pulling with grim-faced, unyielding pressure. Slowly the long-unused door, held shut through a combination of rust and the steady gusting of the wind, opened outward. Sheridan and Franklin moved quickly through the doorway as G'Kar kept it open for them, and then he stepped through as well, allowing the wind to slam the door shut behind them.

"Just a sec," Sheridan told them. "Let me find the power supply. Just hope the solar batteries are still working."

He glanced around the nearly total darkness of the unpromising-looking bunker and, stepping over debris littering the floor, found a button on the wall. *Couldn't be that easy*, he thought, even as he pushed it. He had a flash of apprehension; with his luck, he'd just pushed an emergency self-destruct button that was going to obliterate the entire bunker and, very likely, the whole planet.

Instead the lights around him flickered for a moment and then came on. A moment later there was the slow sound of a motor wheezing to life, and Sheridan sensed the rush of air as the air processors started up.

Sheridan noticed that the outer door was starting to rock

back and forth. Apparently the wind had shifted and the door, having been loosened by G'Kar, was now providing only limited protection from the elements outside. "Dr. Franklin, check the outer door. See if we can secure this place."

Franklin nodded as G'Kar approached Sheridan. He had done much reading up on Sheridan, studied his career, and was most impressed with the resourcefulness that Sheridan had displayed in the battle against the *Black Star*. Much of the trip had passed in silence as Sheridan, lost in thought, had mentally prepared himself for the importance of what they were about to face. Now G'Kar said, "You know, Commander, if we are unable to resolve this war of yours, there is always a place for someone like you among our people. We could arrange a safe haven for you, a few others . . ."

Sheridan shook his head. "Thanks, but if my world goes, I'm going with it."

On one level, G'Kar very likely admired the single-mindedness of this attitude. But the Narn could have used someone like Sheridan. He was adaptable and had a fine military mind. And the Narn were always looking ahead to military-oriented possibilities. But Sheridan seemed to have made up his mind, and G'Kar simply shrugged. "A waste of material. Most unfortunate."

The door sprang open behind them, and G'Kar turned. Dr. Franklin was starkly silhouetted in the glare from outside. "Ah, good, Doctor, I was just telling your associate . . ."

And then he stopped, his voice catching slightly in his throat, for he came to the realization that Dr. Franklin's hands were raised.

The reason for this was quite simple: Franklin was being herded by someone. It did not take a great deal of effort to determine just who that someone might be.

A Minbari entered the room.

Sheridan had seen the few existing photographs of the

Minbari, had a basic knowledge of what they looked like. But that was very different from being face-to-face with one . . . particularly when that one had a gun leveled at them. And it was also different considering that there was something about *this* Minbari in particular.

There was a small stunt that Sheridan's father had taught him many years ago, a means of making eye contact when one is in a situation where it is necessary to firmly establish strength of character and a handle on the proceedings. Rather than simply look straight into the eyes of the individual you are meeting, subtly focus the entirety of your gaze upon his right eye only. Usually the subject will not have the slightest idea that that is what you're doing. But— on a subconscious level—he will sense your vigor and vitality. Perhaps he will even be quicker to accede to whatever it is you have on your mind.

Sheridan did so at that point. He focused the whole of his concentration upon the right eye of the Minbari.

The Minbari returned his gaze levelly, impassively.

And Sheridan felt completely disconcerted. For it brought to mind as well a very common Human saying: The eyes are the window to the soul. And Sheridan could not help but feel that he was encountering a very, very old soul indeed. He was not daunted, but he felt a sense of very quiet awe.

The Minbari, for his part, seemed intrigued by whatever it was he saw in Sheridan's eyes. Perhaps the Minbari had the same saying. Very slowly he lowered his gun, and Sheridan let out a soft sigh . . . but not one, he hoped, that was audible to the Minbari.

Seeing that the Humans and Narn were breathing without any artificial aid, the newcomer slowly removed his own breather.

It was immediately clear to Sheridan, as soon as the Minbari spoke, that he was still struggling with English.

Nonetheless, Sheridan was mightily impressed. It had been only a short while since the Minbari had first encountered Humans, and Sheridan was reasonably certain that it would take him a hell of a lot longer than that to become even remotely conversant in the Minbari tongue.

"A . . . precaution only," the Minbari said, indicating his gun. He tapped his chest once and said, "Lenonn. You . . . Sheridan?"

"Yes," Sheridan said, speaking slowly and distinctly. Things were at a delicate enough stage as it was. The last thing Sheridan, or the entire Human race, needed was for Sheridan to slur his words, have this Lenonn misunderstand and think he'd been insulted, and incinerate the bearers of peace where they stood. "I didn't know you'd been told who was coming."

"We know more than you think," Lenonn replied. He seemed to be speaking with mounting confidence, as if his being able to comprehend what Sheridan said bolstered his faith in his ability to communicate. Then his face darkened. "And I know what you did to the . . ." He paused, unsure of the translation, and turned to G'Kar. "*Drala Fi.*"

"The *Black Star*," G'Kar said to Sheridan.

"Sheridan . . . the Starkiller, you are called."

Sheridan stiffened, the tension in the room seeming to crackle. Granted, Lenonn had described the weapon as a "precaution only," but suddenly Sheridan began to wonder . . . a precaution against what? Against the possibility that Sheridan might try to run because Lenonn was about to exact vengeance for the Minbari who had been blasted to free-floating nuclear-charged atoms? Sheridan abruptly sensed that he was already being presented with what could be a major sticking point, or turning point, in the negotiations. Should he apologize? Plead for mercy, for understanding? Should he say that he panicked, acted rashly? Perhaps even offer up his life in exchange for those he had taken?

Perhaps that was what the Minbari were looking for: someone to sacrifice himself. Someone upon whom all the blame could be placed, whether warranted or not.

There are some Earth cultures which have a person who is known as a "Sin-Eater." When a Human dies, fruits or foodstuffs representing the sins of the deceased are laid out about him. And the Sin-Eater, a societal pariah by definition, comes and consumes the food, taking the sins of the deceased to himself. That way the dearly departed is free to pass on to heaven or to the next life or wherever, untouched and unmarked by whatever wrongs he has committed in his life.

Was that what the Minbari wanted, then? Someone to metaphorically devour the sins of all, and then offer himself up, so that humanity could be cleansed of wrongdoing and be allowed to live?

Or perhaps they just wanted to see a human grovel, face-to-face. Perhaps the pleas of the thousands that the Minbari had slaughtered, their cries for mercy, were insufficient.

Perhaps . . .

Perhaps . . .

Perhaps . . .

All of this went through Sheridan's mind in far less time than it takes me to tell you. To be specific, it was little more than an instant, and in that instant Sheridan determined that, if he was to die, he was going to remain true to himself through to the end.

"We did exactly what they would have done to us," he shot back. "We just did it first."

Franklin looked rather nervously at Sheridan, feeling that perhaps a more mollifying response might have been in order. And G'Kar simply glanced at him as if to say, *Bravely put. At least you'll die with your pride intact.*

With all of those dynamics going on, it was little wonder that Sheridan was surprised as Lenonn replied, "I know. It was necessary." Franklin visibly relaxed. Sheridan kept his breathing slow and steady, and G'Kar . . . well, G'Kar might have been carved from marble for all the expression he showed. He seemed emotionally separated from the moment, as if he could not care less how any of it played out, or even if his own life were forfeit as a result of his involvement with the Humans.

"But I also know many . . . *that* many of my people," continued Lenonn grimly, "will not . . . forget." He paused, letting that sink in.

Years later, in recounting the incident, Sheridan told me that he could almost relate to what Lenonn had said. The Humans apparently memorialized some of their greatest defeats in order to spur them on in battle. *Remember the Alamo!* would be the cry. *Remember the* Maine*! Remember Pearl Harbor!* Somewhere, Sheridan realized, Minbari were shouting, "Remember the *Black Star*!" as a means of inciting each other to battle and glory. And he, Sheridan, was responsible for that. He was no different from those who had destroyed the Alamo and the *Maine*—whatever those were—or Pearl Harbor . . . whoever *she* was.

After a brief time, Lenonn continued, "I speak to you . . . for them. That we may find a way to . . . *Lizenn*?" he said softly to himself. G'Kar started to prompt him, but Lenonn quickly remembered the proper word. ". . . ah, to *resolve* this before more of your kind . . . are killed. We . . ."

There was a sharp electronic beep. The sound was so unexpected in the tense air that Sheridan jumped slightly. It was G'Kar's comm link, and he quickly toggled it. For the first time, Sheridan saw nervousness appear on G'Kar's face. The Narn vessel was under specific orders not to contact him unless it was an extreme emergency, and this was precisely the sort of situation that even the stoic G'Kar did not desire to see turn into an extreme emergency. "Yes?"

"G'Kar!" came the alarmed voice of the ship's captain, N'Fal. "G'Kar! A ship is coming through the gate!"

Franklin glanced at Lenonn, hoping for a particular answer that he had a sick feeling he wasn't going to receive. "Yours?" he asked.

Sure enough, Lenonn didn't say what Franklin wanted to hear. Instead he shook his head and said, "No."

"Do you have a reading on it?" G'Kar asked N'Fal.

Credit Centauri vessels: We are most efficient when it comes to matters of destruction. The Centauri cruiser charged through the jump gate and leaped into normal space, firing as it went. The Narn cruiser never had a chance as our cruiser ripped into it, blasting the helpless vessel apart before the Narns had a chance to offer even the most token resistance. Even as G'Kar, in frustration, shouted into his communications device for a response from N'Fal, N'Fal himself was scattered to the solar winds, along with his ship and crew.

"N'Fal! N'Fal, can you hear me?" G'Kar called.

But while N'Fal was beyond hearing, the Centauri in the vessel above most certainly were not. They picked up G'Kar's desperate summons and, in a burst of interstellar brotherly harmony, tracked it back to its source. Then they let fly with their missiles.

The missiles thudded to the planet's surface, one after another, rocking the ground beneath them and getting progressively nearer with terrifying speed. Sheridan knew that there was nowhere to run to, no shelter to be sought. The only thing that was going to save them was blind luck, and it was what Sheridan was going to have to depend on. "Hit the deck!" he shouted, and he turned to try to grab Lenonn and drag him down to something vaguely approximating safety.

But the roof was falling in on them, literally, and far too

quickly. Sheridan was only a few feet away from Lenonn, his hand outstretched. And he knew, beyond any question, that this was a turning point in the war, right then, right there. Until moments before, the Minbari had been the implacable enemy. Yet at that instant, with potential doom thundering all around them, Sheridan had one thought and one thought only: He himself was expendable, but this Minbari they were facing, this Lenonn . . . he was special. He was brave. He was clearly going against the desire and mind-set of his entire people by secretly pursuing a peace initiative, and if anything happened to him—anything— then the peace initiative was as good as dead.

And so was the human race.

Lenonn staggered, fell, and Sheridan lunged forward with the intention of throwing himself over Lenonn to try to protect him from the falling debris. For all he knew, it would do no good. He and the Minbari would be found together, an almost unrecognizable, pulped mixture of skin, bones, blood, and sinew. Nonetheless, he had to try.

Unfortunately, he was not given the opportunity.

A direct hit upon the bunker smashed in the ceiling, and a hail of debris drove a wedge between Sheridan and Lenonn. Sheridan felt cement collapse down upon him. Something snapped in his upper chest . . . a rib, he suspected, perhaps two, and the pain drove him to the ground. Dirt and dust billowed up all around him. And still he stretched out a hand, his body and heart refusing to acknowledge what his mind already knew: that this was a most hopeless cause. Perhaps it was because Sheridan had been taught by his father, what seemed a lifetime ago, that the only causes worth fighting for were hopeless ones. And he had a feeling that there was no cause more hopeless than this one.

He was right.

The Centauri warship hesitated a moment, surveying the

wreckage from on high. They verified for themselves that their assault had been well aimed, that the target was demolished. They could have gone down to inspect the job firsthand, but there seemed little point. The Narn ship was destroyed, the Narn and the human with whom he was transacting business were likely dead. Even if they lived, they had nowhere to go. There was no point in staying about. And so the Centauri cruiser jumped away into hyperspace, its job done.

I had no idea then, as I've said, that there was a peace initiative being pursued. No idea that there were Humans *and* Minbari on the planet's surface, aided by the Narn who were far more noble at that moment than we could ever have hoped to be. No idea of the immense sin, the thousands more lives, that would be laid at our door . . . at my door.

Nothing breeds more rapidly than ignorance. For the Humans and Minbari likewise had no idea what had truly occurred. Each side assumed it was a renegade arm of its own government. But it was us. And it was my order that destroyed their last chance for peace.

None of that was known to Sheridan. He was not even dwelling on who had been responsible for the attack. Caring about such a thing would have entailed a belief that he was going to survive beyond the moment. And at that point the only thing Sheridan was concerned about was continuing to breathe from one second to the next.

He lost track of how much time passed. Perhaps the pain in his chest even caused him to black out slightly. And in that haze, that "between time" . . .

He saw things.

Things he did not quite understand. Darkness all around him, and something glowing . . . something winged, ever so fleeting . . .

And the glowing, winged form passed Anna, standing in a place that seemed to be nowhere and everywhere. As it passed, Anna was illuminated, and she was glowing and beautiful, and she was the light to Sheridan. He felt himself crawling toward her, not comprehending, but knowing he had to get to her for reasons he could not even begin to articulate.

Then the glowing form passed away, and the last sight he had of Anna was darkness crossing over her face, enveloping her.

And then, slowly, he began to recover his senses. He felt the awful weight and pressure of the rubble upon him, and gritted his teeth as he pushed it off himself. The dust had begun to clear and he was able to see Franklin, performing the same actions. Over in the far corner, G'Kar was likewise freeing himself, although Sheridan noted that it seemed to be with substantially less effort. And while Franklin and Sheridan groaned or moaned with the exertion, not a sound escaped G'Kar's lips. It was as if he was taking whatever pain he was in and using it to focus upon the job at hand.

Then Sheridan saw Lenonn across the way . . .

. . . and saw that he was not moving. His body lay broken, his eyes staring upward, fixed and glassy. He was still alive, but that did not appear to be a long-term state of being for him.

Franklin, who had fared a bit better than Sheridan during the cave-in, had already made it over to the Minbari. He crouched over him, surveying the damage. He was too good a doctor to let the full measure of his awareness be reflected in his eyes, but he knew in a moment that the cause was hopeless. Sheridan hauled himself from the last of the debris that imprisoned him and stumbled to Franklin's side. "How is he?"

The doctor looked over to Sheridan. "Not good," Franklin said. In point of fact he knew that was an understatement, but it is not considered good "bedside manner" to speak other than encouragement in the presence of a patient, par-

ticularly if you think that those moments are going to be
the patient's last. It is far easier to meet one's maker if one
doesn't know one has an appointment scheduled.

"We need him alive," Sheridan said urgently.

And then Lenonn spoke, which startled Franklin slightly
since he thought that speech was, at that point, beyond the
Minbari's capacity. "That . . . may not be . . . possible,"
Lenonn whispered. He looked at them with the eyes of one
who knew he was dying. "I . . . am sorry. I have . . . made
things worse."

"Try not to talk, all right?" Franklin told him. He knew at
that point that the only hope possible was that help would
arrive in time to be of some use. And if Lenonn wasted what
small strength he had remaining in self-recrimination, that
would just increase the likelihood that the only thing waiting in the bunker when help arrived would be two banged-
up Humans, one stoic Narn, and a Minbari corpse. If it
should so happen that help arrived in the form of Minbari,
well . . . that would certainly not be an array that would send
the rescuers into paroxysms of joy.

Lenonn, however, did not seem particularly disposed
toward waiting. "No . . . you must listen," he gasped out. He
didn't seem to be looking at them anymore. Instead it was
as if he was looking beyond them, his eyes focused on a
future that only he could see. "They will come looking for
me . . . and they will blame you . . . for me . . . and the war
will grow worse."

Under the grime that coated his face, Sheridan blanched.
He had envisioned any number of scenarios coming out of
this meeting, but having matters become even worse than
they were was not one that he had anticipated.

Lenonn seemed to focus back on Sheridan for a brief
moment. In a desperate whisper, he said, "Listen . . . carefully . . . and repeat this . . . exactly."

He hissed something into Sheridan's ear. G'Kar leaned
forward, trying to hear, but couldn't. Nor could Franklin. But

Sheridan nodded grimly, jaw set. The words meant nothing to him, and that made him extremely nervous. What if he was hearing a sort of free association floating about in the dying mind of the Minbari? Words, phrases strung together that seemed to make sense to Lenonn, but in fact were nothing more than gibberish.

He wanted to ask Lenonn to clarify, to make clear what it was that he was talking about, but then he heard an awful sound that rose from deep in Lenonn's throat. In an abstract way, he took note of the fact that the death rattle of a Minbari was indistinguishable from that of a Human. It was an interesting, if minor, piece of information, and one that Sheridan would much rather not have acquired.

Franklin looked down upon the unmoving form of the Minbari, and it crossed his mind in a rather bleak fashion that his success rate with Minbari patients was abysmal. Specifically, they'd all died. He hoped that he would have the opportunity to rectify that in the future. He hoped he'd *have* a future. "Did you get it?" he asked Sheridan.

Sheridan nodded slowly, repeating it to himself several times to make certain that it was solid in his memory. He was not sure of what use it would be, or whether it would do him one damned bit of good. But he instinctively knew that, whatever it meant, it might very well be his one opportunity for salvation.

—— *chapter 14* ——

What I am about to tell you now . . . never happened.

That is not to say that it is fabricated, no. No, far from it. The actual events did occur. But what occurs in reality and what occurs officially are two vastly different matters.

On the Minbari cruiser which served the Grey Council, word had slowly begun to filter through various individuals that Lenonn had some sort of a meeting planned with the Narn. There were even further rumors that Humans might be involved, as well. The political ramifications of such a concept were staggering, and Delenn was not quite prepared to cope with them alone. Not yet, in any event.

People began to ask Delenn, casually, if she knew of anything. Now, you must understand, for a Minbari to lie is a considerable sin. They simply do not do so, unless a matter of honor is involved for another individual. Delenn was not completely certain that such a concern applied in this case. To conceal the nature of Lenonn's activities was not a question of honor, but rather one of expediency. Delenn knew that she had wandered into a gray area . . . appropriate, one supposes, considering who and what she was, but nonetheless she found herself wrapped in something of a moral dilemma.

When approached on the topic by Morann, however, she finally chose to respond in the following manner:

"I have heard many conflicting rumors," she told Morann . . . which was true. "And I am also aware that Lenonn has seemed to be most involved with some sort of affairs that he considers to be rather important, and for which discretion is required." Which was true. "Some are saying that it is connected to the Rangers." Which it was. "Others are saying that it is related to the war, and to the Narn, and even to the Humans." Which was true again. She took a deep breath and said, "Now, in my opinion . . . if Lenonn were meeting with the Humans for some reason, I would assume that it is in connection with some sort of fact-finding mission. It is entirely possible that he desires to present himself as some sort of potential ally to the Humans, to make them think that peace is possible."

All of this was absolutely true. At that point, Delenn hesitated, not certain of how to proceed. "That way," she began, and then let her voice trail off, and she looked at Morann expectantly.

His eyes lit with understanding. "Of course," he said with mounting admiration. "That way, it would build within them a false sense of hope. While we prepare ourselves for the final push toward obliterating Humanity, they will be busy convincing themselves that peace is in the offing. Their defenses will be lowered. There will be no more cowardly seeding of asteroid fields, no more sneak attacks. They will grasp at the false hopes presented them, and as a result, when our attacks begin again in force, they will be that much more crushed. The last of their resolve will slip away, their last hope gone, and we will annihilate them with minimal risk to ourselves."

Delenn nodded and, trying to keep the relief from her voice, said truthfully, "That certainly seems a valid interpretation of events."

To Delenn's surprise, Morann seemed almost chagrined. "I am loath to admit this, Delenn, but I, who have been among Lenonn's greatest critics, may have sorely misjudged him. I only wish that he had discussed this strategy with the Grey Council."

"You know Lenonn," Delenn replied. "He must do things his way. Besides, as we both know, we have given him little reason to trust the Grey Council, of late."

"I am very aware of that. But that is going to change, Delenn. You have my word . . ."

At that moment, a member of the religious-caste crew came to the doorway. "I . . . apologize for the intrusion, Satai," he said. His look appeared to encompass both Delenn and Morann.

"It is not a bother. What is it?"

"We have received a distress beacon, from a solo Minbari vessel."

Immediately an alarm began to buzz deep within Delenn. "A solo vessel?"

"Yes. We have verified the registry. It belongs to Lenonn."

"Can you track it?" she asked.

"Absolutely, Satai."

"Take us there. Immediately."

"Immediately, Satai." He bowed quickly before leaving the room. Delenn could almost feel Morann's eyes boring through her. She turned to meet his gaze levelly and say, "What do you think it means?"

"I think," he said, "it means that Lenonn should have indeed consulted us and brought along people to provide cover for him. I think it may be that the Humans have taken from us another of our greatest and bravest. And if that is the case, I shall tear the living hearts from their leaders with my own hands."

And Delenn knew, beyond all doubt, that once again only the truth was being spoken.

The salvage ships arrived on the surface of the planet and found Lenonn's vessel in no time. It seemed that Lenonn—ever the cautious individual, as his entrance with the leveled weapon had indicated—had left his ship with a time-delayed distress beacon. If he did not return to shut it off within a specified period, the beacon would go off automatically. The blasts from the Centauri cruiser overhead had, miraculously, missed striking the ship directly. The ground next to it had been struck and the vessel had half sunk into the wind-blasted surface of the planet, but its beacon was still intact and was doing its job of summoning aid.

The Minbari rescue team looked around. One of them, as happenstance would have it, was Sonovar, my old source for all matters Minbari. It was Sonovar, an individual with sharp eyes, who spotted the caved-in bunker.

Speaking was a problem over the howling of the winds and the breathing devices that they were using to facilitate survival on the planet's surface. Yet they moved quickly, efficiently, their robes whipping around them, and discovered rubble and debris piled high in front of the collapsed door. But for the Minbari, it was only a matter of moments to push it aside and enter the bunker.

They did not know what they expected to find, but it was certainly not the body of Lenonn, being cradled in the lap of a Human. There were two Humans—a darker-skinned one, and the one who was next to Lenonn. That one looked up with a mixture of alarm and, yet, grim determination.

Sonovar spotted G'Kar and said sharply, "Who are you? What are your names?"

"I am G'Kar," he replied to them in Minbari, and then he paused and turned to the Humans. "They want to know your names."

Sheridan froze. It was well that he did, for at that point, he was mere seconds away from death. For he was aware, thanks to Lenonn, that he was known as "Sheridan the Star-killer" to all the Minbari. They would undoubtedly have picked his name out of INN broadcasts that had been bally-hooing the destruction of the Minbari war cruiser to a victory-starved populace, broadcasts that the Minbari would have had no trouble monitoring. They knew his name, they knew . . .

My God, they've probably seen my picture! It was plas-tered everywhere! He realized this with utter horror.

But Sonovar was staring at him with no sign of recog-nition. Sheridan realized that, at the moment, he presented a very different picture from that shown on the INN broad-casts. He was bruised, bleeding, his face smeared with soot and grime. That was combined with the fact that the Min-bari were not all that experienced with individual humans. It was entirely likely that, to Minbari, all Humans tended to look alike.

But if he spoke his name, his true name, that would be more than enough to alert the Minbari to exactly who they were dealing with.

All of this lanced through Sheridan's mind even as Franklin said simply, "Stephen Franklin."

The Minbari turned to Sheridan expectantly.

"John Smith," Sheridan said.

A moment of confusion flickered over Franklin's face, but then he understood. G'Kar, for his part, was already a step ahead of Sheridan, and kept his expression carefully neutral.

Sheridan was wise to act as he did. Sonovar later told me, when he learned, after the fact, just who he had been fac-ing, that had he known the identity of this dirty and dishe-veled human, he would have killed him without a second thought. Indeed, the compulsion to kill the Humans was a sizable one in any event. This was, after all, the race that had slain Dukhat, and was also apparently now responsible for the death of Lenonn.

But there in the bunker, Sonovar felt a flicker of confusion. This was not a simple case of arriving to discover a Human holding a smoking weapon, standing over the body of a Minbari. From the look of the Humans, they had been caught as unaware by whatever attack had been perpetrated as Lenonn had been.

Still, they were responsible in some manner, of that much Sonovar was certain. In any event, it did not matter. Humans were to be killed, slaughtered, regardless of whatever the circumstances surrounding their capture. "No mercy" had been the battle cry of the war. "No mercy." And there was no reason to extend it now.

"Shall we execute them?" a Minbari standing behind Sonovar inquired. G'Kar reacted ever so slightly to the question, just enough for Sheridan to be able to tell what it was that had been asked.

"I need to speak to someone in authority," Sheridan said urgently to G'Kar. "Tell them. Tell them that I have a—"

He did not manage to get the rest of the sentence out, however, for Sonovar found Sheridan's voice to be most annoying. He stepped forward and, before Sheridan could react, swung a fist with blinding speed and struck Sheridan on the side of the head. Sheridan went down, momentarily stunned, unable to collect his thoughts. Sonovar nodded approvingly.

"Well?" the Minbari asked Sonovar once more. He looked at his helpless victims . . .

Helpless.

Sonovar was momentarily annoyed with himself. The Humans had been helpless during much of the incursion against them, but it had been so easy to just blast their ships out of space. To see them face-to-face, to kill a barely conscious Human, or another who was clearly unarmed and nonthreatening . . .

But they had to be executed. No mercy.

Sheridan's entire future and, as it would so happen, the future of the entire battle against an enemy of darkness whose presence would not be known for a decade . . . hinged on the decision of a Minbari whose name Sheridan would never even learn.

"We take them back with us," Sonovar said decisively. His voice hardened. "Those closest to Dukhat, such as Satai Delenn, have never had a chance to look upon the creatures who took Dukhat from us. Perhaps they will wish to ask questions of them. Perhaps they would like to simply see the faces of a race who would take the greatest among us away. They can always be killed. Bringing them back to life after they have been killed is more of a problem." He looked sadly at Lenonn. "Let us bring Lenonn home . . . and give those responsible for his death a short moment of hope before we kill them."

Franklin looked to G'Kar and said urgently, "What are they saying?"

G'Kar considered a moment and then told him bluntly, "Do not ask questions to which you do not really want the answer."

Franklin didn't ask again.

Turning back to the Minbari, G'Kar said, "There are things you must know. You do not fully comprehend what happened here. You see—"

And Sonovar looked at him with as fierce a glare as he had ever summoned. "We are not at war with you, Narn. We are willing to believe that you are a helpless dupe in all of this. But if you say one more word . . . one more . . . you will not only die where you stand, but after we are through with the Humans, we will exact revenge for your involvement upon the Narn homeworld. Is that understood?"

His lips pressed tightly together, G'Kar nodded and said nothing more.

* * *

Delenn was waiting in the corridor of the Minbari cruiser when Sonovar brought in Lenonn's broken body. It was hard for her to comprehend the depth of her own feelings, the immensity of the loss. People such as Lenonn, as Dukhat, had been so filled with life. To see them devoid of it now . . . it seemed almost an obscenity to her.

Sonovar placed Lenonn upon a white, cloth-covered gurney, surrounded by members of the religious caste. Delenn was in the cloak of the Grey Council, her face obscured by it. She felt as if she were falling into darkness, seeing Dukhat and Lenonn at the top of a pit, reaching out their hands to her, but they were so far away and she was plummeting so quickly. Falling into despair and hatred.

What had been the point? What could possibly have been the point of it all?

They had murdered Lenonn. What had she been thinking? She was overwhelmed by guilt as the harsh reality of it crashed home upon her. They had killed Dukhat, and hers had been the deciding vote that sent them to war. Then she had felt guilty, felt uncertain. The words of Dukhat had come to her, telling her that the Humans would be necessary allies, and she had begun to relent. She had enlisted Lenonn . . .

. . . and he had paid the price for what was, once again, her abysmal judgment. What had she been thinking? In Valen's name, *what had she been thinking*?

As they wheeled Lenonn away, Sonovar indicated the three captives who were being shoved forward by other Minbari warriors. "We found these with Lenonn," he said, acting as if they were not even worth acknowledging in terms of sentience. "The Narn, we will send away. We brought you the Humans in case you wanted to question them prior to execution."

Delenn, from within the folds of her hood, was barely able to shake her head, so struck was she by the loss and grief. She had no interest in the Humans at that point. She did not even want to look at them. Did not want to know them, to see them. She simply wanted them gone.

The Minbari began to pull Sheridan and Franklin away, and Sheridan sensed that this individual (he could not determine even so much as her gender, so shrouded in gray was she) was someone whose words would make a difference. "Wait! I have a message . . ." he began.

She didn't hear him. Delenn was familiar with the Human tongue, although she was not quite as fluent as Lenonn had become. At that moment, she hoped she would never hear a word from Humanity again, and so Sheridan's words did not even penetrate her consciousness. She screened him out.

"I said I have a message!" Sheridan repeated more urgently.

She responded now not to the words, but to the tone. She half turned, glanced back at him, her face invisible beneath the hood. She was not waiting for him to speak, really; she was pausing for the briefest of instants, her attention momentarily caught.

"I know . . . what is in Dukhat's sacred place," Sheridan said. "I—"

Even as he spoke, he knew nothing of what he was saying. He did not know who Dukhat was. He did not know what that "sacred place" might be. What he did know, however, was extreme pain. For, with a growl of rage, Sonovar struck Sheridan squarely across the face, then again in the stomach. Sheridan doubled over. The pain from the gutshot, combining with the ache from his ribs, almost sent him back into the state of unconsciousness from which he had only recently emerged.

He fought off the blackness desperately, for he knew that if he lost the capacity to communicate once more, he would never be saying anything again. At least, not in this lifetime.

Sonovar had not understood what Sheridan was trying

to say. But one word had leapt out at him, or to be more precise, one name. The name of Dukhat. To hear that most revered of names uttered by one of the race that slaughtered him . . . the mere act was an obscenity. Having struck Sheridan a flurry of blows, Sonovar snarled, "You dare even speak Dukhat's name?"

He expected Sheridan to say nothing, to lapse into respectful silence. But Sheridan hadn't understood Sonovar's words, and I doubt it would have made any difference if he had. "I know—" he began to say, and again Sonovar struck him. Sonovar glanced in the direction of Delenn, but she was saying nothing. Merely standing there, like a Grey shadow, watching the proceedings.

"Say his name again," Sonovar warned, "and your death will be terrible beyond description."

Sheridan looked up at Sonovar with an expression of pure frustration. *What the hell is this guy's problem?* he wondered, having no idea what it was that was angering the Minbari. With every ounce of will, he said, "I know . . . what is in . . . Dukhat's sacred place . . . I know . . ."

With a roar of fury, Sonovar reached for Sheridan's neck, and there is every chance that he might have ripped the Human's head clear off his body. But that was the instant that Delenn suddenly said, "*Stop!*" The command in her voice was unmistakable, the reaction instantaneous. Sonovar froze in place as Delenn slowly approached with measured tread. She could not quite believe that she had heard the Human correctly; perhaps she had misunderstood him. He could not have been saying what she thought he'd said.

Sheridan still did not see her face clearly . . . and would not for many years to come, although her voice would one day strike a familiar chord with him. Very slowly, not wanting to misspeak or use any words that could possibly muddle her meaning, Delenn said in the Human tongue, "What is in Dukhat's sacred place?"

And Sheridan, who would eventually become rather fluent in Minbari, spoke his first two words in that alien tongue. "*Isil-zha*," he said, wondering if his last words were going to be, curiously, incomprehensible to him. "*Isil-zha*."

Delenn stiffened, as if jolted with electricity. Slowly she surveyed the others to see their reactions. They merely stared at her blankly or in outright confusion. The message meant nothing to them, although it was certainly odd. Just as odd was her stunned reaction. *The future. The Vorlons. The Vorlons are in Dukhat's sanctum.* But only Lenonn and Delenn knew that. Why would he tell the Humans . . . unless it was a message to Delenn to trust them.

Sheridan waited. Waited for what seemed an eternity. Wondering what the term meant to this gray-garbed Minbari on whose word everyone seemed to be waiting.

She turned and said, "Let them go."

Sonovar could not believe it, and Sheridan could tell from Sonovar's expression that something extraordinarily unexpected had just been said. For the first time, he felt just a twinge of hope. "Satai . . ." Sonovar began.

"I said *let them go!*" Delenn said, her voice raised. "There has been enough death today."

She saw no reason to stand around and tolerate the open-mouthed gaping of the other Minbari in the hallway. She walked away quickly. But something made her pause after only a few feet and glance behind her with curiosity. Although Sheridan could not see her clearly, she could nonetheless see him. It was her first sustained look at a Human.

She was surprised to realize that, even with all the grime and dirt on him, even though he was injured and bleeding . . . he was not utterly displeasing to the eye. Then, as quickly as the thought had taken form, she shook it off, turned, and continued on her way.

Franklin, meantime, leaned over toward Sheridan and

said, "*Isil-zha?* What does that mean?"

Sheridan shrugged, shaking his head, but G'Kar told them, "The future."

In the meantime, Sonovar had been rapidly conferring with the others. They spoke in hushed whispers, so quickly that even G'Kar couldn't quite pick up what they were saying. Several of them seemed to be arguing over a particular course of action, but the others were speaking with equal force and invoking the word "Satai" a good deal. Clearly there was some discussion over the notion of disobeying the order that they had been given, and G'Kar wasn't entirely sure which way it was going to go.

Finally Sonovar emerged from the group and approached them slowly. He pulled out a knife, and Sheridan was positive his heart stopped.

Sonovar grabbed Sheridan, whirled him around . . . and cut the bonds that were holding his hands at the wrists. As he proceeded to sever Franklin's as well, Sheridan watched Delenn walk away. He couldn't help but feel that he had just been given the barest glimpse into some sort of dynamics of the Minbari . . . and he only wished he had a better understanding of the personalities involved so that he could fully comprehend it.

A short time later, Sheridan, G'Kar, and Franklin were returned to the bunker. Sonovar brought them there personally, as if hoping that they would do something, make some provocative move, that would give him an excuse to kill them. Wisely, they said and did nothing. They barely even made eye contact. Once he had brought them back there, he simply stood there. It seemed as if he was just glaring at them, but there was more to it than that. He was trying to figure out just what it was about them that had prompted Satai Delenn to release them. He could not see anything special about them. In fact, they seemed rather pathetic.

He turned away, and G'Kar said, "Are you going to alert

the Humans or my people that we are here? That we are stranded?"

Sonovar turned back and fixed him with a glare. "Do not press your good fortune," he warned. G'Kar nodded. The warning could not have been more plain. Sonovar walked out without another word, leaving the three of them alone on a world, surrounded by howling winds.

It was some hours later that another Narn vessel, concerned over having lost touch with the ship transporting G'Kar, finally showed up. All during that time, the men said little or nothing to each other. They simply sat and contemplated their failure.

Morann stormed into Delenn's quarters, shock etched on his face. "Is it true?" he demanded. "Did you actually let the humans go?"

She nodded wordlessly.

"You *let them go*?" It was as if the repetition of the deed could somehow diminish the pure horror of it.

"Yes, Morann, I let them go," she said quite forcefully. "Were you in my position, you would have done the same. And I will tell you something further," she continued, taking a meaningful step toward him. "You will not only support me in this, but you will aid me in altering history. The Humans were never here."

"What?" He tried to comprehend what she was saying. *"What?"*

"That is correct. And not just you. You . . . and your warriors . . . and anyone on this vessel who saw the Humans . . . did not, in fact, see them."

"You want me to lie? To have everyone lie? When it is contrary to everything we believe in as Minbari to do so?" He shook his head and, to her surprise, he looked saddened. "The strain of this war has unhinged you, Delenn. That is all there is to it."

"I am far from unhinged, and you will listen to me carefully. We will do this thing—all of us—for the honor of Lenonn. In the name of his memory."

"I do not understand."

"Listen, then. Lenonn was as proud a Minbari as ever lived, correct?"

"Yes," Morann agreed. Disputes they may have had, but never had he doubted Lenonn's pride or integrity.

"He would have wanted to die well. Also correct? To have died as he had lived, proudly and bravely."

"Yes, but I still don't under—"

"In his last moments . . . he spoke to the Humans. Spoke to them of Dukhat. He said to one of them that the future was in Dukhat's sacred place."

"The future?" Morann shook his head in puzzlement. "The future? How was the future supposed to be in Dukhat's sacred place? Why was he even speaking to the Humans of Dukhat? Why was he giving them messages? It is as if . . . as if . . ."

"It is as if, in his last moments, he lost control of himself," Delenn said. "Lost control of his faculties. Babbled incoherently, jumbled things together, spoke of matters that meant something only to him." She drew herself up. "Is that how we desire for Lenonn to be remembered at the end? Babbling to Humans and treating them as if they were somehow worthy of trust and intimate communication?"

"I—"

"Well? Is it?" she said again, even more forcefully.

Slowly, Morann shook his head. "No," he said. "No, it is not. He deserved better than that. Much better."

"He deserves to be remembered as the warrior he was, who cared about the future of our people. He believed that great danger hovered over us. He desired to be our protector. Let us leave him his dignity at his end."

"So, what would you have us do, Delenn?" Morann said. "The Humans . . ."

And with as careful a deadpan as she could maintain, she asked, "What Humans?"

He was silent for a long moment, and then intoned, "Indeed . . . what Humans?"

She waited until he was gone, and then she quickly left her quarters. She looked neither left nor right, moving briskly, and yet she felt as if she could feel upon her the eyes of everyone she passed. Moments later she arrived at the shrine that Lenonn had created to memorialize Dukhat, and entered it.

She looked around the quarters, her eyes adjusting to the dimness. She saw shadows, large shapes over in the corner of the room. The Vorlons.

"What do I do?" she demanded.

No response.

"I am . . ." Her hands moved in vague patterns. "I am . . . alone. Dukhat . . . gave me knowledge, Lenonn gave me determination. I am surrounded by my people, who wish nothing but to eliminate the Humans in their holy war. I am but one voice . . . one voice . . . they will not listen to me. Even with the help of Lenonn, it would have taken nothing short of a miracle.

"Now Lenonn is gone, and his death has revitalized the hatred that we hold for the Humans. No one will ever trust them, no one will . . . I need . . . help. I need guidance. If you were to show yourselves, if you were to stand by my side . . ."

Again there was no reply.

Her fingers curling into fists, her body began trembling with barely repressed fury, and she told them, "Don't you understand? *I don't know what to do now!* It is . . . it is like trying to stop the roll of waves by standing on the shore and swinging a sword at it! This war has gained greater and greater momentum, and I don't know how to stop it! If I reveal that I was in alliance with Lenonn, then I will lose all credibility within the Council. I am not dealing from strength! I have no strength and I need you to help me!"

She waited. Waited, her eyes pleading for a response. None came.

She moved toward the tall, dark form. "Say something to me! Any sort of answer! Anything! Do not just stand there, silent, knowing all, saying nothing! Do not—!"

Her hands went right through where she thought the Vorlon had been standing. She stepped back, confused, and realized that he hadn't been there at all. That it had been a trick of light. She whirled, looking around desperately. "Where are you?"

The shadows did not move, did not stir.

The Vorlons had gone.

Delenn sank to her knees and softly, ever so softly so that none would hear, she began to sob to herself.

She was alone. All alone in the dark.

Sheridan sat in the office of General Lefcourt. He had been cleaned up, but he still had a haggard expression on his face. Lefcourt looked no happier about the situation. "So you have no idea who attacked you," he said, ticking off each thing he said on his fingers. "You have no idea who this Minbari was, or the significance of what he said to you. And you have no idea why they spared you and Dr. Franklin."

"No, sir." He sighed. "You're free, of course, to speak to Dr. Franklin about it . . ."

"We already have," Lefcourt informed him. "He was of no more use on the matter than you, I'm afraid. Nor was G'Kar. As for the peace initiative . . ."

"We have to pursue it," Sheridan said urgently. "Perhaps there . . ."

But Lefcourt was shaking his head. "No. The Narn are no longer interested in cooperating. They've already lost a vessel over it, and they're not even sure why or to whom. Their suspicion—and I admit it makes sense—is that another arm of the Minbari government secretly decided to destroy the peace initiative."

"I don't know that I agree, sir."

"It's the Narn reading, and we concur."

"But then why did they let us go?"

Again Lefcourt shook his head. "We're not entirely certain. It could be that they did not wish to aggravate the Narn and find themselves fighting a two-front war."

Sheridan looked doubtful. "Look, General, maybe if . . ."

"No, Commander. I'm afraid we no longer have the choice. The Narn, as I've said, are out of the picture, and the Minbari seem no more inclined to talk with us directly than they were before. Which leaves us out of luck and—before too long—out of time."

Never before in his life had Sheridan felt quite that helpless or frustrated. "But if we tell everyone . . . put out a broadcast that said we had an initial meeting with the Minbari . . . maybe we could . . ."

"Could what? Raise hopes needlessly? The mission ended in failure, Sheridan. I know that failure is not something that you cheerfully accept, but in this case you're simply going to have to deal with it. Nor will word of our meeting with the Minbari be considered anything other than strictly classified. We do not need the general populace mourning the loss of a peace that was never going to be. Instead they have to steel themselves and prepare to—"

"Die?" Sheridan asked.

"I was going to say, 'Fight,' " Lefcourt replied.

And, very bleakly, Sheridan thought, *Same difference.*

And so the first official meeting between Minbari and Humans, ever so quietly, evaporated as if it had never happened. Oh, there were rumors, reports that there had been some attempt at a rendezvous, of a Human/Minbari meeting. But it remained merely hearsay. No official confirmation was possible, which was what both sides decided they found preferable.

Instead, as it turned out, a subsequent and rather portentous meeting became considered the "first encounter." I shall tell you of that later.

For now, there was a . . . disturbing incident . . . that I shall share with you . . .

I was walking down a corridor in Earthdome, mulling over the situation and trying to decide just how long it would be wise for me to stay on Earth. After all, the last place I desired to be when the Minbari arrived was upon the homeworld of a race that they had targeted for extermination.

I entered my office and was surprised to see G'Mak, my Narn contact, seated there. He was staring at me levelly, his face unreadable. "G'Mak, " I said slowly. "Did we have an appointment? I do not recall . . ."

"It was for peace," he said.

I did not understand what he was talking about at first. I shook my head in confusion. "Peace? What was . . . ? I don't . . ."

"Peace was an impossibility, you said. Your contacts were very specific, you said." He spoke slowly, dangerously. "You said that, Mollari, and may the gods help me, I believed it." Slowly he was rising from his chair.

Ever so gradually, I began to back up. I did not run, for I did not desire to appear frightened. With a forced casualness in my tone, I said, "Yes, I said that. And what gives you the impression that—"

I noticed that his fingers were flexing. It did not appear, to me, to be a good sign. "G'Kar told me," he whispered harshly. "He told me there were Minbari there. They were waiting to speak of peace. Of *peace*, Mollari. But you put an end to that, didn't you."

I tried to find words. My mouth opened and closed, however, and nothing emerged.

"It was a Centauri ship that destroyed the Narn vessel, wasn't it? That opened fire on the planet below. The planet where *I* told you they were going to be."

"It can't be." I shook my head as if such a motion could dispel the truth. "There . . . is no hope of peace . . . my contacts . . ."

"*Damn* your contacts," G'Mak said. "Damn me for listening to you. And damn you for living, Mollari. As a matter of fact, I think it preferable if you did not."

He lunged for me but missed. I would like to tell you that I was so agile that I easily dodged him. In point of fact, I slipped, and he moved past me without actually coming into contact with me. I spun on my heel, tried to get to the door, and almost made it before he tackled me from behind. We fell through the open doorway into the corridor, G'Mak on top of me, pounding on the side of my head, howling Narn obscenities at me. "We're both going to hell, Mollari!" he howled. "The only difference is, you're going to get there before me! It's on our heads, Mollari, ours!"

I had not fully assimilated the truth of what he was saying. Instead I was too busy fighting for my life. His hands were on my throat, and the only thing that prevented him from breaking my neck was the fact that I had my hands at his wrists, just barely managing to pull them clear. But it was only for a very brief time that I was going to be able to keep an infuriated Narn at bay.

And then a gloved hand came down and grabbed G'Mak by the back of the neck. "What do you think you're doing?" a deep, outraged voice demanded.

Just like that, G'Mak was lifted clear of me. I rolled over onto my back, my face no doubt looking badly injured already, and looked up to see the face of my unexpected savior.

I felt my blood chill.

Understand . . .

. . . many, many years ago, as I have told you—and I am loath to bring it up again, but I regret that it is necessary for you to comprehend—I dreamt of my death. In that dream there was a Narn whom I had never seen before. He had one eye. The other, presumably empty socket was covered by a patch. He possessed a snarl of fury, and his fingers were upon my throat, as were mine upon his, as if we hated each other more than anyone in the galaxy. With a hatred that could shatter planets, annihilate entire races.

Upon looking up into the face of my unexpected savior, I felt a shock of recognition.

It was he. He had two eyes, and there was no fury in them. Merely a cool, mocking look.

My future executioner extended a hand to me, wordlessly, indicating that I should use it to help myself up. I gripped his hand firmly and pulled myself to standing.

As if what I had to say didn't matter, he simply ignored me and turned instead to G'Mak. "What began this?" he demanded.

"It is my business, G'Kar," G'Mak said.

So this was G'Kar. The famous G'Kar, whom I knew through a variety of stories and incidents. G'Kar, the man whom I now believed was going to slay me at some far point in the future.

"I am taking pains to make it my business, as well," G'Kar snapped. "You cannot simply go about assaulting members of other races, even Centauri. They take offense at that for some odd reason." His sarcasm was apparently lost on G'Mak, and I did everything I could to not react. I was too busy hiding my feeling of recognition. And it is entirely possible, I suppose, that he sensed it as well. Or at least sensed something, for he stared at me for a moment before turning back to

G'Mak. "Don't hide the truth from me, G'Mak. What is this all about?"

What was G'Mak supposed to say at that point? Should he admit his duplicity to G'Kar? To do so would be to take responsibility for leaking information to the despised Centauri. For the deaths of all those Narns aboard the transport. For the deaths of untold billions of Humans whose hopes for peace had been dashed. Could he admit to all that?

"Mollari . . . owes me money," he said slowly. "Money . . . lost gaming."

"Money," G'Kar said. "And for that, you would try to kill him. Does it occur to you that, if he is dead, your money will not be forthcoming?"

"It . . . should have," G'Mak admitted. He drew himself up. "Do you desire that I . . . apologize to the Centauri representative here?"

"Well . . ." G'Kar could not suppress a smile. "I don't think we have to go to extremes."

G'Mak turned away, unable to look me in the eyes anymore. I could not blame him, for standing there, I had begun to understand. Whatever self-loathing he might have felt at that moment, it could not be dissimilar to what was going through my own mind. I felt my very soul shriveling over the concept that the Humans might possibly have had salvation at hand. But the prospect had been dashed from those hands by a sweep of my own.

"I am G'Kar," G'Kar informed me with a slight bow. The bow had more of a mocking aspect to it.

I couldn't stop staring at him, and it took me a moment or two to realize that I should return the formal introduction. I made a perfunctory bow in return and said, "Londo Mollari."

"You have something of a reputation which precedes you, Mollari."

"Oh? Do I?" I said, rather tonelessly.

"Yes, yes. I have my contacts, my connections. You would be amazed what I know."

"Is that a fact?"

"Yes." His voice dropped. "I know the truth about you. About your little secret."

For a moment the world seemed to fall away from me. "Oh, really?"

"Definitely." And he sneered. "I know that you cheat at cards."

Relief flooded through me, and then I realized that that was precisely the wrong reaction to show to G'Kar. If I acted as if I were hiding something, then there was every likelihood that he would perceive it and, suspicions aroused, probe further. So, with every bit of acting capability at my command, I drew myself up as if I had been mortally offended. "That is a spurious lie!" I declared.

"I know that you cheat, and how you cheat." He shook his head derisively and made a gesture that indicated I should feel shame. "What happened? Did G'Mak catch you at it? Force you to play on the up-and-up and, consequently, lose?"

"As you say" was my only reply.

I turned and started to walk away quickly. My head was still whirling with what I had learned. A peace initiative. An attempt to stave off genocide, and I had been too narrow-minded, too much the fool to believe it possible. On my head . . . all those deaths still to come, an entire race to be obliterated from the galaxy, and it was my fault.

I tried to tell myself that the peace talks would never have come to anything anyway. That Sonovar had been correct, that the Minbari were still dead set against it. That it was merely the deluded dream of a handful of Minbari who could never have brought matters to fruition.

But I knew. I knew that this was all rationalization, all attempts to assuage my guilty conscience.

They were doomed. Doomed and damned, and it was my fault. All my fault.

Then I heard G'Kar's voice calling behind me. I stopped, turned, and waited for what he had to say.

He wagged a finger at me and said, "Mollari . . . a warning. In the future, I'll have my eye out for you."

For a moment my dream of my death flashed into my mind. The single red eye glaring at me from a face twisted in hate.

"You have *no* idea," I told him, and walked away.

—— *chapter 15* ——

It may seem to you that that is the end of the story. But I assure you, it is not.

At the point where the peace initiative had failed, fifty, maybe sixty thousand Humans had died in the Earth-Minbari War. With their one chance for peace ruined, and Lenonn dead, the war escalated. Over the next six months, two hundred thousand more Humans died. The end of the story? No, not the end at all. The greatest slaughter of all still waits for us. It changed everything . . . everything . . .

The heat . . .

My world . . . my Centauri Prime . . .

When the wind mercifully blows in the other direction, I can pretend to be above it all. But when it blows toward the castle, the heat can be overwhelming, and the smells . . . the charnel smells.

Perhaps I am hellbound. Perhaps I am seeing merely a preview of what awaits me for eternity. Ironic, is it not? I had every window in the palace blocked off because I was afraid that if I came around a corner and saw . . . this . . . unprepared, I would break down and cry. And yet

I spend all my time here in this room. Looking at it.

I see the many buildings, buildings which have existed for centuries. Conceived by the greatest architects of Centauri history. A sort of ongoing record of the growth of the great Centauri empire. For each emperor, for each triumph, for every planet that fell beneath our sphere of influence, there would be a new monument erected, a new building constructed to memorialize it.

That pile of rubble over there? I received my first tutoring there. That pile down at the base of the hill? The home of my best friend. Far in the distance, that incinerated grove of trees? That is where I brought the first woman that I . . .

Women.

In my life, I have had four wives. I cared for them all deeply. But I *loved* Centauri Prime. Loved every street, every tower, every inch of our world. Everything I did, I did for her. And look what we have done to her. Still . . . there is hope. But it will be hard. It will be so very hard . . .

But I stray from the topic?

I am sorry. Accept my apologies. The apology of an emperor—that should certainly be worth something, eh?

Where was I? Oh, yes . . .

The war.

The Humans, I think, knew that they were doomed. But where another race would have surrendered to despair, the Humans fought back with even greater strength.

They made the Minbari fight for every inch of space. In all my life, I have never seen anything like it. They would weep, they would pray, they would say good-bye to those they loved . . . and then launch themselves without fear or hesitation at the very face of death itself. Never surrendering. No one who saw them fighting against the inevitable could help but be moved by their courage. Their stubborn nobility. When they ran out of ships, they fought with guns.

When they ran out of guns, they fought with sticks, with knives, with bare hands. They were magnificent.

Tales of their heroic confrontations ranged throughout half a dozen star systems. The battle of Sinzar, where a wounded Minbari battle cruiser tried to escape, and a crippled Earth vessel rammed into the Minbari, destroying themselves and the Minbari in the process.

The fierce land war on the Flinn Colony, where ground-based weaponry drove the Minbari to the surface, and incredible hand-to-hand struggles ranged across the planet's surface. The Minbari came away from the battle triumphant, but bloodied and bruised.

Word of the Humans raced through all levels of the Minbari. Every caste whispered of it. It is far easier, you see, to destroy an enemy you have demonized. As such, the enemy must have no redeeming value whatsoever.

Remember that the attack on Dukhat had been perceived as the cowardly attack of savages. Savages have no sense of nobility. But the Humans clearly did, and they had further proven, in battle after battle, that they were not cowards. Although they did attempt from time to time to surrender, every rebuff actually appeared to revitalize them. They were determined, as a race, to give an accounting of themselves. It was as if they knew that they could not survive, and that their single goal was to take as many of the Minbari with them as possible. When twenty of their fighter ships were destroyed, the twenty-first would fight with just as much vigor and disregard for his own safety as ever.

I only hope, when it is my time, that I may die with half as much dignity as I saw in their eyes at the end.

They did this . . . for two years. They never ran out of courage. But in the end . . . they ran out of time.

The pilots' ready room—the place where Ganya Ivanov had once heard the announcement that there was someone to see him—had also once hummed with enthusiasm and assurance. The pilots had walked with swagger, with confidence. They were positive that they were the best and the brightest, that somehow, in some way, they would triumph over the aliens who were determined to wipe out Humanity.

As month had followed month, had gone from one year to the next, that confidence had been eroded. The pilots who were there may have been the best and brightest that Earthforce had to offer. More to the point, they were the last. Many of them had seen battle with the Minbari and barely survived to tell the tale. Others had shown up after fights, been part of rescue operations, and seen close up the devastation that resulted from a battle with the Minbari.

They lay on benches or on the floor, trying to catch a few moments of sleep, seeking respite in dreams that were laced with frightening, massive engines of destruction coming for them. Many lay awake, staring at the ceiling, not wanting to risk the dreams. All of them had haunted looks in their eyes.

All but one.

Jeffrey Sinclair sat off to the side, by himself. He was not staring off into space. He was staring into himself, as if all the answers . . . or at least all the answers he needed . . . were there. One of the pilots glanced at him as he walked past, and slowed a moment. "You okay?" he asked.

Sinclair looked at him with calm confidence. "We're going to win this thing, Mitchell," he said.

Mitchell looked at him with something akin to amazement. "You really believe that."

"Yes. I do. And you had better believe it, too." He raised his voice slightly, catching everyone within earshot. Another pilot, Annie Wheeler, who had been one of those lying on the bench staring upward with a hopeless air about her, glanced over at him. Henderson, Lombardi . . . others began to look up at him. He continued, "No battle was ever won by people who believed that their cause was hopeless. Do you have any idea of the wars that have been embarked upon where it seemed clear who the winner was going to be? Any idea how many bodies of surprised nonwinners have littered battlefields?"

They seemed to be listening to him, ever so slightly. Throwing off the shroud of defeat that had cloaked them for so long. Sinclair's mind raced as he considered his next words carefully.

And then he was interrupted by a burst of static. He winced against feedback that issued from the speakers, and then looked up as the overhead screen flickered to life. He heard a familiar voice—the voice of the President, Beth Levy—ask in what sounded like confusion, "Are we on?" Obviously someone confirmed for her that they were indeed, for she continued to speak. "This is . . . this is the President."

He remembered when he had seen her at her Inauguration. Her hair had been elegantly coiffed; she had worn a simple short string of black pearls which had been out of fashion for thirty years—and which promptly came back into fashion as a result of her wearing them. She had been lovely and striking, and possessed of an intelligence that glittered through her eyes.

There was none of that now. Her brown hair was short but elegant, but otherwise she seemed rather unremarkable. In fact she seemed . . . smaller somehow.

"I have just been informed," she said tiredly, "that the midrange military bases at Beta Durani and Proxima Three have fallen to the Minbari advance. We have lost contact with Io and must presume that they have fallen to an advance force."

Sinclair looked around at the others near him. Mitchell still bore an air of quiet determination, but he had known

Sinclair the longest. Wheeler was starting to look beaten
again, and as for the others . . . their eyes were already glaz-
ing over. The eyes that had seen too much war. Whatever
confidence they might have begun to acquire from Sinclair
was evaporating in the face of this new announcement of
hopelessness.

"Intelligence believes the Minbari intend to bypass Mars
and hit Earth directly. They say the attack could come at
any time. We have . . ." Her voice caught for a moment. "We
have continued to broadcast our surrender, and a plea for
mercy. They have not responded. We can only conclude . . . that we stand at the twilight of the Human race."

Sinclair wanted to scream at her. *What kind of speech
is this? Where is the determination? Where are the stirring
words inciting pilots to victory? We need encouragement in
the face of overwhelming odds, not hopelessness!*

Wheeler passed by Sinclair. She wasn't waiting for the
rest of the speech; she knew where it was going. They
locked eyes, and she paused only to put out a hand. He
clapped it once, firmly, in a sort of power grip, and they
both nodded. Mitchell, a short distance away, nodded in
approval as Wheeler walked off. Mitchell followed her a
moment later as the President's words continued to fill the
air.

"To buy time for more evacuation transports to leave
Earth, we ask for the support of every ship capable of fighting to take part in a last defense of our homeworld."

Others were moving out, Sinclair's attempts at spirit-
raising forgotten or simply deemed irrelevant. Some of them
couldn't even look Sinclair in the eye, as if they were
letting him down by being convinced that they could not
win.

"We will not lie to you," Levy continued. "Survival . . . is
not a possibility. Those who enter the battle . . . will never
come back. But for every ten minutes we can delay the

enemy advance, several hundred more civilians may be able to escape to neutral territory."

To her credit, she did not add that there was no guarantee the Minbari would honor the concept of "neutral territory." They might very well follow the last of Humanity wherever they ran and obliterate them. That seemed to be the plan, after all. Still, the pilots knew. Knew that even the smallest shred of hope was likely a futile one. But at least it gave them something to fight for. Sinclair shouldered his load, took his helmet, didn't even bother to glance up at the President as she continued, "Though Earth may fall, the Human race must have a chance to continue elsewhere. No greater sacrifice has ever been asked of a people. But I ask you now to step forward one last time . . . one last battle to hold the line against the night."

Sinclair was the last one out. He glanced around the pilots' waiting area one final time. And even at the last . . . he refused to believe that he wouldn't be back.

We'll find a way, he thought, and walked out.

The President's final words—"God go with you all"— were spoken to a deserted room.

John Sheridan was going out of his mind.

At that point he was serving aboard a battle cruiser called the *Hector*, part of a small convoy of vessels that had learned of a planned Minbari incursion against a colony in the Triad sector. It had been a two-day journey via jump gates to arrive there, and it was only once they had arrived in the Triad sector that word was received of the Minbari push toward Earth itself. So the *Hector*, upon learning of the last desperate defense of Earth, immediately turned around and started to head back, but Sheridan knew he wasn't going to make it.

He thought of the evacuation going on, of his parents and Elizabeth desperately trying to get to evacuation vessels.

He had begged his father to relocate the family to some-place remote, someplace that even the Minbari wouldn't find. But the elder Sheridan had refused, saying that there was no such place, and besides, running wasn't his style. John Sheridan had alternately cursed and pleaded with his father to change his mind, but nothing had managed to convince him. Typical. So typical.

And John thought of Anna as well. Was she gone? Was she safe?

In the intervening two years, he had seen her—on and off—and their relationship had grown, blossomed and devel-oped. Somewhere along the way, Sheridan came to the realization that—had he been someone with a normal life—he would certainly have married the woman by now. That was how strongly he had come to feel for her. That alone meant more to him than he would have previously thought possible.

Was she safe? Were any of them?

Earth was dying and he wasn't there to defend her.

He barely slept for the entire voyage there, and by the time he arrived, it had ended . . . but not in a way that any-one had expected.

It would later be called the Battle of the Line. Twenty thousand ships and fighters, arrayed in a last-ditch effort to defend the homeworld of Humanity. A homeworld that had survived the trauma of birth . . . meteor strikes . . . ice ages . . . and, most challengingly, the abuse heaped on it by the race that first began crawling on the surface barely half an eyeblink earlier, as the planet itself reckoned time.

In point of fact, the homeworld would survive this debacle as well. The Minbari did not care about the blue-green planet itself. The world, as far as they were concerned, could continue in its rather dreary orbit around its sun until time itself came to an end.

But the people—as far as the Minbari were concerned—were doomed.

Truth to tell, we all believed that as well.

I had long before retreated to Centauri Prime, knowing that the Earth was a lost cause and knowing that I was—in some measure—responsible for that. I kept mostly to myself, every so often monitoring the progress of the battle. When word of the final battle came, I sat in my home and stared out at the green, rolling hills of Centauri Prime and wondered in a very oblique fashion what that would be like. To fight a hopeless battle against impossible odds. To know that one's world would likely soon be in flames.

Some advice to you, my friends: Never idly speculate. Because someone out there notices such things, and takes a perverse pleasure in providing concrete examples. As you can tell, considering that . . . once again . . . the wind has shifted.

—— *chapter 16* ——

The Minbari fleet was a very different affair from the desperate last defenders of planet Earth. Whereas the Earth-force fleet clearly displayed results of the many battles they had been through, the Minbari vessels looked unperturbed. As they cruised through hyperspace, heading for their final assault on Humanity, one would simply have been unable to tell that they had been involved in a wearying, two-year-long war.

At least, that was the picture on the outside. On the inside, it was a very different story.

In Delenn's quarters, a single candle provided illumination.

Over the last two years, Delenn had descended further and further into darkness . . . literally. It was a reflection of what she was enduring spiritually. When the door opened, she did not even have to bother to turn to see that it was Morann. These days, he was the only one who ever came to see her, and then it was only to provide her with updates as to the battle.

"We are almost within range of the homeworld of the Humans," he told her. He waited to see if a response was forthcoming. None was. "The Grey Council should be assembled to see the end of our great campaign."

At first she spoke so softly that it was almost impossible to hear her. "What glory is there in eliminating an entire race, Morann?"

She turned to face him and was surprised at what she saw. There was incredible exhaustion etched on his face. She realized that it had been some time since she had last seen him, and the change in him was quite evident. She suspected he had not been sleeping much, if at all.

Was it that the campaign was simply more difficult than he had anticipated? It was one thing to wage war against a helpless enemy, but the Humans had proven surprisingly ingenious and resilient. The cost to the Minbari had been considerable in terms of lives and resources. Indeed, among the populace there were secret mutterings of becoming tired of the entire business. But these mutterings were kept secret, for none could forget that the war was being waged in the name of Dukhat.

Or was it something more, Delenn wondered. More than just the physical toll? Was there a psychic cost as well? A depletion on the Minbari as a race, as if their own souls were being drained in the endeavor?

Morann considered the question. "Glory?" he mused, wondering out loud to himself as much as he was speaking to her. "Not as much as in the beginning." He seemed to make an effort to shake off the exhaustion. "It has been a long road, Delenn. But we are nearly at the end of our holy war."

"Yes . . . but are we any longer holy?"

He actually seemed amused by her response. "Why is it, whenever I see you, you never speak other than to ask questions?"

And now it was Delenn's turn to speak out loud to herself, with Morann listening to her inner turmoil. "Because questions are all I have left. After today, I think they are all I will ever have."

"Then at least bring your questions to the Council. We must all be there at the end."

There was something in his voice. Something in the way that he had suggested she bring her questions to the Council. It was almost as if he were encouraging her to question, to dispute their purpose.

She wanted to probe more deeply into what was going through his mind, but she did not have the opportunity, for she found herself watching his retreating back.

She remained in her quarters, pondering the situation for a moment, and then she walked out the door.

It was very likely her imagination, but the corridors around her—which once had seemed almost suffused with warmth—now seemed cold and uninviting. There seemed to be no one around, which was unusual. She drew her Grey Council robe closer in around herself, for she felt as if there was a chill in the air . . .

She walked past Dukhat's shrine . . . and stopped.

She had not gone there since that time two years previously, when she had gone in looking for guidance from the Vorlons and found none to be forthcoming. She had no idea what prompted her to stand outside the room. Nor did she have any true notion of why she decided to walk in. Perhaps, she reasoned, it was in order to give her one last, brief connection with Dukhat before they finished this ghastly business that was being conducted in his name.

When she entered, she thought that the room seemed . . . different somehow. Slightly brighter. But there were still long shadows creeping across the floor, the walls. She glanced toward the corner where she had last thought she saw a Vorlon standing. She sighed, started to turn away . . . and then, just out of the corner of her eye, she saw it.

It moved. She had to convince herself that she hadn't merely fancied it, as she had the last time. It had really, genuinely moved. In a low voice, barely daring to hope, she said, "Are you still here?"

The shadow stopped moving, and her heart sank. She turned to leave . . .

. . . and Kosh was standing behind her.

"We have always been here," Kosh said in that odd musical manner of his.

She did not question. She realized, in the end, that questioning was pointless, particularly when it came to the Vorlons. Some things simply had to be taken on faith.

"I've failed," she said. "In a little while, the final slaughter will begin." She began to circle the room. "I know the others do not want it. Even Morann is tired of war, tired of blood . . . but the war has taken on a life of its own, and it will continue to its bloody end no matter our feelings. I think the others need only a reason to delay or reconsider, but there is no such reason. And we are out of time."

She waited for them to say something, and continued to wait. They volunteered nothing. They simply remained inscrutable within their encounter suits. It really wasn't much of an improvement over when she had come to the room and discovered it empty. Finally, despairing of learning anything useful from the Vorlons, she started to leave the room for what she firmly felt was the last time.

"The truth points to itself," said the Vorlon who had the more rounded edges to his encounter suit.

Slowly she turned and looked back at them. "What?"

"The truth points to itself," he said again.

"I . . . don't understand."

The other Vorlon spoke up. The one who seemed oddly more menacing for some reason. **"You will."**

She shook her head, still uncomprehending. "But—"

"Go now," the second Vorlon said.

And the first one . . . the one whom, Delenn realized, she felt less disturbed by, said, **"Go. Before it is too late."**

She did not understand, but she felt she had one hope: that
somehow, sooner or later, the advice from the Vorlons
would mean something to her. But she prayed that it would
be "sooner," since the Human race did not appear to have
much in the way of "later."

The Earthforce fighter pilots were not certain which direction the Minbari would be coming from. Squadrons were
spread out in all directions along the various spatial planes,
looking, watching and waiting for some sign of the Minbari
advance.

Alpha Squadron was busy cruising its designated sector.
Hecht in Alpha Seven had his sensors on full, scanning the
stars, trying to see if any of them were moving. Then he
suddenly received a warning on his instrumentation. He
locked it down and said briskly, "Alpha Seven to base. I'm
picking up energy emissions on the horizon."

He heard the voice of the fleet commander come back,
"Alpha Seven, scout ahead. See what's out there."

Hecht had every intention of proceeding with the utmost
caution. He was usually something of a go-getter, Hecht was,
and ordinarily liked to be first for things. He had no desire,
however, to be the very first person to die in the Battle of the
Line. "Affirmative," he said. "Any bogeys on the screen?"

"Negative, Alpha Seven," replied Fleet Command. "All
other squadrons, maintain radio silence until Alpha Seven
checks this out."

Hecht swung his Starfury around and moved off in the
direction of the energy emissions. For the briefest of moments, he considered the fact that when Humankind first
embarked on space travel, a voyage to the moon had occu-
pied many days. Now, with Earth at his back, he was approaching the moon and would be passing it in a matter
of seconds. He remembered, as a cadet, going to the Neil
Armstrong museum on the moon; the one that had been built

around Armstrong's first footprints. He had placed his
foot in Armstrong's track, as all visitors were permitted
to do, and he had been pleased to see that, appropriately
booted, he fit precisely. It gave him a sort of connection to
those without whose efforts he would never have become a
Starfury pilot.

"Closing in on trace emissions," Hecht said as the moon
began to fill the view just outside his Starfury. "So far nothing. Might be just an echo or a . . ."

Then he saw them coming. It was a horde of Minbari
fighters, swarming up and over from the other side of one of
the moon's mountain ranges. They shot straight upward and
then looped around as Hecht shouted "Aw, hell!" before re-
covering his professionalism and announcing, "We've got a
scouting party! Repeat, we've got a scouting party! Hostiles
on approach! Locking on!"

He swung his ship desperately around, trying to get away
from the incoming fighters and seek the relative safety of
the fleet. But even as he opened up the throttle and fired the
thrusters, he knew that he was accomplishing too little, too
late. He was blasted from behind, had barely enough time to
see his starboard engine erupt, and think, *Yup, figures, now
when I don't want to be, I'm first,* just before his ship blew
completely apart.

Jeffrey Sinclair, or—as he was designated—Alpha Leader,
shouted over his comm unit, "Alpha Seven!"

"He's gone!" called Wheeler, who had seen Hecht's ship
go up.

Sinclair's hands clenched more tightly on his controls.
His jaw set grimly, he ordered, "Stay in formation! Hold the
Line! No one gets through, no matter what!"

"Understood," Mitchell shot back. And then, with alarm,
he called, "Alpha Leader, you've got a Minbari on your tail!"

Sinclair had been momentarily distracted, hadn't even

noticed his own rear sensor readouts. That had been unforgivably sloppy; without Mitchell's shouted warning, it could have cost him everything. Sinclair opened up his controls wide and the Starfury angled sharply away as the Minbari fighter moved in pursuit. For a brief moment, Sinclair hated to admit that he admired the quality of flying exhibited by his pursuer. Sinclair prided himself on his ability to execute evasive maneuvers, but this Minbari pilot was right on his tail, matching him move for move.

What allies they would have made, he thought, and then sent his fighter angling rapidly away as blasts from the pursuer exploded in space around him.

Delenn had never before quite regretted the obscuring covering of the Grey Council hoods as much as she did at that moment in time. She would dearly have loved to be able to see their faces, to look into their eyes. Convince them through sheer force of will to call off this madness before it was too late.

But she could hear their replies in her head. *Yours was the decision, Delenn. You ordered "No mercy." Have you not the strength of character to see it through?*

So she said nothing as they stood within the Council chamber, watching the unfolding battle on the screens overhead. "It is time," Morann said. "Tell the others to jump."

The Minbari cruisers moved forward, preparing to make the leap from hyperspace into normal space. Preparing for the final push that would wipe Humanity from existence.

The explosions rocked Sinclair's Starfury as he banked sharply to the right, and his pursuer was still after him.

But he had not yet been squarely hit, and Sinclair was beginning to become suspicious. He knew his capabilities, knew how long luck should hold out before a hit was scored. He shouldn't have been questioning his luck that he was still alive, but still . . .

Then something clicked in his mind, just as he heard Mitchell's voice across his comm unit, saying, "I'm on him!" Sure enough, Mitchell's Starfury had broken off from its position and was diving down toward Sinclair.

"No!" Sinclair shouted. "Mitchell! Stay in formation! It might be a—"

Sure enough, the Minbari pursuer suddenly peeled off as space before him rippled and shimmered, and he was even certain he sensed a reverberation—an impressive trick in the vacuum—when jump points formed all around them.

"Oh my God," Sinclair whispered. And if his God was hearing him, then it was quite evident that he was choosing to turn a deaf ear.

Through the jump points they came, roaring out of hyperspace, Minbari cruisers launching fighter vessels the moment they dropped into normal space. And more fighter vessels—numberless as the stars, it seemed. In a perverse way, it was almost a thing of beauty. In the same way that one can look at a tornado and admire in it the devastating craftsmanship of the Great Maker, even as one runs in terror . . . in awe of its hideous glory. So was it when the Minbari fleet arrived. A perfect, sweeping engine of destruction was the fleet, a vast blanket of death to be hurled upon the last defenders like a burial shroud.

They came and they came and when it seemed as if there could not possibly be more, another jump point would open and more ships would burst forth. The jump points would blossom like flowers and spit out their poison seeds, more and more. And as every Earthforce pilot would think that they had reached the ultimate pit of despair, and that the sense of overwhelming futility could not be greater, at that moment, still more appeared. It was beyond comprehension, beyond reason. These were not simply enough vessels to destroy Humanity. There were enough to obliterate them ten times over. It was as if the Minbari had launched an attack intended not only to wipe out the current crop of Mankind, but to assail them with such force that the entire race would be annihilated back to the point when the first of them had crawled out of the primordial ooze.

Credit the Minbari with consistency. True believers in the reality and sanctity of the soul were they. They wanted Humanity's collective soul to witness the power and might that they had unleashed, the whirlwind that they had reaped, and they wanted that soul to wither and die.

All in the name of Dukhat. All in the name of nobility.

Madness. Madness.

Sinclair heard the voices of his fellows. Heard Keogh and Knauerhase, Weider and Feit, Cohn and Scannell, and they were shouting over one another.

"They're everywhere!"

"Can't stop 'em!"

"My God, they came out of nowhere!"

"They're locking on!"

And one after another they were blown out of the sky, sliced to pieces. Everywhere Sinclair looked it was the same hideous scene, repeated over and over. It didn't matter how skilled, how battle savvy, how well prepared, how confident. They were being torn to ribbons.

Mitchell's Starfury raced toward a nearby cruiser, and Mitchell shouted, "I've got a clear shot!"

"It's a trap!" Sinclair shouted, automatically laying down covering fire at the same time.

"I can take it, I can take it!" Mitchell shouted.

"Mitchell, break off! *Break off!*"

In the end, Mitchell was right. He did take it. But what he took was a single bright green blast from the Minbari cruiser, slicing through his Starfury and carving it in half. Sinclair watched helplessly as one of his most experienced and dedicated wingmen was blown into oblivion.

Space around him was becoming thick with scraps of metal, with scraps of bodies. Legs and arms, and a head floating by, staring at Sinclair with dead eyes.

And it was at that moment . . . at that very moment . . . that Sinclair, for the first time, stopped believing. Stopped waiting for a miracle to occur. Stopped thinking that somehow Humanity would survive it. He realized that he had believed in the ultimate triumph of his race simply because the concept that Humanity's time in the galaxy had ended was simply too vast a concept for him to grasp.

They were going to die. All of them, they were going to die, as helpless as ants being ground under the heel of a colossus. And once all the defenders were gone, the Minbari would chase down the last of the Humans, and that would be all.

No more great hopes or dreams or plans. No more Human babies to be born, no more women to walk with the sun shining upon their faces, the gentle winds of Earth blowing their hair or rustling their skirts, no more weddings, no more books to be written, stories to be passed on.

Just one great, big funeral to which all were invited. A massive fire upon which all of Humanity would be tossed, and the smoke from the pyre would reach to all worlds throughout the galaxy as if to say, Do not ever, *ever,* cross the Minbari, or this will be the result. And no power that exists will be able to help you.

It was at that moment that Sinclair completely gave up.

And it was the very next moment that he gritted his teeth, ran his weapons to maximum, and plunged back into battle.

Men such as that, you see, do not doubt themselves for very long.

Delenn had wondered if, when the final moment came, she would be able to watch. That question was answered for her, far more promptly than she would have suspected, as she quickly turned away from the sight of Earth vessel after Earth vessel being destroyed.

"They fight bravely," she said with quiet admiration. "They cannot harm our ships. But they continue to try."

Morann shrugged. "Whether they fight or not, they will die anyway. So really, is this bravery, or simple desperation?" He paused to watch the slaughter continue and shook his head. "Foolish."

"But brave," Delenn insisted, and she made no effort to keep the awe from her voice. "In Valen's name . . . so brave . . ."

She had to do something. Something . . . unexpected. But she had no clue as to what.

And then, as if listening from outside herself, she heard herself say, "We should bring one of them aboard for questioning." Morann looked at her quizzically. By way of explanation, she continued, "If our next step is the final assault on their world, we must know their defenses."

It seemed an odd request to Morann. What final defense could they possibly have that would have a prayer of halting the Minbari fleet? If anything, *this* was their final defense. It could not possibly be a trick or subterfuge; no one would be insane enough to commit this much firepower to a mere ploy.

Still and all, it made little difference to Morann. "Very well, Delenn," he said. "Choose." He looked back to the battle's progress and added, "But quickly. We're fast running out of candidates."

Delenn looked at the vessels assailing them. Which one? In Valen's name, there were so many, moving so quickly. Which single life was to be spared, albeit temporarily? What criteria could she use?

She sensed—she did not know how, but she did—that the survival of one, and perhaps two, races, depended upon her making a prudent choice. But she had no means of . . .

And then one vessel broke away from the others and was driving itself straight toward the Minbari cruiser. It was one of the single-man fighters. The cruiser's weapons could easily destroy it; for that matter, even if they did nothing, the explosion of the fighter against the cruiser's hull would likely have little effect.

Still, it showed . . .

. . . it showed spirit.

And the voice of the Vorlon echoed in her head. **The truth points to itself.**

She had no clear idea why, and wondered if she would ever truly know. But she pointed to the rapidly approaching Starfury and said confidently, "That one."

And in so doing, in that one moment, she changed the outcome of the current war, and affected not only the outcome of a war to be fought years later, but also a war that had occurred a thousand years previously.

A rather impressive feat, that.

A flurry of white beams ripped out from the belly of the cruiser, snaring the Starfury. It halted the ship in its path and then drew it, implacably and steadily, toward the Minbari cruiser. Morann bowed slightly and said, "I will see to the interrogation."

He left Delenn and the rest of the Grey Council to watch the slaughter.

As Sinclair fought to maintain control of his fighter, his onboard computer informed him of his vessel's plight. "Aft stabilizers hit," it said. "Weapons system at zero. Defensive grid at zero. Power plant nearing critical mass. Minbari targeting systems locking on."

The thought of being a helpless target in space, waiting either to blow up from internal stress or to be blown apart by the Minbari, was completely unacceptable to Sinclair. In a way, I think that the debate as to whether it was bravery or foolhardiness is a moot question. In Sinclair's case—and I suspect that it may have been true for any number of the last defenders as well—it was simply anger. Anger that overwhelmed fear, or self-preservation. Rage against the dying of the light.

"Not like this," Sinclair said furiously. "Not like this. If I'm going out I'm taking you bastards with me!" He snapped at the computer, "Target main cruiser! Set for full-velocity ram! Afterburners on my mark . . . *mark*!"

The Starfury blasted forward on its final run.

The Minbari cruiser loomed before him, larger and larger still, and he could not believe the size of it. It just seemed to get bigger and bigger, and he suspected that his full-impact strike would very likely not even be noticed by the occupants of the ship. But the rage overwhelmed him and he blasted forward, hoping only that his ship would hold together long enough to smash into the Minbari ship.

He threw his arms up reflexively in self-protection as he prepared for impact . . .

. . . and suddenly his ship was enveloped in light. Light that blasted out from the underside of the Minbari cruiser. It took control of his Starfury. He grabbed at the controls, trying to take back command, but the ship ignored him. He squinted against the intensity of the white glare, thought he saw something, forms waiting for him, and a quick flash of . . .

. . . wings . . .

. . . and then they were gone as his Starfury suddenly jolted to a halt. He was having trouble focusing his blurred vision, but a quick survey of the instrumentation told him that his vessel was completely dead. And he was too, he had to be.

Then the cockpit of his vessel was pulled open, and strong hands were pulling him from it. He struggled furiously in their grasp, but he had as much success against them as his fellow pilots had had against their ships.

They all looked identical to him. All bald with bone crests, all with utterly implacable expressions. For all the good that his fighting against them did, he might as well have not even bothered. But he continued to struggle, to shout questions, to make demands. No fear, as I have said.

Something was held up to his face and a burst of gas was pumped at him. It filled his nostrils, filled his senses, and he felt the world beginning to unravel around him. Immediately he realized that he had been drugged, but the awareness did nothing to solve his problem.

He was placed upon a gurney and wheeled into the heart of the cruiser. Faces blurred past him as, in his drugged haze, he said, "Why are you . . . doing this . . .?" But no answer was forthcoming. Little surprise there: They didn't understand what he was saying, nor would he have comprehended an answer.

They brought him to an interrogation area. A crossbar was hanging overhead, and it was clear that they were preparing to lash him to it. As they removed him from the gurney in preparation, he noticed—even in his dazed and confused state—a single, gray-clad Minbari standing there, apparently staring at him. It was hard to make out anything beneath the hood.

The Minbari held up something in front of him . . . a small triangle. Sinclair didn't know what it was, but assumed it to be some sort of weapon, or an instrument of torture, and he had absolutely no intention of simply standing around and allowing them to use it on him. As they grabbed one of his hands to tie him up, Sinclair suddenly and unexpectedly pulled free. He swung a fist around, knocking the triangle out of the hands of the startled Minbari.

It clattered to the floor and there were shocked gasps from all the Minbari around him. He had no idea what he had done, nor did he care. The rage was still strong within him, still burning brightly, and all he wanted to do at that point was hurt the Minbari and continue to hurt them, in any way and manner that he could manage.

So disoriented and drugged was he that he did not even feel the first blow that landed upon him. The second blow, however, definitely registered, as did the third and fourth. The gray-clad Minbari, clearly infuriated at the offense, clubbed Sinclair several more times while one of the others picked up the triangle that Sinclair had so cavalierly knocked to the floor.

From the reverential manner in which they treated it, it became quickly evident to Sinclair—even in his drug-induced confusion—that this was something incredibly valuable to them. He had no idea what it was or why they considered it vital, and he didn't care. *Hurt them hurt them hurt them* tumbled through his skull, and curiously it was accompanied by a second thought, namely, *Why? Why? Why? What do they want? Who am I?*

Apparently deciding that sufficient recriminations had been made for the sin of striking down one of their most sacred relics, they attached him to the crossbar, which then held him helpless. The cold glare of twin lights shone down upon him. The gray-clad Minbari held the triangle up to Sinclair once more. Sinclair's arms and legs strained against the bonds, as he fought against his body's own weakness, but he wasn't able to manage any sort of offensive action other than to spit in the Minbari's general direction. It landed on the floor, and the Minbari paused, looking at it with curiosity. As a sign of disrespect, it was not especially successful, since the Minbari were not familiar with it as such. The Minbari likely considered Sinclair's grand gesture of defiance to be little more than a sort of biological curiosity.

The gray-clad Minbari held up the triangle, uncaring of anything that Sinclair might have to offer by way of further truculence. It glowed . . .

And the Minbari gasped. Even Sinclair heard it. He had
no idea of the significance of it, but it was clear that something had surprised the Minbari. He could not even begin to
guess what it was.

"Why are you . . . doing this?" he asked once more, and
then his head slumped forward in exhaustion as the gray-
clad Minbari dashed from the room, heading straight for the
Council chambers.

Delenn had seen all she could tolerate.

She was moving quickly down a hallway, trying to put
as much distance between herself and the Council chamber
as possible. She had given no explanation for her abrupt
departure. And part of her didn't care that the others would
be wondering what the problem was. In fact, she wanted
them to know. She wanted them to know the depths of
loathing and disgust she felt for what her people, her race,
had become.

She stopped for a moment and leaned against a wall to
steady herself, to try to compose herself. That was how
Morann found her. She did not realize that, at that moment,
he was the more shaken of the two of them.

She knew that Morann had just come from interrogating
the prisoner. She wondered if the prisoner was still alive,
but then she figured, *What difference does that make? If
he's not dead yet, he will be soon!*

"Report to me if you wish," she said tightly. "But I have
seen more death than anyone should ever have to see. I will
see no more."

"Delenn," Morann began to say, and it was only because
of her own distraught mood that she did not catch the
strange intonation in his voice.

"If you wish to conduct the final destruction of Earth, I
will not watch, I—"

"Delenn!"

This time the tone brought her up short. She had never heard him like this: a combination of panic and fear and urgency echoed in his voice. She stared at him in confusion. He didn't speak so much as have words tumble out of his mouth. "I . . . we were using the triluminary to probe the Human, and . . ." She waited expectantly, but he seemed unable even to frame his thoughts. It was as if he was faced with something so massive, so incomprehensible, that he could not even wrap his consciousness around it. Shaking his head in exasperation at what he saw as his own ineptitude, he finally said, "You should come and see. I'll get the others. You should all come and see."

Within minutes they had assembled in the interrogation room. Delenn saw the bruised and battered Human hanging there and wondered why in the world he had come to that state. A probe by the triluminary should have been painless. Had Morann simply beaten him up out of a sense of revenge? In Valen's name, how much revenge did Morann need to exact?

But he looked anything but vengeful at this point. He was looking up at the Human with . . .

. . . awe? Yes . . . yes, that was it. Delenn couldn't believe it. Morann was awestruck. By a Human. By a member of the race that had slain Dukhat, that was responsible for Lenonn's death. He looked for all the world as if he were about to genuflect. What could possibly have transpired to bring Morann to such a state? Had a Vorlon appeared, hovering above the Human—was that what had shaken him? No . . . no, his attention seemed entirely focused on the triluminary. And now another member of the Grey Council, Koplan, was coming forward with the relic, as if Morann did not trust himself to administer the probe and needed someone else to verify something for him. But, verify what?

And then she heard whispers coming from Morann. Something about Minbari souls . . . about Valen . . . about . . .

No . . . no, she couldn't have heard him correctly. Snatches of conversation at best. What he was saying . . . the consequences of it, the hideousness of the holy war if that were the case. The destruction of the most profound aspect of Minbari culture. The implications would be staggering.

The triluminary glowed as soon as it came into psychic contact with the Human. Delenn looked to the results, and her eyes widened in shock. She saw the reactions of the others, saw them literally stagger upon realizing what it was they were seeing. She threw back her hood, as if to do so would change what it was that she was seeing. The Human gazed at her through half-closed eyes, his head swimming, but she took no notice of it.

"The triluminary confirms it. The Human . . . has a Minbari soul," she whispered. "And not just a Minbari soul. The soul . . . of . . . Valen . . ."

Oddly, Morann looked ever so slightly relieved. Clearly he had doubted his very senses on this matter and needed independent verification to fully accept what the triluminary was revealing. "I still can't believe it," he said, "but the triluminary is our most holy relic. It cannot be questioned."

Delenn was shaking her head in slow disbelief, still trying to fully comprehend all the ramifications of the revelation.

"Minbari do not kill Minbari. It is our greatest law. Valen must have been reborn into this form to tell us that the Humans are important . . . important to the next phase, the coming Shadow War." Morann's head whipped around upon hearing this. Clearly it had not yet occurred to him. Not only was he trying to deal with the notion that they had slain all those creatures with Minbari souls . . . hundreds of thousands of violations of the Minbari's most sacred credo . . . but on a more personal basis, the "return" of Valen now lent incredible support to the point that Lenonn had been trying to make two years previously.

Delenn saw him murmuring to himself, "So wrong . . . how could I have . . . been so wrong . . . ?" But there was no time to indulge Morann in his fit of despair. Quick action had to be taken. "We cannot destroy them," Delenn said urgently. "In Valen's name, and the one who is Valen's shadow in this life . . . we cannot kill them. Tell the ships to stop firing. Tell them, Koplan. Tell them now."

Koplan quickly passed the triluminary to one of the nearby members of the religious caste and bolted from the room.

"What do we . . .?" Morann gestured helplessly toward the battered Human. "What do we do with . . . how . . ."

And then, to their shock, the Human spoke. "I won't . . . tell you anything," he said through swollen and bleeding lips. "Nothing . . . just . . . my name . . . is Jeffrey Sinclair . . . captain . . . serial number . . . one . . . five . . ."

"What is he babbling about?" Morann asked in confusion.

Delenn shook her head, only vaguely beginning to comprehend. She walked slowly to the Human, staring up at him. Now he seemed to focus more fully on her face. He continued to recite some sort of meaningless number, and then started to repeat it. "He is . . . telling us minimal information," Delenn said. "It may be some sort of . . . ritualistic introduction."

There was a bleak humor to it all. "All my life," Morann whispered, "I have wondered what it would be like, to connect in some way to Valen himself. To encounter an incarnation of him. I never dreamt it truly possible, though, and certainly, not like . . . like this . . ."

Delenn gazed at the Human. "You know, he even . . . even looks like Valen, in a way. Like the pictures of him. Looks like him around the eyes . . . and nose . . ."

"Don't be ridiculous, there's no resemblance at all," Morann said, more sharply than he would have liked. She glanced at him and, apologetically, he waved it off. "I am sorry, I . . . there is much for me to understand . . ."

"For all of us, Morann, and we need time for the understanding." She looked thoughtfully at the Human a moment more. "He called himself Sinclair." Hearing his own name, the Human looked up, but Delenn did not address her remarks to him. Instead she said briskly, "We must eliminate his memory of these events, Morann. Whatever he may remember, whatever he may have heard, consciously or subconsciously, we must eliminate from his memory."

"And do what with him?" Morann pushed. "Just . . . just release him? Release the soul of Valen to go back and live among the Humans?"

"We will keep watch on him, Morann . . . somehow. After all," she said ruefully, "this is a Human being who has been aboard a Minbari cruiser and lived to tell the tale. A Human who, it will become quickly apparent, somehow is connected with the end of the war. He will be something of a celebrity among his people, I would think. It should not be especially difficult to keep track of him."

"And what of the Humans themselves, Delenn? We have halted our attack. But now what? What do we say?"

She did not hesitate. "We tell them that . . . we surrender."

There was a burst of protest from the other members of the Grey Council, confused conversation, shouting one against the other, no one even bothering to pull aside their hoods because there was such confusion. Morann, shouting above the others, said, *"Surrender!?* We are the Minbari! Surrender is a sign of weakness. Surrender to the Humans? We will look weak, uncertain. We have—"

"Have what? A reputation to consider?" Delenn snapped back, and her fury began to mount. "Look at what has happened to us, Morann. All of you, look. Look at what we have done. Broken our most sacred law to a degree not even imaginable. Tormented and tortured the physical carrier of the soul of Valen. *Of Valen!*" she thundered.

"Lenonn warned us, and we did not believe. Our own conscience warned us, and we did not believe. And now you are concerned with how it will look to the Humans, to the

rest of the galaxy, if we surrender? How it will *look*? In
Valen's—" She stopped, pointed to Sinclair. "In *his* name,
think of what you are saying! Think of where your priorities are! We have spiraled into the pit, Morann! We are
wallowing in the darkness, the soul of our race blackened
and stained, perhaps beyond redemption, and you are concerned about how something will *look*?"

She shook her head furiously. "It is the only way, Morann.
If it injures your warrior's spirit, your warrior's pride . . .
well . . . good. It injures mine as well, and I am no less
guilty than you of this abomination. Let the galaxy wonder.
Let every sentient race debate until the end of time why the
Minbari surrendered on the eve of their triumph. Let them
call it mercy, let them call it cowardice, let them call it one
of the great mysteries of our age. *I don't care.* And neither
should you. Now send out the word to the Earth government, and may Valen have mercy on all our souls, because
I do not know if anyone else will."

The warrior caste reluctantly, finally, painfully went
along with the surrender order. One of them, Neroon, would
never truly forget or forgive until the moment of his death,
and another, armed with a Changeling Net and a grudge,
would attempt to destroy Sinclair years later. But that is yet
another story.

Sinclair did not understand any of what was happening.
Everything was blurring together in his confused and
drugged mind.

He looked through hazy eyes at the group of excitedly
talking Minbari who were near him. At the same time, his
mind seized upon the beating he had taken at the hands of
one of them. He felt as if they were all assaulting him, all
of them coming at him from all sides, reality and fantasy
jumbling together.

And he focused on one of them . . . one of them with

its hood torn aside. Male or female or maybe some other gender entirely; it was difficult for him to tell.

Eventually they cut him loose from his bonds, laid him more gently down upon the gurney. He stared up at them in bewilderment. It was almost as if they were treating him with . . .

. . . respect.

Reality and fantasy tumbled together for him, colliding in his mind, and it would take a great deal of time to sort it all out.

Time that, miraculously, had been given him. To him . . . and to all of Humanity.

— *chapter 17* —

The Sheridan household had been in some disarray. This father and mother had madly scrambled to pack all that they could carry in preparation for the evacuation. And then, just as quickly and abruptly, the need had ceased. The Minbari had surrendered, for no reason that anyone could discern.

When John Sheridan ran into the living room, as if he had dashed all the way from the depths of space to his parents' front door, he found it in that state. Never had he found any clutter to be quite so beautiful. He embraced his father and mother, and his sister ran in from the next room and nearly bowled him over as she leapt into his arms.

"I have so many questions!" his father said, and his mother echoed the sentiment. No one knew or understood the reasons for the last-minute salvation of the Human race, and everyone was asking everyone else their opinions, theories, and details as to whatever gossip they might have heard.

"So do I," John replied. "I have just as many questions as anyone. I have—"

Then he stopped, for he heard a familiar footfall behind him. He turned and saw her: Anna, his beloved, standing in the doorway.

"But there's one question more important than any of the others," John said meaningfully as he looked at her. He held his arms open to her, and quickly she crossed the room and fell into his embrace as if she were meant to be there for all time.

And she whispered her answer: "Yes."

General Lefcourt could not quite believe that he was across his desk from a Minbari.

She stood there with a number of other Minbari surrounding her. She did not sit, and so Lefcourt stood, as well. He'd be damned if he'd take any chance of offending her. Now was not the time to put the collective nose of the Minbari out of joint.

To Lefcourt's right stood President Levy, looking an odd combination of pleasant and apprehensive. "General Lefcourt . . . Ambassador Delenn. You . . . do prefer the title 'Ambassador'?"

"One of your titles is as another to us," Delenn said, sounding a bit arch. She surveyed them slowly.

"As I told all of you in yesterday's debriefing, General," the President continued, "Ambassador Delenn says that she and her people would like to make . . . reparations. Their surrender has been unconditional and I believe their offer of help is entirely sincere."

"I'm . . . most glad to hear that," Lefcourt said. But he couldn't quite take his eyes off Delenn's face. There was such an air of mystery about her, a sense that something was being hidden. "Ambassador, if you don't mind my asking . . ."

"If this is about the surrender . . . I do."

He put up his hands defensively. "Okay. Okay, fine. Not a problem for me."

"Do not," she said as much to Levy as to Lefcourt, "ask me again why we surrendered. Nor ask any of us. For some it is a sore point, and continued inquiries will only exacerbate it. Now, we have many plans. Plans that will enable us all to help each other." She glanced around. "May I ask, where is Jeffrey Sinclair?"

"He's being . . . debriefed," Lefcourt said carefully.

Delenn half smiled. She knew what that meant. She knew it meant at least a preliminary psi probe. Well, let them. They'd never find the truth of it, buried so deep within him that no TP would ever get at it.

"That will not be a problem," she said reasonably. She pictured his face and, yes, it was true . . . saw Valen's. "I can always catch up with him later. I suspect, you see, that we will have plenty of time to do so. Now, let us get down to business."

President Beth Levy presented little resemblance to the haggard, dispirited woman who had previously addressed her people, when it seemed as if it would be the last time she would ever speak to them. Through the window of her office, the sun filtered as if making a point of welcoming a new day. "Today," she said, "the Senate has approved funding to begin construction on the Babylon station, located in neutral space between several major governments. Together, we stood on the eve of destruction, the result of a terrible, terrible mistake. We cannot afford to make that mistake again. The Babylon station will provide a place where we may work out our problems peacefully. It is, we believe, our last, best hope . . . for peace."

But, like all good things, it took a while to work it out. The first three stations were destroyed while still under construction. The fourth . . . disappeared . . . not long after it went online. Exasperated by all the difficulties, they decided to make one more attempt. The last of the Babylon stations. The name of the place . . .

. . . was Babylon 5.

— epilogue —

I have absolutely no idea how long I have been speaking.

The children . . . Luc, Lyssa . . . still stare up at me, entranced by the narrative. Even their nurse, Senna, is upon the floor looking up at me with childlike fascination. I am afraid to break the spell, but break it I must. For my throat is sore, my head aching. The sort of ache from which only a good, stiff drink can relieve me. I reach for my imperial seal, which Luc silently hands me.

"There," I say slowly. "You have had your story. You must go now. I have . . . things to do."

The children seem reluctant, and they look to their governess for guidance. Clearly they feel that, if she offers some sort of protest—asks to stay a time longer—I will relent. And who knows? Perhaps they are right. But instead she has already gotten to her feet, and she bows slightly. "I hope they were not an inconvenience, Majesty."

"No," I tell her sincerely. "Thank you for allowing me to see joy one more time, before it gets too dark to see anything anymore."

I do not tell her, of course, the resolution I've made.

The thing that I know I must do. I do not tell her that I know the darkness is not far off, an hour or two at most. And yet she seems to sense it, sense what's on my mind. Sense that I do not expect to be upon this planet—this planet which I have so bitterly disappointed—much longer. As she senses it, she feels a need within her, a need to somehow . . . connect to this pathetic shell of a man that I have become. A once-great man, who has taken on too much of a burden in this life, and is ready to lay it down.

She reaches out, and gently touches my arm.

What do you want?

That question comes back to me. Comes back to haunt me as it has so many times in the past years.

My thoughts turn once again to Morden, on whom I dwelt earlier. Morden, who asked an assortment of key people on Babylon 5 that very question: What do you want?

I have been searching, even as I spoke to the children, to recall my exact response, word for word. I believe I have it now.

There I was on Babylon 5, in a post that was generally considered to be a dead-end joke. I drank, I gambled, I debauched, and I thought I watched my career wither away. I felt as if I were the living incarnation of everything that the Centauri empire might have been, and no longer was. And when Mr. Morden asked me what I wanted, I replied:

"Do you really want to know what I want? Do you really want to know the truth? I want my people to reclaim their rightful place in the galaxy. I want to see the Centauri stretch forth their hands again and command the stars. I want a rebirth of glory—a renaissance of power. I want to stop running through my life like a man late for an appointment, afraid to look back or look forward. I want us to be what we used to be. I want . . . I want it all back the way it was. Does that answer your question?"

It did. It answered his question, and sealed not only my fate, but the fate of all of Centauri Prime. For the Shadows whom Mr. Morden represented exploited my hopes, my dreams and desires, and used us to launch a chaotic war that almost brought the galaxy down around us.

The Humans have a saying: Be careful of what you wish for. You may get it.

Great Maker, I got it.

I wanted so much . . . so much . . . and I . . .

. . . I never truly understood . . . what was important . . . never . . . I . . .

I look at the lady Senna, and in a low voice, a voice that might once have been alluring when spoken by a young and handsome man, I say to her, "Dear lady . . . I would love to walk with you on a beach . . . somewhere. For just five minutes." I feel tears welling in my eyes, and I fight them back. It is the single greatest battle of my life. "How strange, to have come this far, and to want so little."

I turn away from her, for I do not know how much longer I can keep my eyes dry. A dear, sweet woman. Two lovely children. They could have been mine. They are the life I turned away from, the life of a different man . . . a lucky man.

"Children." My voice is low and hoarse. "Will you remember this story? Will you remember me?"

"All my life, Majesty," Luc says in wonderment.

I nod. It will have to suffice. "Then go."

But Luc suddenly seems less than willing to depart. "What happened to Sheridan and Delenn?" he asks. "What about the end of the story?"

"Sheridan," I say slowly, "became the president of a great alliance, Delenn ever at his side. And the story . . . is not over yet. The story is never over. Now go."

Senna takes one child in each hand, and she starts to head out of the room.

And Lyssa, the child who never spoke, turns and suddenly utters what is possibly the longest sentence that Senna has ever heard from her. It is, of course, the age-old question, even more fundamental than "What do you want?" Indeed, I should have anticipated it.

"Did they live happily ever after?" she inquires.

"Lyssa!" Senna says in surprise.

The child seems determinedly oblivious of the effect she had on her nurse. Instead she repeats, insistently, "Did they live happily ever after?"

"That . . . remains to be seen," I say after a moment.

The last Centauri woman I will ever see ushers the children, and herself, from my presence.

I am alone once more. Alone with the empty room. With the emptiness of my own soul.

I pick up a small control device and aim it at a hidden screen. The view flares to life, and suddenly I have, floating before me, an image of two people in a cell.

Sheridan and Delenn. She is embracing him furiously, looking for all the world as if she would break him in half. She is speaking to him in a hurried, desperate half whisper.

"They're allowing us one last moment together before . . ." She stops, unable to say the words, and then she switches thoughts. She smiles, nods with a bravery that I can only admire. "It's all right, John. I accepted this fate a long time ago. They cannot touch me. They cannot harm me. I'm not afraid. Not if you are with me. Our son is safe. That's all that matters. John . . . I love you." She embraces him with a passion born of a sense of doom.

Yes . . . their son was safe. At least . . . safe from me.

I pick up a bell and ring it. Moments later I say to the guard standing there in response to it, "I need another bottle. I will need several more bottles. Then wait one hour . . . and bring the prisoners here."

Then I am alone once more.

Delenn and I had come to an arrangement, you see. I went to her earlier, when she was alone in her cell. My interrogators had been after her for a while to give us certain information with which she was not forthcoming. When she laid eyes upon me, looking exhausted and worn, she had the appearance of a hunted animal. Hunted and haunted.

"I want information, Delenn," I told her.

"Go to hell, Londo," she shot back.

"You have picked up some intriguing phrases from your husband," I said approvingly. "I will go to hell soon enough. I do not want any information that will endanger your future, Delenn. I want only to know of . . . the past."

She was clearly suspicious, since my associates had brought her there with much darker objectives, but I convinced her that my agenda at that moment was different from my ministers'. I desired simply to possess certain pieces of knowledge. Certain scenarios to which I was not privy in the past, which were known only to Delenn. The information I needed in order to understand and assemble the history which I have just recounted to Luc and Lyssa.

In exchange for providing me with what were, to her, useless and outdated facts, I swore to her that her son would never suffer harm at the hands of myself or the House Mollari. That he would, in fact, be under the protection of my House, for now and ever . . . presuming anything was left of it. She doubted me at first. Who could blame her? But I indicated to her that I had promised G'Kar, under different circumstances, that I would free his homeworld from Centauri domination if he cooperated with me. He did, and I did. So how could I be less honest with Delenn?

So she told me. Filled in the pieces for me. My interrogators she told nothing. Me, she offered what were, to her, details concerning matters of no consequence. But they meant everything to me, for now I know.

You see, just like anyone else . . . I desire to know . . . the entire story. Know it, and pass it on to those who are interested. Deserving. For a story is only as good as the audience that desires it.

I raise my glass in a toast, the last of my drink, and I say, "To the future . . . my old friends." And I drain the contents.

Footsteps can be heard, returning briskly. I recognize the stride. How could I not? After all these years, it is impossible for me not to. I look up and there he is, holding several bottles on a tray. I waggle my fingers and say, "Come here."

Vir approaches, his hair streaked with gray.

Nearly two decades ago, it was predicted by a noted seer, the Lady Morella, that—of Vir and myself—one of us would become emperor upon the death of the other.

My death, I believe, is not far off. Not if I handle matters correctly. And Vir is looking hale and hearty. So I think it fairly obvious how that prophecy is going to turn out.

"You will drink with me, Vir?" I ask.

"No, if it's all the same to you," he says. I think of the old days, when his voice always seemed to have a slight tremor to it. No more. Now he speaks with confidence . . . and just a hint of perpetual sadness. He waits, desiring to know how he can serve me, just the same as always.

"I have decided to work on a history, Vir," I tell him. "And I have decided that you will write it with me."

He appears surprised. Clearly he did not know what to expect, but it was not that. "I will?" he asks.

"Oh, yes. It will be quite comprehensive. Unfortunately I do not think I will have overmuch time to complete it. I would like your help in achieving that. You were there for most of it. I think you are fit to do the job. If you wish," and I made a magnanimous gesture, "you may put your name first in the credits. For I strongly suspect, you see, that it will be published posthumously."

"I see," he says.

"I shall spend the next hour," I tell him, as I proceed to pour a drink, "giving you some details . . . some highlights . . . for I have been discussing it at length recently, and it is all fresh in my mind. You may record it however you wish. Expand upon it, put it into chronological order at your convenience. Then you will leave me, for I will meet with Sheridan and Delenn."

"Are you . . . are you . . ." He could not even frame the words.

I shake my head. "I . . . do not wish to discuss it, Vir, for reasons I cannot explain at the moment. For I am watched, you see, all the time . . . even here. So let us instead discuss matters of scholarship . . . and let the rest sort itself out.

"And Vir . . . you will let the people know. Let them know there was to be more than a world in flames. That there was supposed to be . . . should have been . . . greatness. With all the sacrifices, with all the people who have died, you would think we were entitled to that.

"You will carry on for me, Vir. It will be among the last orders I give. You will carry on and tell the story to others. It will be uplifting . . . or a warning . . . or simply a rather Byzantine adventure, depending upon how it's told and who is listening, I would imagine. And in this way, the story will never end. You will do this thing for me, Vir?"

With true tragedy in his voice, he replies, "Of course I will."

"Thank you," I say. "Thank you, my old friend." I pat him on the hand and lean back, feeling the warmth of the liquor already beginning to fill me.

I shall drink myself into oblivion . . . and shortly thereafter, my soul will follow.

Vir waits for me to speak, a recording device in his hand. "Where . . . where do you wish to start?" he asks.

Where to start?

Where else, of course? In the beginning . . .

I look out upon the burning remains of Centauri Prime, steady my hand so that I can permit the liquid to cascade down my throat . . .

. . . and I begin to speak. "I was there, at the dawn of the third age of mankind."

I had such dreams. Such dreams . . .

JOIN FORCES.

THE OFFICIAL

BABYLON 5™

FAN CLUB

"...These are your sons and your daughters,
whose loyalty has never wavered,
whose belief in the Alliance has forced us
to take extraordinary means.

For justice, for peace, for the future...
we have come home."

-John Sheridan

Earth's Last Best Hope:
www.thestation.com
P.O. Box 856 N. Hollywood, CA. 91603

ANNOUNCING THE PAST, PRESENT AND FUTURE OF...

BABYLON 5™

ALL NEW EPISODES
BABYLON 5: THE FIFTH SEASON
WEDNESDAYS 10PM (ET)

THE SERIES: SEASONS 1-4
BABYLON 5
MONDAYS-SATURDAYS

© 1997 Turner Broadcasting System, Inc.
A Time Warner Company. All Rights Reserved.
BABYLON 5, names, characters, and all related indicia are trademarks of Warner Bros. ™ and © 1997 Warner Bros.

Coming soon:

BABYLON 5™

THIRDSPACE

by Peter David
based on
the original screenplay
by J. Michael Straczynski

In the depths of hyperspace, a squad of Starfuries makes an astounding discovery that could affect the destiny of the civilized universe. But have the pilots from the embattled space station uncovered the threshold to a new age . . . or a gateway to hell?

As they recover a gargantuan alien artifact floating derelict in space, both Captain Sheridan and archeologist Elizabeth Quijana know it is a gold mine of possibilities. But the telepath Lyta is the first to sense the danger, when her mind is assaulted by swift, crippling images of unspeakable terror. And as research teams attempt to penetrate the mysteries of the mammoth machine, Babylon 5 is thrust toward a terrifying confrontation with the monstrous dimension of Thirdspace . . .

YOU MISSED THE BIG BANG.
HERE'S YOUR CHANCE TO SEE
HOW *ANOTHER*
AMAZING UNIVERSE WAS BORN!

Deep in outer space, in the year 2258, diplomats, traders, hustlers, and travelers from every corner of the galaxy rub shoulders aboard the Babylon 5 space station...while back on Earth, in the year 1997, dedicated viewers monitor every moment of it!

Now take the ultimate behind-the-scenes look at the hottest outer-space drama to hit television in decades. **CREATING BABYLON 5** is the total companion to the Hugo Award–winning series, featuring:

- •Inside information on everything from plot development to groundbreaking special effects.
- •Interviews with the main cast members, key production technicians, and series creator J. Michael Straczynski.
- •Page after page of stunning photography and essential detail about the *Babylon 5* universe.
- •A complete listing of episodes from the first four seasons, *exclusively in this edition.*

CREATING
BABYLON 5

A Del Rey Trade Paperback
Available now

DEL REY® ONLINE!

The Del Rey Internet Newsletter...

A monthly electronic publication, posted on the Internet, GEnie, CompuServe, BIX, various BBSs, and the Panix gopher (gopher.panix.com). It features hype-free descriptions of books that are new in the stores, a list of our upcoming books, special announcements, a signing/reading/convention-attendance schedule for Del Rey authors, "In Depth" essays in which professionals in the field (authors, artists, designers, salespeople, etc.) talk about their jobs in science fiction, a question-and-answer section, behind-the-scenes looks at sf publishing, and more!

Internet information source!

A lot of Del Rey material is available to the Internet on our Web site and on a gopher server: all back issues and the current issue of the Del Rey Internet Newsletter, sample chapters of upcoming or current books (readable or downloadable for free), submission requirements, mail-order information, and much more. We will be adding more items of all sorts (mostly new DRINs and sample chapters) regularly. The Web site is http://www.randomhouse.com/delrey/ and the address of the gopher is gopher.panix.com

Why?

We at Del Rey realize that the networks are the medium of the future. That's where you'll find us promoting our books, socializing with others in the sf field, and—most important—making contact and sharing information with sf readers.

Online editorial presence:

Many of the Del Rey editors are online, on the Internet, GEnie, CompuServe, America Online, and Delphi. There is a Del Rey topic on GEnie and a Del Rey folder on America Online.

Our official e-mail address

for Del Rey Books is delrey@randomhouse.com (though it sometimes takes us a while to answer).

✎ FREE DRINKS ✎

Take the Del Rey® survey and get a free newsletter! Answer the questions below and we will send you complimentary copies of the DRINK (Del Rey® Ink) newsletter free for one year. Here's where you will find out all about upcoming books, read articles by top authors, artists, and editors, and get the inside scoop on your favorite books.

Age _____ Sex ❑ M ❑ F

Highest education level: ❑ high school ❑ college ❑ graduate degree

Annual income: ❑ $0-30,000 ❑ $30,001-60,000 ❑ over $60,000

Number of books you read per month: ❑ 0-2 ❑ 3-5 ❑ 6 or more

Preference: ❑ fantasy ❑ science fiction ❑ horror ❑ other fiction ❑ nonfiction

I buy books in hardcover: ❑ frequently ❑ sometimes ❑ rarely

I buy books at: ❑ superstores ❑ mall bookstores ❑ independent bookstores
❑ mail order

I read books by new authors: ❑ frequently ❑ sometimes ❑ rarely

I read comic books: ❑ frequently ❑ sometimes ❑ rarely

I watch the Sci-Fi cable TV channel: ❑ frequently ❑ sometimes ❑ rarely

I am interested in collector editions (signed by the author or illustrated):
❑ yes ❑ no ❑ maybe

I read Star Wars novels: ❑ frequently ❑ sometimes ❑ rarely

I read Star Trek novels: ❑ frequently ❑ sometimes ❑ rarely

I read the following newspapers and magazines:

❑ *Analog*	❑ *Locus*	❑ *Popular Science*
❑ *Asimov*	❑ *Wired*	❑ *USA Today*
❑ *SF Universe*	❑ *Realms of Fantasy*	❑ *The New York Times*

Check the box if you do not want your name and address shared with qualified vendors ❑

Name _____

Address _____

City/State/Zip _____

E-mail _____

babylon5

**PLEASE SEND TO: DEL REY®/The DRINK
201 EAST 50TH STREET NEW YORK NY 10022**